KATE M

A man of will
meets a woman
of deceit...

To SEDUCE
An ANGEL

"A writer to treasure."
—SABRINA JEFFRIES, *New York Times* bestselling author

BERKLEY SENSATION

$7.99 U.S.
$8.99 CAN

ISBN 978-0-425-24369-5

5 0 7 9 9

EAN

"In addi
the story
tion and
whets re

"This ins
romance while skillfully tantalizing readers with hints of
what's to come."   —*Library Journal*

"A well-written book with an interesting hero and an unusual
heroine."   —*The Romance Dish*

"It's a somewhat breathless—but very enjoyable—ride."
—*San Francisco Book Review*

"There is lots of humor and page-turning action for exist-
ing and new fans of Kate Moore."   —*Fresh Fiction*

"Fast-paced, witty, and highly satisfying. I enjoyed every
last word . . . Kate Moore really delivers with *To Save the
Devil*."   —*Romance Junkies*

"I enjoyed reading this story and look forward to reading
more of Ms. Moore's work."   —*Night Owl Reviews*

continued . . .

Berkley Sensation Titles by Kate Moore

TO TEMPT A SAINT
TO SAVE THE DEVIL
TO SEDUCE AN ANGEL

To Seduce an Angel

KATE MOORE

BERKLEY SENSATION, NEW YORK

THE BERKLEY PUBLISHING GROUP
Published by the Penguin Group
Penguin Group (USA) Inc.
375 Hudson Street, New York, New York 10014, USA
Penguin Group (Canada), 90 Eglinton Avenue East, Suite 700, Toronto, Ontario M4P 2Y3, Canada
(a division of Pearson Penguin Canada Inc.)
Penguin Books Ltd., 80 Strand, London WC2R 0RL, England
Penguin Group Ireland, 25 St. Stephen's Green, Dublin 2, Ireland (a division of Penguin Books Ltd.)
Penguin Group (Australia), 250 Camberwell Road, Camberwell, Victoria 3124, Australia
(a division of Pearson Australia Group Pty. Ltd.)
Penguin Books India Pvt. Ltd., 11 Community Centre, Panchsheel Park, New Delhi—110 017, India
Penguin Group (NZ), 67 Apollo Drive, Rosedale, Auckland 0632, New Zealand
(a division of Pearson New Zealand Ltd.)
Penguin Books (South Africa) (Pty.) Ltd., 24 Sturdee Avenue, Rosebank, Johannesburg 2196,
South Africa

Penguin Books Ltd., Registered Offices: 80 Strand, London WC2R 0RL, England

This is a work of fiction. Names, characters, places, and incidents either are the product of the author's imagination or are used fictitiously, and any resemblance to actual persons, living or dead, business establishments, events, or locales is entirely coincidental. The publisher does not have any control over and does not assume any responsibility for author or third-party websites or their content.

TO SEDUCE AN ANGEL

A Berkley Sensation Book / published by arrangement with the author

PRINTING HISTORY
Berkley Sensation mass-market edition / September 2011

Copyright © 2011 by Kate Moore.
Excerpt on pages 287–291 by Kate Moore copyright © by Kate Moore.
Cover art by Aleta Rafton.
Cover design by George Long.
Cover hand lettering by Ron Zinn.
Interior text design by Kristin del Rosario.

ISBN: 978-0-425-24369-5

BERKLEY SENSATION®
Berkley Sensation Books are published by The Berkley Publishing Group,
a division of Penguin Group (USA) Inc.,
375 Hudson Street, New York, New York 10014.
BERKLEY SENSATION® is a registered trademark of Penguin Group (USA) Inc.
The "B" design is a trademark of Penguin Group (USA) Inc.

PRINTED IN THE UNITED STATES OF AMERICA

10 9 8 7 6 5 4 3 2 1

To my sisters and sisters-in-law—
Nancy, Joan, Sarah, Kimberly, Lynn, and Jeanie—
heroines all and champions in life's resilience Olympics!
And to Lord Roderick Philoughby
for his support and inspiration.

Now, gods, stand up for bastards.

—*King Lear*

Chapter One

꙰

ENGLAND, 1824

Emma faced the two gentlemen in front of the massive stone fireplace. A painting on the wall above the gray stones depicted a hunting dog pinning a spotted fawn in agony between his forepaws. Emma's sympathies were with the fawn.

They had her pinned, the duke and his nephew. The Duke of Wenlocke, tall, gaunt, and imperious, his face as unyielding as granite, leaned heavily on a black cane. His gnarled hand curved over its golden head like an eagle's talon. His other hand clutched a document.

"This is the girl?" His haughty gaze sent an icy wave of alarm over her. "She doesn't look like a murderess to me."

Emma willed her knees to remain steady. It took steady knees to run.

"Oh, she's the one, Uncle. Emma Portland." The other man, the duke's nephew, the Earl of Aubrey, turned from prodding a great log with an iron poker. A shower of sparks vanished up the flue. *If only escape were that easy.*

"What's your age, girl?" the duke demanded.

"Twenty, Your Grace." Her voice came out thin and reedy, unrecognizable to her own ears over the pounding of her heart.

The duke's gaze fixed her to the spot. "Stuck a knife in some fellow's ribs, did you?"

Don't deny it, Emma. She clenched her fists in the folds of her shawl. Let them think her a murderess. Let them stare as if she were a beast in a menagerie to be baited.

"She's accused of the deed, Uncle, not convicted. I'm sure she'd rather do a favor for a pair of gentlemen than face the law." Aubrey had a smooth voice and a powerful body, his muscled thighs bulging in skintight riding breeches, his calves sheathed in gleaming black leather. Emma had seen him return his pretty mare to the stables with bloodied sides. She had not imagined that he noticed her.

The duke's stare pierced her. "She'd better. I'm done with the law and courts. Hang all lawyers. I want that *whore's get* out of Daventry Hall and back in the gutter where he belongs."

He shook the paper in his fist at Emma. "You know what this is, girl? A request for the king's pardon. The duchess wants me to sign it. If I don't, you'll be had up before the justices at the next assizes in Horsham."

Emma drew a sharp breath and blinked hard against a sudden sting in her eyes. Somehow in spite of all their care, the law had connected her with the spy's death. She knew what that meant. Once more she and Tatty had been betrayed. Her thoughts raced back through the long chain of coins and jewels pressed into willing palms and hasty bargains made with low characters. Their enemies might have bought off anyone on sea or land in the thousand miles between home and England.

"You'll hang, you know." The duke handed the paper to Aubrey. "Read it to her."

Aubrey circled her, making a slow deliberate perusal of her person, the privilege of a man with power. A mad desire to pick up her skirts and run passed in an instant. She would not make half the distance to the library door. She would never make the first set of stairs or the grand entrance or the drive, let alone the unfriendly woods below Wenlocke Castle. Escape took care and planning and, above all, luck. No one knew that better than Emma. How many times had she and Tatty and Leo tried and failed in seven years until their jailers had hanged Leo.

Aubrey stopped so close to her she breathed his scent, a heavy male mix of musk and leather with a tang of sweat.

"Not pleasant to contemplate, is it? Much better to hide here at Wenlocke, teaching servants' brats. That's what you do, isn't it, Miss Portland?"

Her downward gaze caught at the flimsy paper in Aubrey's hand. A pardon meant that the duchess, her grandmother's friend, still believed in her. When she and Tatty had reached Her Grace, all their difficulties had melted away. Until now. Now the duchess had gone to London to visit her daughter. Tatty was on her way to a ship at Bristol. There was no one at Wenlocke to help Emma. Still the duchess's wishes must count for something. "The duchess kindly gave me a position."

"Don't think to hide behind Her Grace, girl," the duke snapped.

"But she's done it for weeks, Uncle. Look at her. With her pink cheeks, golden curls, and round blue eyes, a man thinks butter won't melt in that sweet mouth, but that's a lie, isn't it?" Aubrey lifted her chin, the cutting edge of his nail against her throat. Her stomach roiled at the touch. "You're a lie, Emma Portland. There's a dead man in Reading whose reeking corpse says you're someone else."

His broad back was to his uncle. He let go of her chin and reached down and dealt her breast a swift, stinging blow with a flick of his middle finger.

Fear cramped her insides, but Emma knew better than to show it. She had wanted to be a girl again, but she'd made a mistake to brush the walnut dye out of her hair and scrub her skin and accept an old figured gown from the duchess, sweet and clean and scented with lavender and verbena from the clothes press.

"Listen to Aubrey, girl." The duke's voice brought her gaze back to him. "If you don't want them to break your pretty neck and feed you to the crows, you'll do as he says."

Crows. She steadied her treacherous knees. *Don't think about crows, Emma.* Tatty and the babe must reach the coast and the waiting messenger.

The fire crackled. Outside, a March gale howled against the windows. The Englishness of the place, which had seemed so warm and comforting when she first arrived at Wenlocke, now seemed chillingly cold. The baroque grandeur of the room dwarfed her. Its dark oak cases held thousands of morocco-bound tomes with gold-tooled spines, crushing slabs of history and law. The English liked their law to do the killing. They did not send assassins to kill babes in their cradles as her countrymen did, but they would hang the merest child for stealing.

Aubrey called it a favor, but Emma knew better. The prickle of the small hairs of her neck warned her. He and the duke wanted her for some ruthless business because they believed her to be a murderess. She could tell them what a joke that was. Tatty, older than Emma by three years, was the fearless one. Leo had always admired her for it, married her for it. Her brother and her cousin had been well matched in courage.

It had been Emma's duty to kill the flies and spiders in the cell she'd shared with Tatty. Once Emma had even been so bold as to kill a rat. But if these gentlemen knew the truth about her, if they saw that she would be of no use to them, they would simply give her over to the law. And the crows would get her.

Aubrey handed the paper to the duke. His voice turned coaxing. "We want you to teach a different group of brats. That's all. Here, read this notice." Emma swung her gaze back to him. This time he offered her a newspaper, and she was pleased with the steadiness of her hand as she took it. Inside her everything quaked as if she would shake apart in spite of the name she had taken for herself. *Portland* for the stone and *Emma* for the lover of the great English hero Nelson. She had vowed to be as unshakeable as her new name.

The paper was folded open to a small notice inquiring after a schoolmaster. *Private instruction wanted in letters, mathematics, and geography. References required. Inquire at Daventry Hall for interview.*

Emma handed the notice back. Asking a suspected murderess to tutor children in a private gentleman's house was not the favor Aubrey meant. "What makes you think this person will hire me?"

She did not know where her boldness came from. Tatty would say a cat pent up becomes a lion.

Aubrey watched her with a twisted smile. A ridge of vein marred his smooth broad forehead. "We will send impeccable credentials with you."

Aubrey's smile was the slow, complacent smile of power. Emma waited for the trap to close.

"In return, you must do something for us. It's simple really. I'll keep a man in the village. He'll tell you what to do, and you'll report to him everything you discover about your new employer's habits and plans."

"I must spy?" She tried not to betray any relief. They had not asked her to kill anyone. *Still she would have to report to a man, Aubrey's man. Aubrey would know where she was. Escape would be very, very hard.*

"Or hang if that's your preference."

"On whom must I spy?" Her mind raced. Let them think her agreeable. Let them think she could be bought with a piece of paper. There would be time while she spied for them for Tatty to reach the coast and Emma to plan another escape. She was the planner, not Tatty.

"On the Marquess of Daventry."

"A lord?"

"Whore's get." The duke's cold voice insisted.

She turned to him. The lines cut deep in his harsh face. The hooded eyes were unreadable. "May I know why I am to spy on this lord?"

"He's an enemy of this house, Miss Portland."

"Is he dangerous, then?"

"He's damned hard to kill."

She stared at the duke, but his closed expression revealed nothing. Emma's brain could make no sense of it—to send a schoolmistress to spy on a dangerous lord. "For how long must I spy?"

"As long as it takes. And we may ask you to obtain certain items for us, certain papers and objects."

They wanted her to spy and steal. "You will sign the pardon request if I spy?"

In answer the duke tossed the paper aside. The weary gesture told Emma all she needed to know about her predicament. The duke's unsteady leg buckled, and Aubrey took his arm to help him to a leather chair. Emma understood the gesture. The duke relied on Aubrey now, and Aubrey only waited to take power as it slipped from the duke's grip.

"When do I leave?"

"Today."

Chapter Two

❧

DAVENTRY Hall stood on a low rise with a wide view of surrounding woods and fields, still bleak and bare in March. An arched bridge over a smooth-flowing blue river led to a curving drive. Four stories of warm golden stone rose with the stern and stately symmetry of an earlier century to a series of flat roofs with nearly a dozen small towers domed with copper cupolas blue-tinted with age. Hundreds of windows caught the afternoon light.

Emma saw at once that the house had no defenses to keep out an army. Apparently the English believed themselves protected from attack by their little ribbon of choppy sea over which a man could easily row. The house's only defense was its unobstructed view. A spy could not escape undetected in such an open setting.

The gig from the inn rocked to stop under a two-story porch that projected from the main house. Its weathered stones, carved and ornamented with columns and tracery, gave the impression of a hundred staring eyes. Emma was glad to step inside.

When she explained that she was expected for an interview, a cheerful manservant in a plain brown suit led her up a stairway dark with heavy old timbers to an ancient stone chapel. Entering its shadowy vaulted nave, she experienced a moment of confusion.

On Sundays when their jailers took them to chapel, she and Tatty had counted the painted cherubs on the ceiling with their tiny fluttering wings, peeping around clouds or dangling their bare feet over the architecture. Here the ceiling had apparently crumbled with age, dumping frescoed cherubs onto the floor. She looked down to see sturdy fallen angels lying tangled on one another, round limbs protruding from snowy linen, rosy cheeks and tumbled curls in a jumble.

At her footfall on the stone, the heap of angels stirred.

A midsized angel opened one blue eye and peered up at her. "'Oo the devil are you?" he asked with a surprisingly earthly accent.

His words prompted other angels to stir and scramble to their feet in a row. Emma counted seven earthbound angels, staring openly at her. They came thin and round, dark and light, rough-hewn like carved figures, or rounded with curls about their rosy cheeks, not angels after all, but barefoot boys in white shirts and gray wool breeches. One last angel lay on the stone floor. He was no cherub.

A thin lawn shirt, open at the throat, clung to a powerful chest and shoulders. One sleeve was sheered off completely, exposing a gleaming muscled arm like living marble, and a lean hand gripping a great sword. The words of a childhood prayer—*archangel defend us*—rose to her lips.

The warrior angel rolled to his bare feet in a fluid move, tall and lithe and fierce. His shirt billowed about him. Charcoal wool trousers hugged his lean hips and legs. He took Emma's breath. Angels such as he had fought each other for the heavens with fiery swords when Lucifer revolted.

His bold gaze met Emma's and held.

"I came about the position," she told the angel. She had no idea what his place on the household staff was, but the boys around him must be her intended pupils.

He leaned his folded arms on the hilt of his great sword and regarded her with frank interest, a sardonic lift to one brow. "I don't remember advertising for anyone with your qualifications."

"I beg your pardon. *You* placed the notice in the paper?"

"*You* are hardly the expected result."

Emma blinked. "*You* are Daventry?"

"None other." He bowed slightly. "You are E. Portland?"

Emma tried to pull her wits together. She was talking to a man, not an angel, a dangerous man who was hard to kill. She found herself babbling her qualifications, real and false. "Emma Portland. I speak French, German, and Italian. I know Latin, maths, and geography. Do you wish to see my credentials?"

"Can you teach?"

"Of course."

"Let's find out." With an effortless sweep of his bare arm, he brandished the sword in the air. Emma retreated a step before she realized the sword was made of wood. "To the schoolroom, lads."

The ragged cherubs erupted into motion and noise, surging around her. In a blink they had snatched her reticule and letters of reference and whisked them away. She could see her bag bobbing from hand to hand above their heads as they disappeared up the dark, narrow stair.

"After you, Miss Portland." The warlike angel lord, whatever he was, grinned at her discomposure. It was not a good start. Her escape plan was not in place. She could not go back to Aubrey's man at the inn. She needed this man to hire her, not to mock her.

THE girl turned an assessing gaze on the schoolroom. Dav had held no proper lessons there since his old tutor Hodge had left. The books he'd purchased for the boys lay in a heap in one corner. Their slates were scattered about the floor. He had continued to read to them a tale of exploring the great pharaohs' tombs. The result of that tale dominated the room—a dark pyramid built of desks and chairs that nearly reached the ceiling. A tunnel led to the interior of the structure, where the boys had disappeared.

Dav doubted she would last the afternoon, and a stab of disappointment accompanied the thought. He needed someone to take charge of the boys. They could not play games forever as if time would stand still for perpetual youth. But his idea of a tutor was nothing like this girl. From the letter he'd received, he had expected E. Portland to be a shabby scholar with his mind on the ancients. He should have told her at once that she wouldn't do for the job and arranged her escort back to wherever she came from. Even now he should stop her before his band ate her for luncheon, but it would only be polite to offer tea before he sent her away.

He righted a chair in the back of the room, straddled it, and waited to see what she would do. The sword had startled her, but now she ignored him, her brow puckered in a little frown of concentration, as she removed her plain black bonnet and gloves. She was thinking, stalling for time, he suspected.

Her hair, gold as sunbeams and springy as waves, was pulled back from her face with only a few curls escaping. A part of him just wanted to look at her. She undid the strings of her cloak. He hadn't seen the style, but he recognized an old, secondhand garment when he saw it, like the velvet coat he had in his wardrobe, a garment with a past. The cloth was faded rose wool, and the collar had a fringe like the petals of a wilted rose. Her gesture in removing it spoke of pride even when necessity made one bow.

He imagined helping her undo it, a missed opportunity. Gentlemen did such things, didn't they? And he was a gentleman now. The courts had made him one in spite of his grandfather's opposition. Daventry. He'd actually said the name rather easily.

Under her cloak she wore a dove gray muslin gown, too loose for her light figure. An overdress of pale sky blue closed under her bosom and gave some shape to the gown. Her eyes were vivid against that blue. Something about the dignity of her bearing had made him expect elegance, and not a woman in a secondhand gown applying for a humble household post. The upward tilt of her chin with its slight dent seemed regal, a dent made for a man's thumb.

Inside the pyramid the boys squirmed and positioned themselves to spy on her. At any moment he expected them to erupt from their hiding place with wild whoops. He prepared himself to step in and put a comforting arm around her shoulder. If she sensed the boys meant mischief, she didn't show it. She circled the pyramid, collecting slates and pencils and stacking them on a chair facing the dark entrance.

When the room grew quiet, she stopped and touched the pocket of her gown, as if she had something tucked there. He smiled to himself. If she had something there, a good luck talisman perhaps, and still possessed it, the lads had lost their touch. Lark and Rook could lift the feathers from a strutting cock, and he'd not miss them.

Her gown fell back in its near-shapeless line, and she folded one hand over the other, a gesture of perfect self-containment. It irked him. He felt his fists tighten on the sword and his jaw clench that she should be an expert at retreating into herself. It spoke of a past about which he wanted to know nothing.

Her voice, low and sweet and surprising in its authority, interrupted the thought. "Once upon a time," she began.

He did not know the story. It was like the old stories he had heard as a child, but unfamiliar too. He doubted it was English at all. A part of him believed she was making it up on the spot, or at least altering it to suit her audience, for there were seven sons of a poor woodcutter and his wife who had no more money. The wife took a threadbare cloth and wrapped it around the last of the bread, and they sent their two oldest sons out into the world.

Dav thought he could listen to her voice if she talked about laundry, and he certainly did not mind looking at her. The story continued with the journey of the woodcutter's sons.

"Off they went down the road, and passed men working in the fields, and building a great church, and selling goods, but no one offered them work. As they sat at noon to eat their bread, a flock of little brown birds landed in the branches above and hopped about their feet. The birds chirped and chirped."

Here the storyteller paused and wrote upon a slate, her

pencil making a birdlike cheep. She put the slate aside and resumed the tale of the hungry boys, who ate and went their way, leaving the empty cloth but not a crumb for the birds. As the sun was setting, they met an ogre, and the storyteller lowered her voice to a gruff growl. " 'What do you have to say for yourselves?'

"When the woodcutter's sons replied, 'Nothing,' the ogre said, 'Then you'd best come work for me.' He led them to his house at the edge of a wood and opened an oaken door crossed with iron bars. 'In here,' he invited. The boys stepped forward, and he shoved them down stone steps and locked them in darkness black as pitch."

In the way of such stories the second pair of sons met the same fate as the first. They, too, waved away the birds and left behind their mother's scrap of cloth but shared no crumbs. Again the girl wrote on the slates. Again the woodcutter's sons had nothing to say for themselves when questioned by the ogre, and down into the cellar they went.

She paused, and the room held its breath. Her gaze didn't waver, but Dav felt her awareness of him. He had tightened his grip on his sword. She told the story as if she knew just what it was to be locked in that fairy-tale cellar, and she made him feel it, too, his heart beating in his chest. When she began again, his hands relaxed.

"At last the woodcutter and his wife were so hungry they sent their youngest sons out into the world with bread tied in neat bundles. These three passed the men in the fields, the church builders, and the busy market, but no one offered them a job. Hungry and weary they sat on a log to eat their bread. When a flock of birds flew near, the youngest said to his brothers, 'Listen, the birds want to speak.' He held out his hand with crumbs upon it. A bird hopped down at once and pecked them up. And when the three brothers rose to go on their way, they brushed the remaining crumbs onto the ground for the flock."

This time when she paused, Dav knew that she had reached the turning point. Now the brothers would get it right. Kindness, that was the point of the story, he felt sure, an easy moral lesson and there an end. He felt disappointed.

Her concentration was perfect. She seemed so caught up in the world of the story that she did not notice rustlings and whispers from inside the pyramid.

Consciousness of her femaleness thrummed in him like the low vibration of some powerful machine. Her gown seemed insubstantial, like cloud or water, loosely clinging to her form. He liked the look of her springy golden hair that might escape its bonds and her wide blue eyes and the way she wavered between trembling courage and contained purpose. He put her age at twenty or so. It occurred to him that she would have to be a prodigy to have the scholar's knowledge of languages and maps and math she claimed to have.

"The last three of the woodcutter's sons soon met the ogre, who asked them, 'What do you have to say for yourselves?'

"The youngest opened his mouth to answer when the flock of birds flew round and set up such a din of beating wings and chirping that a person could not hear himself think. The ogre shouted and waved and drove the flock to the rooftop except one bird who settled on the shoulder of the youngest son and chirped in his ear."

The girl stopped speaking and put down the slate in her hands. Her voice dropped as if she had come to the last words of the tale. Dav could sense the edge of anticipation in the boys. She stood contained and cool, unmoved by the tension of the unfinished story.

"Well, wot happens?" came a voice from within the

pyramid. Slaps, grunts, and rustling hushed the speaker. Someone whispered, "Let 'er finish it."

Dav did not know whether to be amused or annoyed that she had engaged him in this test of patience. She had violated the fundamental rule of storytelling by leaving the woodcutter's sons trapped in the ogre's cellar and her audience unsatisfied.

He could call a halt to the lesson and thank her, but if he did so, he, too, would not know the story's end.

He was sure the boys could see her, but she gave no sign of impatience. Again there was movement in the pyramid, and Robin, at eight, the baby of the band, poked his blond head out of the tunnel. "Please, miss, are you going to say wot 'appens?"

In a flash Dav realized the unfinished story had been her strategy all along. But she showed no sign of triumph at this first victory. She was patient, Dav would give her that.

"Only you can finish the story."

Robin crawled out and sat at her feet. Savage whispers hissed at him from the tunnel. "'Ow can we finish yer story?"

She looked as solemn as the little boy. "Each must answer the ogre's question."

"'Ow do we know wot to answer?"

Swallow's head emerged. "Robin, ye nodcock, it's wot the birds say, isn't it?"

The girl handed Robin a slate. "I've written their words for you on these slates. There's a word for each to tell the ogre."

Jay and Raven crawled out next, a matched pair of ruffians at ten. She handed out more slates.

Finch came out, bringing her bag. He gave it to her and accepted a slate in exchange. The boys sat, looking at each other's slates without speaking until a voice from within the pyramid muttered, "Idiots." Dav knew their dilemma and wondered if they would admit it to a stranger.

At last Swallow admitted, "We can't read."

Lark and Rook slid out of the tunnel and stood, arms crossed over thin chests. "And wot do we care? Words don't slay ogres."

"Besides Daventry can read. As long as we've got 'im, we don't need 'er." Rook looked to Dav for support.

Instant debate started.

"She could stay until she teaches us to read."

"But only seven words."

"A week, then."

"'Oo wants a blinkin' girl around for a week? Girls, useless as warts."

Dav held up his sword, and they fell silent. "We vote then. Who wants to keep her for a week?"

"A fortnight." The girl's voice shocked him. There was an unmistakable hint of desperation in it that woke all the instincts that had kept him alive for three years in the streets of London. She was not the ancient scholar he'd expected, nor was she what she appeared to be.

"I will stay a fortnight. No less, or not at all," she declared firmly. She had control of herself again, except for her eyes.

He felt the boys' gazes on him. He knew the smart thing to do, the thing his brothers would advise. But his street self was awake in him now, alert to snatch any good thing that came his way. She was a prize, a windfall from a passing wagon, a treasure washed in on the tide. The desperate flash of need in those blue eyes told him so, told him that whoever had once possessed her had let her go. She was his for the taking. He would have the end of her story.

"Miss Portland, you may have your fortnight. Prove

yourself a worthy tutor to my boys, and you may have the position." He made it sound like a gentlemanly request, reasonable and aloof.

She did not thank him, but he did not miss the relief in her eyes.

"Tea, lads. Take the sword," he ordered. Lark took the hilt, and Jay and the others lined up to carry the long blade. Where he could lift it with ease, the weight of it made them stumble awkwardly, like pallbearers shuffling solemnly under their burden.

Dav was left with the beautiful stranger he'd hired without a glance at her credentials, wondering irrelevantly, where she would sleep.

Chapter Three

❦

THE sound of the boys berating one another as they maneuvered the heavy sword echoed up from the stairs. Perpetually hungry, they would head directly for the kitchen to pester Dav's old cook, Mrs. Wardlow, for cakes or beef pies. Miss Portland had held them spellbound with her story for as long as they could be held.

He led her to a bare little room beyond the stairs with some idea that the room would suit a tutor. But he saw at once that he could not put her there. The room was bleak, but strategic. He passed through it often to escape the house. No doubt it puzzled her.

He was alone with her now, free to look at her as much as he liked without anyone's notice or suspicion, free to touch if he wished.

He watched her try to compose her features. The blue of her eyes, darkened by the agitation of the previous moment, brightened with relief. Naturally he wondered at it. Her faded, overlarge gown suggested an empty purse and the likelihood that she'd soon be or had been reduced to beggary, a fall from respectability that could be fatal to a woman. She pulled the old rose cloak back about her and tied the ribbons at her throat with hasty fingers as if to protect herself from his scrutiny. He knew concealment when he saw it.

He had little private experience of women. His history was against it. Taken at thirteen and kept for two years by his kidnapper, he had missed any time of innocent curiosity about females. Free at fifteen, he had formed his band of urchins and worked at survival. They had been nearly inseparable for five years, first in the streets of London, then in his mother's house. But he had not become a monk. He had no objection to enlarging his experience of the female sex with this woman who had fallen into his power.

He could see that the details of her story did not add up. Her elegant person in the ill-fitting clothes and her capacity for invention did not match her regal posture and desperate desire for the position. He did not think her a fortune hunter, but he could not say what she was. She seemed to have a dogged resolve that only necessity could teach. She had put herself into the story she told. Of that he was sure, though who her ogres were, he could not guess. Her wary eyes said she knew a world more dangerous than any schoolroom.

Emma squeezed her palms together to contain a giddy rush of relief. She had time. The fortnight stretched endlessly before her, time enough to plan a major campaign, and she had only herself to free, not Tatty or the babe. But it was hard to feel triumphant with Daventry's heavy-lidded gaze on her. His eyes puzzled her, a cool and silvery gray, like a lake surface at dawn with everything hidden underneath.

When she looked into those eyes, she could not tell his age. His face was too severe to be youthful, his manner too cool. His face was rather like a statue of eternal youth, carved in stone. Straight brows, deep-set eyes, sharp-cut lips. The boys for all their scrawniness had the soft round-edness of boyhood in their faces. But in Daventry's face there was no softness except in the loose wheat-colored hair that framed it. She now saw darker strands under the wheat to match his brows and lashes.

Her first impression of him as a warrior angel lingered. His white linen shirt with its missing sleeve gave him the look of a robed angel with bared limbs. His sword arm, curved, powerful, and bare drew her unwary gaze. Each time her gaze slid to the dense bulge of muscle there, she thought of angel defenders at the gates of heaven and hell. Looking into his eyes, she thought there was nothing those eyes had not seen.

Emma was not so naïve that she didn't know the duke and Aubrey meant to destroy him. They had not directly asked her to kill him, but they had chosen her to spy because they thought her wicked and unnatural, a woman capable of murder. She would have to lie as if her life and his depended on it, lie to him and lie to them. It would take a weaver's skill to keep all the strands of the story straight. Lying on the spot was easy enough. Lying to an angel struck her as a dangerous and unwise.

"Do you have a trunk, Miss Portland?"

Emma blinked at the harmless, necessary question. His gray glance was detached. He did not seem to be distracted by her person as she was by his. She did have a trunk. Aubrey had arranged one for her as he had arranged a past, a convenient history she could bring out when questioned.

She nodded. "At the inn." She could not repress a quick shudder. Sending for her trunk would signal Aubrey's man, Mr. Wallop, that their plan was working.

"Cold?"

She shook her head, and the tie of her cloak gave. The worn garment slipped from her shoulders, and Daventry reached to lift it back into place. His fingers caught the strings, and in the face of his nearness, his unsmiling concentration on her cloak strings, she dropped her gaze. Her consciousness of him shifted. His bare wrist, strong and masculine in its structure, dusted with springy golden hair, was under her chin. His hands tugged the strings straight. The gesture seemed to enclose them in an intimate space. Emma stared helplessly at his wrist circled by a faint white pucker of skin as if a girl's awkward stitching had raised a rough seam there.

He stood as close, closer to her than any man had stood. Under the thin lawn shirt, his chest rose and fell with his breathing. Her body did not flinch or recoil at his nearness. Instead it quickened and hummed with life. She looked at the scar, which plainly spoke of pain, of a time when he'd been injured or helpless. The helplessness of it lured her closer. Her fingers closed of their own volition around the place, and she drew her thumb along the white ridge.

He froze at her touch, the backs of his fingers warm against her collarbone, where her pulse leapt. Emma had trained herself in stillness to avoid careless blows, but now she held herself still to invite this man's touch as if the mere brush of his fingers woke a hunger in her skin for warmth.

She felt herself lean toward him, the way ponies in the fields on a cold night leaned against one another for warmth. His hands moved away, and she recovered her distance. They stood in a bare little room that smelled of dust and disuse. Daventry was not helpless but very much in control. She had no reason to trust him, and he certainly should not trust her. Tatty would say—*To trust is good. Not to trust is better.*

Emma, who knew the look in a jailer's eye, the one that said, *I can do with you as I wish,* did not know what to make of Daventry's expression. She looked at his mouth. A mouth could tell a lot, but it was a mistake to look at his mouth. A warm flush rose in her cheeks as she tried to understand his mouth. There was dominance there, surely. After all, this palace was his. He ruled here, but she detected no cruelty, no threat of punishment. Knowing amusement perhaps, as if he understood her better than she understood herself.

She took a steadying breath. "I should like to discuss the terms of my employment."

That sardonic lift of his brow came again, making him seem annoyingly older than Emma. "Ahead of yourself, aren't you, Miss Portland? I haven't yet examined your credentials."

"I have them here." Emma reached to hand him her papers. She needed to take charge of the conversation some how, to make it brisk and pointed, and not be sucked down into the kind of bodily languor his nearness evoked.

After a pause he took them. "What terms of employment did you imagine were open to discussion?"

"Schoolroom hours, your aims for the boys, when and where I may prepare my lessons, and my days off."

"Days off? Before you've begun?"

"I shall want every other afternoon for a walk to the village."

"Someone will drive you." The lines around his mouth tightened.

"I must walk. For my health." She could hear the lie in her own voice and fervently hoped he could not. Every other day she was to report to Aubrey's man Wallop. Her real employers would have their information.

The closeness of the previous moment vanished. Emma felt his withdrawal into the stone youth who could not be touched.

"Pull that bell rope." He waved a careless hand, dismissing her. "Someone will come to lead you downstairs. My housekeeper, Mrs. Creevey, will find you a maid."

Emma felt disposed of, as if the moment of closeness between them had never happened. She should not care. To glimpse his past pain, whatever had made the scar, would not help her escape.

"Take supper with me and the boys, and then we'll talk again about the terms of your employment, after I've examined your papers." He bowed briefly, stepped around her, and vanished through a narrow paneled door.

Over his shoulder Emma saw a flash of sky before the door closed and a draft of cold air swirled around her. She pressed a hand to her breast to slow the erratic beat of her heart. She was in a plain room on an upper floor of the hall. Her employer had just stepped through a door into the sky.

D AV strode across the gray slates of the hall roof, letting the March wind blow away whatever unreasoning desire had overtaken him in the girl's presence. The lowest level of the great roof stretched across the front of the hall between the two great wings. His family worried that he roamed the roof, but among its chimneystacks and turrets his balance was swift and sure. The vast rooftop, nearly an acre in size, was his. He would wager the hall that his grandfather had never set foot on the roof. Dav had seen it on his first approach to the house and felt a surprising release of some tightness in his limbs of which he had been barely conscious. The wide expanse with no walls was for him the hall's saving feature. No one else came up there except himself and the boys.

If he'd lost his balance, it was in hiring Emma Portland. He had acted purely on impulse, on a startling desire to have the girl in his bed. With his fingers on the worn flannel of her cloak he had imagined them skimming the silky smoothness of her breast under the cloth with a vividness that shook him, a desire that instantly undid his family's long effort to bring him back from the streets. She was alone in the world, unprotected. She had wandered into his keeping. A gentleman, he knew, would regard such a woman as completely untouchable, but he'd been ungentlemanly from the start.

The crazy thing was that such a mad desire would also please his brothers. They feared that he was too damaged to want a woman in spite of some careful efforts to revive his wounded sensual appetites and one memorable evening they had arranged for him with a professional. Well, he could tell them they had succeeded. He wanted the new tutor in his bed.

He had had to touch her, and then he had had to leave her before he became more obvious and even more foolish. She had unnerved him by touching his scarred wrist as if some instinct of hers knew the real man. Cuffs and coats hid his past easily enough in most company. But today because the boys had been restless without their regular lessons, he had given in and led them in a pirate game, more like the life they'd led in the streets than the one he was training them to live. For an hour he'd forgotten Daventry and gone back to being "Boy," their leader, as he had been in London, in those years when he'd had no name.

Faced with Emma Portland he had not known who he

was. He had acted out of his street habit of seizing an opportunity the moment one appeared. Take first. Think second. Yet hiring her separated him from the boys, making him not their leader so much as their guardian with power to shape their lives. It had to be. It was one more step in becoming Daventry, his grandfather's heir, not Kit Jones, the boy he'd once been, son of London's most notorious courtesan.

He stopped halfway across the roof and slid down its slope to the low balustrade. The wind blew hard, sweeping away the last clouds of the storm that had passed. It whipped his hair about his face and made his shirt flap like a loose sail.

It would take his family no time to get the news of his hiring the girl. Every caution of the past four years since he had been reunited with his mother and brothers had been designed to protect him from his grandfather's malice. Everyone who served him was a guard as well as a servant.

The old duke, who, when he discovered Dav's existence, had ordered him kidnapped, continued to threaten Dav's mother and older brothers. Wenlocke seemed to know every move of Xander's business and Will's career and endlessly put blocks in their paths. Whether Xander and his partners sought patents and charters to bring gas lighting to more streets and cities in England, or Will struggled to create a modern police force for London, the Duke of Wenlocke interfered.

The family had built protective layers in all their dealings with the world. Hiring Emma Portland broke the main rule of staying alive—let no stranger near. He laughed at himself. It was precisely the interruption his safe life needed.

They all expected the old duke to die, but he lived on, possibly on hatred itself, and while he lived he threatened them all. They claimed not to mind. Dav's sisters-in-law made jokes of the large footmen who accompanied them everywhere. His brothers assured him that the whole family was in the fight. But Dav was going to change that. Since they'd won in court and he'd come to this house, he had been studying how to free them and himself from the old man's hold.

His oldest brother Xander had given him the wooden sword and told him to wait. Xan had the sword made with an iron-weighted hilt so that Dav might strengthen his arms. In the beginning he could barely lift it above his waist or swing it with any speed. Now it was as light to him as a sword of lath. His palms were callused and his grip strong, but in conversation with Miss Portland it had suddenly seemed a boy's weapon, not a man's. He had been quick to send it off with his wards.

It had served its purpose. Now he wanted to be free of it, free of his family's caution. Whatever they thought, he was ready to take on his grandfather. Tomorrow Henry Norwood, his old solicitor, who had led the battle against Wenlocke in the courts, would bring Dav an account of all of his grandfather's actions against him. And Dav would plan the defeat of his grandfather.

He crossed the roof to the south side. His wards needed a tutor. He'd hired one. He'd acted on his own, and he would handle the consequences.

He would shake off Emma Portland's influence. The next time he saw her he would make sure he was armed in gentlemanly and civilized trappings. He would have her credentials investigated. He had given her the fortnight she wanted. Then she would be gone from his house and his mind.

Chapter Four

❧

E MMA counted off a full five minutes before she opened the door through which Daventry had vanished as if he were indeed an angel warrior who could ascend the ether. She took the knob in her hand and slowly turned until she felt the mechanism engage. A fraction of a turn more, and the door opened with a barely audible click. She would practice. She must be flawless in door opening if she meant to escape. In the meantime a spy must spy. Tatty would say that if you wanted eggs for breakfast, you had to endure the cackling of chickens. *At least until the French army came to consume them all.*

There was no sign of Daventry, only a wind-scoured stretch of gray slate roof across the front of the house. At least he had not simply stepped on a cloud. The roof had levels above levels. Directly in front of her a narrow portion about a yard wide stretched along the base of an upper wall. To her right the slates sloped steeply down to a low

balustrade. Above the upper wall was another roof with towers and copper cupolas turned verdigris with age and wide,
tall chimneystacks, each topped with a row of distinctive
round pots like chess pieces for an ogre. The wind blew
sharply, scattering threads of smoke from the chimneys
and whipping her skirts about her legs so that she gripped
the doorframe.

The airy, unconfined space with only sky and wind for
walls made her giddy. There was a door opposite to the
south wing of the house, but no other way up or down that
she could see. Apparently Daventry had simply walked
through the air, as another man would stroll through a
salon. But he was no ordinary gentleman. He unsettled her
with his sword and his scars, his quick intelligence and his
knowing looks.

She shivered and stepped back inside. She must treat
Daventry Hall as just another prison. Escape, that was her
goal. She knew what to do. In a rough wooden chair in the
sparsely furnished room, she sat and used her nail to pull a
loop of thread from the hem of her blue overdress. When
she had eased a long enough piece from the fabric, she
broke it off and wound it round the doorknob. She and
Tatty had learned such tricks to mark their way about their
prison. As their gowns frayed, they'd grown cleverer and
bolder, using different colors and different knots to map a
path for their escape.

Emma used the knot for a door that led nowhere. The
Castello di Malgrate had had dozens of such doors, bricked
over when it had become a prison. No light penetrated its
interior through the walls, only through the vast open
courtyard in the center where the executioner did his work.

Once she had counted her steps and marked the doors of
Daventry Hall, she could escape in the darkest night.

When she had wound and tied her thread, she rang the bell. Mr. Creevey, who had led her to the chapel, appeared and led her down the dizzying stone stairway with ancient dark timbers that doubled back on itself to the entrance hall. Emma counted sixteen steps in each flight.

Emma waited where Mr. Creevey left her, thinking of the work she had to do. Overhead and around her the vast household loomed, a grand maze for a trapped mouse like herself.

At last the housekeeper and a maid appeared. The housekeeper, Mrs. Creevey, was a tall woman with deep red hair peeking out from under her white cap and alert hazel eyes. Her majestic bosom strained against the moss-colored bodice of her gown. A dozen keys jangled at her waist. With her was her daughter, a girl not much younger than Emma herself with a wide, vividly freckled face, prominent hazel eyes, and rusty brown curls under her cap. She had her mother's bosom but none of her beauty.

Mrs. Creevey looked Emma over. A severe frown drew her brows to a sharp vee. "Daventry has irregular ways, miss, for a man of his station. It is not my place to alter them, but I run a regular household. Of that you may be assured. There will be clean linens, hot food, and properly laid fires. Ruth will show you to your room." She turned to her daughter. "Now, mind your tongue, Ruth." She strode off.

The girl dropped Emma a curtsy. "Your trunk's arrived, miss, and His Lordship says you're to have the blue room."

Ruth led Emma back up the stairs to the floor below the schoolroom and opened the door to a room such as Emma had not entered since her childhood, a room for a princess. Walls as blue as a clear sky rose to a high white ceiling. A large tester bed with a simple white coverlet was canopied in chintz hangings patterned with vivid red chrysanthemums.

The white moldings had gilt edges, and on the vast carpet gold ribbons intertwined on a cream field. Light from the soaring windows made Emma blink.

It was nothing like the modest room in the servants' wing to which the duchess had assigned Emma at Wenlocke. No wonder Mrs. Creevey had frowned so at her. The elegant room was far above Emma's position as temporary tutor to a group of rough boys. But it must mean nothing to an eccentric rich man, such a room. What did he care where his wards' tutor slept when his splendid house had dozens of rooms? He lived here alone with servants and those lost boys. She knew them. They were the fruit thieves and port rats of her childhood, scrambling and squabbling over a few coins tossed from a passing carriage. As a child she had never envied them, until they remained free when she and Tatty were locked up.

The puzzle was how such boys had come to live here in this palace of a house. She wondered if they and their master were under some enchantment and thought how Tatty would laugh such an idea to scorn. Nothing magic about money, Tatty would say. Emma would teach them, but she would keep her distance. She would not love them as she had begun to love the sweet children in the duchess's school.

"Ruth, is there a governess's room somewhere?"

"Was, miss, a little old room upstairs next to the schoolroom, but with seven boys, all the upstairs rooms are filled. There's old Hodge's room, that was the grinder, but that's in the other wing by the library. You'd be right lonely on that side of the house. Nobody goes there much except Daventry, and the family when they come. Mum thinks . . . but I should not say what mum thinks."

A lumbering man, with a heavy brow and shoulders

wide as a hay cart, brought Emma's trunk into the room.
Emma froze. The fairy-tale room came with its own ogre.
His hands were as big as Emma's head. Ruth showed no
fear but directed him to stand the trunk in the dressing
room as if it were nothing to order a giant about.

"No need to be afraid of Adam Digweed, miss," Ruth
assured her. "He won't hurt ye. He protects Daventry is all."

"Protects him?" So Daventry knew the threat against
him. She had no doubt that Adam Digweed would crush an
adversary first and interrogate the corpse after.

"Ye must have heard the story, miss. It's been in the
papers for months. Mum didn't like it, but Da saved the
papers to read us all the Chancery Court doings at Sunday
supper. How Daventry came to be lord here after years of
being lost in London and how his own grandfather hates
him something fierce."

"Are those papers still about, Ruth? I'd like to read the
story." She hoped Ruth wouldn't see the obvious flaw in her
request. If she were who she claimed to be, she would
know a scandal that filled the London papers.

"Bless me, miss, Mum tossed them on the fire first
chance she had."

"But you could tell me the story."

Ruth's mouth opened. The girl was a talker. Her natural
disposition was trusting and open, but she clamped her lips
shut tight.

"Mum would have my head if I started speechifying like
they do in Parliament. Now, miss, we'll get ye settled and
ready for supper in a trice if ye'll give me your trunk key."

Emma fished the little key from her bag and handed it to
Ruth, who made quick work of opening the trunk, then
stopped dead and turned to Emma.

"Beg pardon, miss, but is this the right trunk?"

Emma followed Ruth's gaze, and they stared together at a gold silk gown with a bodice that was no more than a twisted rope of blue and gold that would never conceal Emma's breasts. The dress was wicked, a dress made for seduction, light and fluid and made to rustle and whisper and cling. Tatty at seventeen had told Emma fourteen all about seduction. Seduction, Tatty said was the art of bringing men to their knees, and women must practice it only on men they loved to distraction.

Emma had protested that there were no men to seduce, only their jailers and Leo. She had wanted to know then how a woman could learn such arts without any men. Tatty had laughed and promised that her first free action would be to find Emma the right man to practice on. Emma thought of her heart racing at Daventry's touch and her own need to put her fingers to his scarred wrist. Apparently Emma's heart had the sense of a loon. Daventry could not be the right man. Mixing spying and seduction was like setting the table and inviting bad luck to take the best seat.

"Don't you have the prettiest gowns, miss?" Ruth was saying.

Emma studied her trunk again. She might have thought it the wrong trunk, a mix-up at the inn in which the gowns of a fashionable lady of leisure and license had been sent with Emma, but it was plainly the trunk on which Wallop's hand had rested as he warned her, *You play by Josiah Wallop's rules now, missy, or you hang.*

"My last employer gave me her old gowns."

"Lordy, miss, she was rich as a queen. I'll just hang this one in the press, miss."

"Thank you." Emma turned away to let Ruth unpack

while her brain worked furiously at what Aubrey meant by putting such gowns in her trunk. He did nothing unintentional or careless, but the rich gown did not fit the story they'd invented for Emma at all. Emma's few gowns from the duchess were plain muslins and kerseymere wools of modest, high-necked cut. She had managed to take just two with her though they suited the version of her life Aubrey had put in her papers. Those papers said she was a vicar's daughter fallen on hard times since her father's death. Aubrey had been amused to give a murderess such a history. He had made her study the false documents in the carriage.

Emma could hear Ruth uttering sighs of admiration over the clothes as she hung them up. The rich gowns made no sense. Emma was supposed to be a vicar's daughter who would never own such clothes. A spy should be invisible.

She stared out the windows. White clouds billowed in towering formations in the bright sky. Beyond a stand of somber dark trees the view stretched away north toward distant purple hills. The unfamiliar English landscape rose and dipped in a rolling stretch of countryside as unlike home as a desert. There were no silvery olives or rows of tall slender cypress or groves of oranges. There were no mountains, only fields and woods in shades of coffee and chocolate with hints of new green in the hedges and ditches. She missed the warm gold and deep green of her native country and its clear geography with the mountains to the east and north and the sea to the south and west. England seemed a brown and gray coverlet with a hundred dips and turns and no straight paths. She and Tatty had lost their way a dozen times before they'd come to Reading and met the spy.

Emma touched her pocket, feeling for the little pin she kept there, for luck. In two weeks those woods might begin to green with the spring, but even then they would hardly offer the leafy concealment she needed. Perhaps she would have better luck on the other side of the house.

Tatty always said they just needed luck to escape, but Emma knew that luck was useless without a good plan. A good plan mixed patience and opportunity with distraction. With the right mix a woman could escape. Without it she was crow meat.

"Beg pardon, miss, but what will ye want to wear to dinner?"

Emma came to stand beside Ruth. The maid had filled the press and closed up the trunk. Nothing seemed right for a servant invited to take supper with her employer. The bright silks had low bodices, elaborate sleeves, and skirts flaring from narrow waists. The shoes were even more elegant and twice as useless. Aubrey's choice dismayed her, dainty slippers to match the silken gowns. It was not a wardrobe to escape in.

She turned to Ruth. "I suppose I must wear this dress."

Ruth put her hands on her hips and looked Emma up and down. With sudden decision she turned to the press and pulled out a poppy-colored India muslin with sprigs of gold. The short full sleeves would bare Emma's arms, and the bodice was shockingly low, but the dress would not cling immodestly like the gold one.

Ruth looked on the dress with favor. "If we tuck some lace in the bodice and put a wrap about your shoulders, it will not be so . . ."

"Low?"

"Right, miss. Now if you'll let me, I'll do you up proper."

"If you tell me Daventry's story. I know you're dying to."

Ruth grinned. "Oh, miss, you'll bring the wrath of Mum down upon me sure."

"Is she very hard on you, Ruth?"

"Not as hard as on me sisters Violet and Hyacinth. Mum called me Ruth because she said two wicked foolish girls were enough in one family. She saw I was born to be plain and no beauty, so maybe I would not take after my sisters, but she says I've a way with ladies' things."

"I'm grateful to have you, Ruth."

Emma let Ruth help her out of her worn gown and into the poppy-colored muslin. Ruth seated Emma on a cushioned bench and began to brush Emma's hair, her movements brisk and deft as she arranged Emma's curls in a loose knot at the back of her head. Working with her hands seemed to free Ruth's tongue.

"Daventry won't let us call him *lord*, but he is one just the same, a marquess and all. His mother is a great beauty, Miss Sophie Rhys-Jones. Mum says we've got to treat her with respect, but she's got a scandalous past for sure. When Daventry's father fell in love with her, he had to marry her in secret. Then he went off to India and died. So Daventry grew up in London instead of here. He never knew his father. They say he did not even know his parents had married. He thought he was baseborn."

"His mother did not tell him the truth?"

Ruth paused with the brush and shook her head. "They say she couldn't, miss, because of his grandfather, that's the duke. He's a powerful, cold old dragon. He was dead against Daventry's mamma, so she kept the marriage secret for near thirteen years even when she was a widow. She and Daventry's father came here for their wedding night. My mum was in service then, just married herself. She says she never saw a husband and wife so happy."

Emma nodded. Only youth could explain it, for Mrs.

Creevey did not seem the sort of woman who would notice the happiness of young lovers.

Ruth teased a few curls about Emma's ears. "Years and years later the secret got out. Someone told the old duke he had a grandson. And our Daventry was snatched right off the streets of London."

Emma knew why. She had heard the icy voice full of disdain pronounce Daventry to be a *whore's get*. Still she had to ask. "Snatched?"

"Just a boy he was. It happened during an exhibition mill with the champion, old Tom Cribb. Hundreds of gentlemen came, and our Daventry was there, too, with his older brother. He wanted to be a miller even then, same as now."

"A miller?"

"A miller's a prizefighter, miss, one who's handy with his fives, you know. Gentlemen are all mad for milling."

Emma wondered if it was the prizefighting that explained his scars. She could not ask about them without admitting that private moment between herself and her employer. "Go on, Ruth."

"Daventry was on his way home with his oldest brother Sir Alexander when some ruffians attacked the king himself in that old yellow coach of his, and while Daventry's brother fought them, Dav vanished—stolen, right off the streets. The family searched for years to find him."

"And where was he?"

"Living in the lowest streets with that band of his."

Emma tried to make sense of it. First he had been stolen, then he had been free and living in the streets, but he hadn't returned to his family. "You mean the boys I'm to teach? Are they all orphans?"

Ruth nodded. "Or might as well be, since no one knows

their proper names. Daventry's been searching the records of all the churches and workhouses to see if he can find their parents."

"How did he find them?"

"Collected them from the streets."

"But he dines with them?"

"Most nights, miss. He's teaching them to be gentlemen, like him."

"What happened to the man who stole him?"

"Died, miss, of an apoplexy, just like that. That's how Daventry escaped."

With the word *escaped* another darker thought came to her about those scars. Whoever had taken him had not killed him but kept him in captivity. She shivered, and Ruth bustled off to find a shawl for her shoulders.

She had asked for his story, just to know the facts, but some facts, once known, could not be unknown; they became white puckers on the smooth skin of memory.

"And how old was he when his family found him?"

Ruth tucked a pale gold-and-blue shawl around Emma's shoulders. "Well, he's twenty, now, so, he must have been sixteen or thereabouts. He went back to his family, and his mamma told them the truth about her marrying a marquess and all, so they went to court to get Daventry his proper title."

"Did his grandfather accept him then?"

"Oh no. The old dragon fought every inch of the way. He put terrible things in the papers about Daventry and his mamma, poor lady. He hates them something fierce because . . . well . . . because the poor lady was not respectable, you know. Years and years it was in the courts until the old duke lost, and they gave Daventry this house, which was his father's house."

"And when was that, Ruth?"

"Last November it was. All his father's people who had been in service before were called back. Some came like me mum, but most were too old or too afraid."

"Do you fear him, the old duke?"

"Don't think about him much, miss. He's as old as a Roman and far away and not like to think about such as me." Ruth stepped back. "Now look at you, pretty as a princess."

The words jolted Emma. She had not looked in mirrors for a long time, and no one had done her hair except when she and Tatty had put the dye in theirs.

The face reflected back at her seemed not herself, but a startlingly vivid creature, almost a woman. She looked again, taking inventory of her own features, her blue eyes, her plain straight nose that neither tipped up nor turned down, her small tight mouth, her dented chin. Perhaps all released prisoners experienced such a startling moment of self-recognition, meeting themselves face-to-face in the mirror.

If a person looked every day as the years passed, she would hardly notice her face changing. Maybe Emma noticed now simply because of the shock of the gown, poppy-and-gold muslin as bright as a sunset. The gown and shoes and shawl were lies, but at least her hair was a truth with its endless waves like an unquiet sea. If Daventry looked closely at her, he would know she was not the woman she claimed to be.

When she didn't move, Ruth gave her a bit of encouragement. "The hall's a big old pile, miss, but ye'll soon get used to it. There's a stair at the beginning and end of each wing, and a long gallery on the ground and first floors to take you from north to south. There are footmen everywhere, and someone'll help ye, sure."

Chapter Five

❧

THE dining room of Daventry Hall filled the southwest corner of the ground floor. Its windows from wainscot to ceiling looked out on the approach to the house over a tree-dotted lawn that stretched down to the lazy blue stream and the arched bridge over which Emma had come.

Daventry stood at the head of a long stretch of table gleaming with silver and plate and glowing from candles.

Whoever he was, warrior angel or lost boy, he was unrecognizable in his new guise as polite host. A black ribbon at his nape neatly tamed the overlong hair, like wind-darkened wheat, which had framed his face in loose waves. Fine black wool, white linen, and silk in subtle shades of gray and gold, like his eyes and hair, concealed his limbs and his scars. Again his age eluded her in spite of Ruth's story. Though he could be no older than Emma herself, everyone in the room moved at his command. One gray-eyed look quelled his young companions, as wild as Emma thought them. Tuned to his every expression, they stood behind their green leather chairs like carved figures as servants arranged dishes on a side table. Like him they were attired as gentlemen in coats and shirts and neckcloths.

Daventry's gaze met hers, a further reminder that he was a man skilled in concealing his true nature. His story, the story Ruth had told, lay like submerged wreckage in those lake eyes of his. What the elegant clothes could not disguise was his height and breadth of shoulder and the piercing look that made him formidable. Her own disguise of borrowed gowns, false papers, and fictions seemed inadequate.

Adam Digweed, a shadowy bulk in the corner behind Daventry, made a rough-hewn contrast to the display of rich columns and intricate plasterwork.

Emma turned to the boys. They separated her from Daventry and the lurking menace of Adam Digweed. The bigger boys were ranged on one side, the smaller boys with Emma on the other. The boys' eyes, both curious and hostile, flashed in her direction. Once Daventry nodded, they sat and two footmen began to serve.

One of them set a large flat bowl of creamy soup garnished with bits of green in front of her. She wanted to run her fingers around the smooth, unchipped rim of the lovely china bowl. The silver of her spoon gleamed softly in the candlelight. But when the rich steam from the soup reached her, it stopped her hand. She no longer saw the elegant dining room. Another time and place claimed her, and she could not lift her spoon. Emma smelled jail, smelled fish and salt and the stink of the sea, heard the ceaseless rush of water over the rocks.

"It's haddock, miss." They all looked at her. She made the effort to lift her spoon and offered a polite smile. The boys lifted theirs, poised, waiting for her to begin. She made herself dip the spoon into the bowl and couldn't continue. The fish smell choked her.

All heads turned to Daventry. He nodded, and they began to eat.

"You don't like fish soup, Miss Portland?" her host inquired. He nodded to a footman who removed her bowl. At Wenlocke in the servants' hall no one had noted the peculiarity of her taste.

She looked up, feeling Daventry's alert scrutiny in spite of the mild tone of the question. It was she who should be noticing what he ate and did not eat, not the other way about. "I don't care for it, L . . . Daventry."

One of the boys spoke up: "I'll eat it if you won't, miss. I'm Finch. Mrs. Wardlow doesn't let us waste 'er cooking." She remembered him, the thinnest by far of all the boys. He had an anxious look and held one hand in front of his mouth as he spoke.

"I hope I haven't offended Mrs. Wardlow."

"Maybe you like a fried bloater better'n soup, miss. The best fish is a good bloater," offered Robin, the rosy-cheeked boy with hair like curling straw, who had been her first questioner.

"No, thank you, Robin."

The oldest of the boys spoke up. "Well, are we going to talk about the soup all night because she don't care for it?" He had sullen good looks with dark reddish hair, a full mouth, and knowing eyes.

Daventry turned to him. "Choose a topic, Lark."

A boy with chubby cheeks and a mop of glossy brown hair wanted to know: "Can we ask 'er questions?"

Daventry looked at Emma. "You may ask, but she's our guest tonight, so introduce yourselves."

"But she's not a guest, is she?" Lark immediately challenged. "If she takes your money."

"To put up with you lot. You weren't uncivil to Hodge, so I'll thank you not to be uncivil to Miss Portland." It was a clear command with a snap in it.

For some moments tense silence ruled the table, but as the boys continued to eat, the food seemed to restore their ease.

The next speaker had coffee brown hair that fell in a straight line across his brow. He was the one who had admitted earlier that the boys didn't read. "Beg pardon, miss, I'm Swallow. What will ye teach us?"

"Reading, mathematics, and maps." A footman served Emma a portion of fowl. Something she could eat.

"Wot's the point of reading, miss?" The skeptic was Lark with his haughty profile and long lashes.

"To know things for yourself and not to have to depend on another person's report." Emma could see that her answer was not what he'd expected.

"How long does it take to learn reading? We'll have to sit in the schoolroom all day, right?"

"What schoolroom hours did you keep with your previous teacher?" Emma asked.

A snort was the only reply. The hostilities had begun, and Daventry had not curbed them. It occurred to Emma that he was testing her to see if she had the experience to know how to handle her student's resistance.

AFTER the meal the big man, Adam Digweed, took the boys to play at games. Daventry led Emma to an elegant drawing room like the inside of a jewel box. Its walls, covered with gold brocade, displayed mellow-hued paintings of past lords and ladies in heavy gilt frames. The furnishings, saber-backed chairs and long settees, all silk and damask covered, were equally rich in rose and pale blue and gold. A carpet of deeper blues and reds in oriental patterns swirled underfoot.

Daventry offered her a seat on a long gold silk settee by the fire and took a seat on the opposite sofa. A footman hovered, setting out a tea tray. Emma sat as she'd first learned to sit at five or six in a room only a degree more ornate than the one around her. Her spine was straight. Her hands rested lightly in her lap. She studied her employer from under her lashes.

He arranged his cuffs over his wrists, no sign of the warrior angel in his appearance, as if the past he covered up had no hold on him now. He seemed an aloof gentleman, resigned to the task of making after-dinner conversation with an unwelcome guest. The footman left them. The silver teapot sent a fragrant vapor into the air.

"I read your papers. Tell me, were you educated at home or at a school?"

"I had a governess and later a tutor." That was one way to describe Tatty.

"Your former employers praise your remarkable scholarly achievements for one so young."

"I devoted hours and hours to study." Because Tatty refused to waste a moment of their jail time. Because prisoners become experts in counting and storytelling.

"And chose to leave your family. Did they have other expectations for one so young?"

"My parents and my brother were gone. I had to provide for myself." She looked down and found her hands clenched.

"No property remained?"

"Without a male heir it went elsewhere."

He stood to pour her a cup of tea with an awkward carefulness of attention to the business like a man remembering the steps in a dance. Watching his studied care with the teapot, Emma remembered his easy, careless wielding of the huge sword.

When he handed her the cup and resumed his seat, he seemed almost bored, looking at her out of heavy-lidded eyes. Emma balanced the delicate cup and saucer in her palm. She wanted to tell him something shocking, something to make him really see her. *You know how it is when a foreign army invades your nation and traitors sell you to save their skins or line their pockets.*

Golden clocks on the mantel suddenly tolled the quarter hour with sweet chimes, and Emma allowed herself an inward laugh. She should be glad he found her false story boring. He was not supposed to look too closely at her fictions.

He stirred himself enough to ask another question. "Tell me about your previous school. A foundling school, was it?"

"The Grimston School." As soon as she said it, she detected a change in his expression. He remained at ease, leaning back in his chair, but the gray eyes were no longer remote, but sharply alert.

"In Grimston?"

Grimston was wrong somehow, and she did not know how, nor could she change it now. She had to carry on with the story as it came to her. She was careful neither to confirm nor deny the name of the place. "Mr. and Mrs. Robert Merton ran the school until Robert became ill, and Mrs. Merton devoted herself to his care. Naturally, she had to close the school."

"What became of the students and the other teachers?"

"Mrs. Merton found situations for the older students. The younger ones went to orphanages."

"And the teachers?"

"It was a small school, just myself and two others. We parted. They, too, are seeking positions." Emma ventured to take a sip of the tea.

"How were the children treated at the Grimsby School for Foundlings?"

She almost choked. He coolly offered the altered name. So that had been the error. He waited for her to correct him. She swallowed her tea. She had mixed up the English name of the town. *Grimston. Grimsby.* The endings sounded equally English to her ear. She had no idea which was right. She had supposed all the names in her false papers to be inventions, but apparently only the Mertons were a fiction. Grimsby must be a real place, and one that he knew.

The trick was to keep going, to mix truth with the lies. It was like paying one's shot with promises. There would be a day of reckoning. She lowered her cup to the saucer. "Everyone had shoes and sufficient food and plenty of outdoor exercise and singing."

"Singing, Miss Portland?"

Emma smiled to herself. He thought he'd caught her in another falsehood, but not this time. "Do your boys sing?"

"They whistle. Do you recommend singing?"

"I do." She sat a little straighter to deliver him a truth. "You can't mope when you sing. When a lesson is hard and students are struggling, I find a song restores their spirits and makes them willing to try again."

"What songs did you teach your students?"

"They taught me their favorite tunes." She would not be trapped again naming names of English songs he might know.

"Did you study music yourself?"

"No." There was another truth. No pianofortes for girls in prison.

That seemed to silence him while the little clocks went on measuring the awkward moment with indifferent ticks and whirs, and Emma waited to see whether he would keep her for the trial period or not.

She had begun to think the clocks in the room had wound down when he spoke again.

"What time tomorrow do you wish to begin?"

"I think it's wise for boys to take some exercise before they are made to attend to lessons. Do they ride or fence? What? Why do you smile?"

"Did your foundlings fence, Miss Portland? There are no fencing masters in London streets. The boys box, and they do play at games."

She studied the lovely porcelain in her hands. She and Tatty had had tea sets to play with just as fine. Sipping tea from a delicate cup and sitting on a golden settee, she'd made another mistake, thinking of Leo's boyhood training, not the life of orphans and street urchins. Her education was full of gaps, an odd mixture of rules and tricks and truths picked up in palaces and prison. Nothing for it but to go boldly on. "I recommend an hour of games for boys each morning." She announced it as a philosophical principle of education.

He stood with an instant shift from languid ease to command. "Let me get you paper and a pen, and you can write a plan of the day for them. I'll see that everyone helps to keep the boys to your hours."

"Thank you."

Emma took the pen and paper he offered. When she had written out her plan, he led her by a stair up past the chapel entry to the room he'd chosen for her.

"The room suits you?" her polite host asked, once again distant, detached.

She nodded.

"I hope you'll find it convenient to be here below the schoolroom. Good night, Miss Portland."

Inside her room Emma leaned against the door. Her brain hurt from juggling truth and lies. She would just lean and rest for a moment before she summoned Ruth to help her undress.

In the corridor a neighboring door opened and a gruff voice spoke. She recognized it as belonging to the big man, Adam Digweed.

"Don't like ta leave ye alone, sir."

"I'm never alone, Adam."

"Who's to keep watch while I'm gone then?"

"The boys and I will look out for each other. Take these papers to Will. He'll investigate Miss Portland. If there's anything amiss in her credentials, Will can find it out."

"Yes, sir."

"Show him this bit in her handwriting. It doesn't match the original letter, and I'd like Will to see what he makes of the change in handwriting."

"Odd that she takes such a dislike to fish if she's lived in Grimsby, sir."

"No accounting for taste, Adam."

"That's as may be, sir, but Grimsby's famous for the fish."

Emma held her breath. Her hands curled until her nails dug into her palms. She strained to catch the end of the conversation over the rapid pounding of her heart. She had misjudged Daventry entirely. She had believed he had genuinely hired her, and that she was the deceitful one. She had trustingly put her hand to the paper he offered, but he didn't believe her in the least. She had had little time to study the documents Aubrey had created. The English names meant nothing to her, but after she had rejected the soup, Daventry instantly caught her error over the town.

He had been testing her. She would be investigated, exposed. She might not have much time. His servant could be in London in half a day. She unclenched her fists and made herself take a slow breath. Sending inquiries north about her fictitious school would take longer. She knew nothing of the English post or English roads or of how thorough Aubrey's planning had been. If only Tatty's message had reached the duchess before Aubrey had discovered Emma. If Emma knew that Tatty was safe, she could leave. She could put the walnut dye back in her hair and take to the road.

Until she knew Tatty was safe, her masquerade was needed. With it she bought time for Tatty to reach the rendezvous and board the ship for America and a new life for herself and Leo's son. The first spy was dead. When the news of it reached home, another would be sent. In the meantime, she was a fugitive from English justice. As long as their enemies searched for Emma, Tatty and the babe were safe.

The door next to hers closed. She heard the big man's footsteps in the corridor. A new thought hit her, striking in its clarity. Daventry had given her the room next to his. Once again her impression of him turned upside down. He was suspicious of her papers. He would send his own personal ogre to investigate her, but he was not indifferent to her person as he appeared in the golden drawing room. Tatty would say his choice of a room for Emma meant only one thing. Emma agreed. More bad luck.

Chapter Six

❦

"D AVENTRY'LL sack 'er if we don't heed her lessons."
"He won't sack 'er."
"Why not?"

The urgent voices stopped when Emma turned the knob on the schoolroom door. As quiet as she was, they heard the lock click. She needed more practice yet. When she entered, Lark's sullen gaze swept once over the others. There was no question that, away from Daventry, Lark was their leader.

The pyramid was gone, and the desks and chairs had been arranged in two rows. She motioned the boys to sit, and they slouched into their seats. Scrubbed faces and combed hair did not mean willingness to learn. Emma was pretty sure that all of them were not against her, but Lark was, and the younger ones would not defy him.

Lark's deep reddish brown hair framed a sullenly handsome face. He looked to be fifteen with a distrustful gaze that dared her to try to reach him. "Are you going to finish your story today?"

"You are when you've learned your letters." Emma stood straight and still and told herself that Lark's resistance was a good thing. It would keep her on her guard. She had felt too safe in the duchess's employ.

"You think you can snap your fingers and make us learn 'em in a fortnight?"

"You can learn to read what's on your slate."

"You mean we'll be like circus dogs, trained to jump on your command."

"Not at all. We'll see what you already know and add to your knowledge." She refused to lose her composure.

"But wot's the use of learning one word?" Jay asked.

"Depends on the word."

"Daventry knows hundreds of words. He reads a great many books, big ones." Robin was clearly loyal to his hero.

"Dull ones on the law," Lark mocked.

"But he's not dull." Finch's defense came from behind his hand.

"He's a prime gun in the ring, miss, handy with his fives," Swallow assured her.

"She doesn't know what you're talking about, Swallow."

"It's prizefighting, isn't it?"

"Yes, miss, and Daventry's teaching us, too, every week when his brothers come," Jay told her.

Rook held up his slate. "Why don't you just tell us our words?"

"Because you'll not gain independence that way."

"What if I do this?" Rook deliberately rubbed his jacket sleeve over the slate, wiping it clean.

Emma shrugged. "I can write it again, or you can write it yourself when you know it. Words are like that. Once you own them, you can spend them any time you like."

"Will reading make us rich like Daventry?" Raven asked.

"It will let you make your way in the world." She would make them no false promises.

"Will Daventry send us away when we can read?" Robin asked.

"Oh no. I'm sure he means you to have a home with him as long as you want it." She looked into seven unconvinced faces with sharp chins and doubting eyes. What did her assurance mean? They knew the world to be a precarious place.

Lark summed up the judgment of the group. "You don't know anything useful, do you?"

"Nevertheless, Daventry has made me your grinder for now."

"For now, Miss Portland. Grind away." He neatly reminded her that it was a trial period. Daventry's man was off starting an investigation of her false credentials and his urchins were testing her. At night she was well guarded. By day she would be confined to this bare room with Daventry's wards. She could hardly plan her escape if she didn't know the house, its inhabitants, and its patterns. She looked at the wary faces turned her way, and a strategy came to her. She would use her lessons to search the house.

"Stand up," she ordered them.

She began with Robin. "How many arms do you have?"
"Two."

"Finch, how many legs do you have?"
"Two," he answered through his fingers.

Emma turned to Swallow. "How many legs do Finch and Robin have together?"

She avoided Lark, and in a few minutes she had the younger boys counting and adding and multiplying—arms and legs, eyes, ears, and noses, hearts and tongues, heads and feet. Doing mathematics. Until a breathless Robin finally complained that they were running out of things to count.

Emma resisted the temptation to smile. She had them sit down.

"What's next?" asked Raven.

"Next, we measure," Emma declared.

They measured each other with fingers, hands, and arms, and the schoolroom, using their bodies. The room was ten Robins long by four Swallows wide. When she had trained them in counting and measuring, she gave them each a slate and a pencil and had them lead her through the hall. Each new room had objects to count and measure and record while Emma made a note of where they met footmen on duty and where each staircase led.

In the south wing, they had to show her Daventry's library. Plainly they expected him to be there. They gathered at the open door looking in, and Emma knew that she was truly spying, trespassing in a space that was his. The shelves had been raided, leaving books tilting against one another across the gaps. Open books covered the carpet like flagstones. The number of volumes, stacked one on top of the other, suggested an insatiable, curious mind at work. They crowded every surface so that there was no place for a companion to sit or stand. Daventry obviously worked alone.

A passing footman stopped to tell them Daventry was in the hall with a visitor from London.

Jay shrugged. "Dav might be a great reader, but it looks like a dull lot of words to me. No pictures."

"Anyway, miss," Finch assured her, "he's great with his fives."

"Where does he box?"

"Oh, we've a ring out back, miss," Raven told her. "His brothers come once a week."

Swallow chimed in with more praise for Daventry. "Soon, he's to have a real match, and Lark says we can bet on him, and because he's an unknown, we'll clean up."

Lark gave Swallow a withering stare for that comment, and Emma urged them on to another room.

By the end of the morning she knew where the sleeping quarters were for the boys and the servants. She had seen most of the vast house, with its countless doors and windows, and knew her employer's haunts. The boys hurried her along from wonder to wonder until they came to a door on the upper floor of the south wing.

Swallow reached to open the door, when Lark stopped him.

"We've got to show her the roof. That's the best part of the house." Swallow defended his position.

"You boys go out on the roof? You could fall."

They laughed at her. "We'd never fall, miss. We've walked 'undreds of roofs in town."

Lark turned away. "The roof is not for her."

Swallow looked at the others. They hung their heads. They had enjoyed showing her their world. Robin had taken her hand and she'd allowed it, but now he dropped her hold. She said nothing.

"We could vote." Swallow offered.

Lark shook his head. "The roof is for us and Daventry. No one else." His flat tone settled the matter.

Emma stepped forward then. "Good work this morning, boys. Afternoon lessons at one."

* * *

D AV spent the morning after he'd hired his new grinder
with Henry Norwood, his family's solicitor, the man
who had led the court case against Wenlocke.

Norwood brought Dav a full report on his grandfather,
the Duke of Wenlocke. For seven years the duke had been
trying to destroy him and injure his mother and brothers
and their families. Dav had wanted to know the whole of it.
Will and Nate Wilde, the young man Will had rescued
from thievery, had done the investigative work in town
among the low hirelings the duke had employed over the
years, and Norwood had followed the duke's legal attacks
through the courts.

Norwood assured Dav that other copies of the report
existed in safe places to be read should any accident befall
Dav himself or any member of his family.

A few gaps remained in the picture, but Dav thought he
now mostly understood his grandfather's long campaign to
destroy him. It had begun with a man named Archibald
March. Once considered a great philanthropist, March had
in fact been a notorious blackmailer. March had controlled
the banker Samuel Evershot and through him gained access
to the private financial and personal dealings of hundreds
of the bank's clients.When March uncovered the truth of
the secret marriage between Wenlocke's son and a courtesan, he recognized the power he held over the Duke of
Wenlocke.

Dav had tried many times to imagine the conversation
in which March informed Wenlocke that a boy named Kit
Jones, youngest son of an infamous courtesan, was actually Wenlocke's legitimate grandson and heir. He imagined
his grandfather in his London club first annoyed at March

as an inferior who presumed to disturb his peace, then shaken by this threat to his power from a despised source. Whatever the actual circumstances of that conversation it had led to March's arranging the kidnapping of a thirteen-year-old boy.

The hired brute who kidnapped Kit Jones had been an out-of-work plasterer named Timothy Harris. At least once, Dav knew from acute and painful memory, March and Harris had met. The words of that conversation were fixed in his mind. *The boy disappears—you understand, Harris? Aye, Mr. March.*

Dav did not know what March had intended, but in Harris March had chosen an imperfect tool. Harris had not killed Dav but had made him his prisoner in the darkest heart of London, chained to one bed after another for two years. In the last room they came to on Bread Street, an old woman, Mother Greenslade, had been Dav's savior and his tormentor, bringing him cake that made his stomach ache but that sometimes was his only food for days.

When Harris died unexpectedly, Dav had escaped. Mother Greenslade had unlocked his bonds before the death cart arrived, and he had gone up to the roof of the building and found a new world on London's rooftops. There he had begun a new life.

Once he learned to manage on his own, he started collecting other abandoned boys. He taught them his pathways across that airy terrain, and the tricks of navigation from roof to roof across the sooty old city. Soon he had a band capable of gathering everything that dropped from passing wagons or washed up on the banks of the Thames.

In time his old home beckoned, but when he went to look at it, he saw only his brother Xander in an empty house blazing with light. His strongest feeling had been that he no longer belonged there. The family he had known was gone. The boy he had been did not exist. He could not recall that boy.

Still the house drew him when night came, and he had settled his gang in some corner of London. Then one evening a young woman leaning on her balcony above the garden changed everything. He did not know what to make of her until he learned she was Xander's bride and she was in danger.

While his band held aloof, most of the denizens of London's darker neighborhoods allied themselves with one or more of its criminal factions. Boy thieves knew their fences and brought their hard-earned coins back to one high mobsman or another. One of those thieves, a boy named Nate Wilde, was spying on Xander's bride and following her about. Wilde lived in the Reverend Bredsell's school for boys at the top of Bread Street. Dav had known from the first that the place did not train boys for honest positions in the world.

So he'd kept an eye on his new sister-in-law. If he could not bring himself to go home, he could at least help his brother Xander to be happy. He and his band had been watching the day a pair of hired fists dragged Xander's wife, Cleo Jones, into a carriage with March and drove to Bread Street, where they locked her in a cellar to face certain death from an accident arranged by March.

Helping to save Cleo Jones was the first thing Dav had done in years that made him feel any connection to his family. But he was not Kit Jones any longer, and his family of boys needed him more than his first family. So he had stayed in his world that night. It had taken his brother Will's reckless courage to bring him back. Will, who always took the fight right to his enemies, had discovered the secrets of March's brothel and had walked into Bredsell's school, where Dav and Robin and Will's love, Helen, were trapped and held. When Will took a bullet from March, Dav had acted—killing the man who had arranged his nightmare.

But stopping March had not stopped Wenlocke. Stopping Wenlocke was the unfinished business of Dav's life, and Norwood's report would help him find the way to do it.

A T one the boys were in their places, but their fidgety unsettled air alerted Emma that the good feeling of the morning was forgotten. A trick was coming. A trick on her, she supposed. She touched the pin in her pocket for luck.

They'd rearranged themselves, and she made note of the switch. She could distinguish Jay and Raven from one another now, by Jay's tendency to speak first, and Raven's habit of running his sleeve under his nose. She made a slow circuit of the room, stopping at each boy's desk to point to a letter on his slate and sound it out. As she moved, she became aware of a small regular noise coming from Robin's desk, a creak, like a squeaky hinge opening. Robin leaned forward, his arms around his slate, concealing the source of the noise. Finch hid a grin behind his hand, and Raven gave Jay a hard nudge.

When she stopped at Robin's desk, he lifted his head and released his hands, and a small brown creature sprang up from his slate and collided with Emma's chest. She started and held out her hands to break its fall. A toad dropped into her upturned hands. It pushed away from her palms with cold, dry feet and landed on the floor. The boys were up, laughing and shouting, to follow its lurching walk across the room. When it met the wall, it turned and faced the ring of boys, a small, frightened thing breathing rapidly.

Emma whistled once, and they fell silent and turned to her.

"You can whistle." Swallow was impressed.

She stepped into the circle. "You're frightening it."

"What is it?" asked Finch.

"It's Robin's baby *dragon*." Lark condemned the little creature to absurdity with sarcasm.

"Robin, you nodcock, dragons aren't real." Jay gave Robin's shoulder a shove.

Robin looked at Emma, his eyes big and pleading. He wanted the homely creature to be something wonderful and magical, and his mates wanted to remind him that the world was an ordinary place and that what you thought miraculous was common and ugly.

"Where did you find him, Robin?" Emma kept her tone light and disinterested, but she knelt down to look at the little creature more closely. He was brown and speckled and as lumpy and ugly as his fellows had always been, but he was a living thing. Robin squatted beside her.

"He was hopping about the long gallery after lunch. I think he was looking for a new cave. I'm going to make him a cave in my room."

Jay laughed. "Dragons can't live in a house, Robin."

"Where would a cave be around here?" Robin asked.

"This dragon will like a cave by the river, I suspect. Can you scoop him up gently, Robin?" Emma rose and turned to the others. "Afternoon lessons at the river, meet me at the bottom of the north stairs in ten minutes."

No one moved.

"Have you got old clothes and boots?" There were nods all round. "Go."

Still no one moved.

"We don't swim," Finch said his fingers pressed to his lips as usual.

Emma did not let herself smile. "Well, we won't go in the river, just to the riverbank to find a home for Robin's friend."

Lark snorted.

Robin had the toad cupped in his hands and offered it to Emma. "Can you hold 'im for me, Miss Portland?"

"Of course."

They dashed off, and she was left with the toad and Lark.

Lark's frown darkened his expression. "What kind of grinder are you? You going to let him think dragons are real?"

"What kind of friend are you to kill his pleasure in a living thing?"

Lark knocked his chest with his fist. "I'm his best friend. Dragons aren't real, but it's a blinking real world we 'ave to live in, our sort. Not this place." He flung his arms out to indicate all of Daventry Hall. "This place. Yer reading lessons. They're not for us."

Emma held the toad, its frantic pulse racing. She thought Lark oddly named for a boy afraid that the simplest joy might be snatched from him any minute.

"The world you speak of may have few delights. It may be hard on boys, but if today Robin has a toad and a river to delight in, I ask you to let him have his delight."

"*De-light*. Now there's a word that our kind of boy don't hear in London. Is that one of the words on your slates, grinder?"

* * *

D AV parted from Henry Norwood at three. He needed the roof. He had been patient with hours of legal talk while thoughts of his new grinder intruded. He would read Norwood's full report in the days ahead, looking for the places in it that would show him how to beat his grandfather. He headed up the north stairs and met Emma Portland coming down them. She had something cupped in her gloved hands that claimed her whole attention so he had a moment to look at her without her notice.

An old black bonnet covered her bright hair, but when she looked up, blue was what he saw. He tried to recall what had made him so suspicious of her the night before.

"What have you got? You're like to break your neck if you don't mind the steps and your cloak."

"Oh, it's you."

He blocked her way. "No one else. What's in your hands?

"Robin's baby dragon. Do you want to see it?"

He raised a brow. She lifted her cupped hands and it felt like an invitation, so he fitted his hands around hers. As soon as he touched her, he knew he had been wanting to touch her since yesterday. She tilted her upper hand slightly so that he could see the creature huddled inside.

It was a toad, a common toad, brown and speckled, knobby and squat. Its amber, jewellike eyes stared unblinking. She held it as gently as possible, but the frightened creature's pulse quickened. Dav felt the rapid beat of his own pulse, glad for the concealing linen around his throat.

"Looks like a toad to me."

She closed her hands and looked up at him, the blue dazzling. She gave a slow reproachful shake of her head as if he were a thickheaded student.

"What? Are you an admirer of toads?" He hardly knew what he was saying with her hands still cupped in his.

"He's quite handsome if you think of him as a dragon."

"But homely if you're in the toad faction."

She withdrew her hands from his. "Well, I'm in the dragon faction, and we're going to find this fellow a proper home on the riverbank."

He looked at her again. He'd just shared a light moment with her, and he'd thought the only brightness in her spirit was in that hair.

"Don't fall in." He stepped aside, and she passed him, but it was another minute before he remembered whether he had been going down or up.

F ROM the roof he could see the faded rose of her cloak against the browns and faint greens at the edge of the river. The green surprised him. He'd arrived at Daventry Hall in late November and come to expect a perpetual winter landscape, like the rooftops of London. He liked a muted landscape, another reason to prefer the roof of the hall to its luxurious rooms with their brocaded walls in rich colors. In London he could read colors from leaden and ashy grays to umbers and deep coffee browns to rusts and coppers, and know the heat and texture of a rooftop. Here in the country, where he could not roam freely from rooftop to rooftop, he had learned to drive. The bare fields bounded by ditches and leafless hedgerows had at first been blank slates of earth, but now he was learning to pick out the marks of a harrow or a plow and identify the bits of stubble clinging to the clods.

Below him at the river's edge the boys chased after one another and sent birds flapping into the air. His gaze followed the red cloak and black bonnet, and he felt the scene sink to dullness when they disappeared below the bank. He was surprised at the difference that bit of red made in the empty rolling landscape.

He regretted that he would not dine with the boys and their tutor but with his estate manager and the local vicar, who wanted to consult him on a matter of tithes.

Chapter Seven

❧

O N her third afternoon at Daventry Hall Emma set off for the town. On the way she tied a thread to those places in hedges and trees where she might later conceal the items needed for her escape. Adam Digweed had not returned to the hall, and each night Emma fell asleep waiting for the man in the room next to hers to succumb. She could not match him in wakefulness and doubted that he actually slept. He walked the roof. He read insatiably. He didn't sleep. She knew little more about him than she had learned that first day. What she did know—that he cared for a ragtag band of boys—was not something to tell his enemies. She formulated her report to Aubrey's man as she walked.

The village of Somerton sat on a rise above the same river that flowed past the hall. Wood-timbered buildings with overhanging upper floors lined Bridge Street on one side of the green. Rows of plastered cottages extended

down the side streets, and a tall old church with a spire sat
back in a large churchyard opposite a brick town hall. The
Bell, where she was to meet Aubrey's man, was a white-
washed building with a prominent bow window and a busy
yard. A redbrick malting house stood on one side and the
town shop on the other.

Josiah Wallop leaned back from a pigeon and beefsteak
pie in one of the inn's private dining rooms when Emma
arrived. His imposing girth stretched the closure of a purple silk waistcoat below a brown-stained napkin tied about
his neck. His doughy face had a broad genial expanse like
the face of a prosperous farmer with ruddy cheeks, abun-
dant black side whiskers, and multiple chins nesting in his
linen, but his eyes were sharp and sly and the tufts of his
brows rose like wicked tongues of black flame. No other
man in Somerton wore purple silk.

Wallop looked her over.

Emma did not know any English farmers, but she knew
jailers. You could tell a good guard from a bad guard by
the way each handled the fish soup. It was always fish soup.
The good guards were the indifferent ones, the ones bored
by the long stretch of hours in the Castello di Malgrate.
They were cardplayers who would place bets on the liveliness of the fleas. They shoved the soup forward into the
cell and went back to their next wager.

The scrupulous guards with neat uniforms and trim
moustaches were not half bad, either. They played by the
rules, were punctual to the minute in their routines and pre-
dictable in all their movements, even to the glance of their
unseeing eyes. They set the soup down warm or cold in the
same spot every evening. New guards, green ones who did
not know yet what power was theirs, were the best of the lot.
They sometimes brought a bowl filled to the brim.

Bad guards were a different lot. They expected a little bite, a bribe for bringing the soup into the cell. A prisoner with nothing to offer could watch his soup sit on the cold stones until yellow islands of congealed grease floated in the broth. The worst guards were the dictators, the pashas of the prison, who let girls know what would happen to them if they didn't obey orders. They spit in the soup.

In Emma's judgment, Josiah Wallop combined all the worst guards in his large person. He would insist on his little bite and then spit in your soup. He pretended to check on Emma as a chance acquaintance he'd helped along the way. The waiter left, closing the door behind him with a firm tug, that popped a cupboard door open a crack behind Wallop. It gave Emma a bad feeling to see that thin black crack as if the cupboard watched her, too.

"So you got the position, eh?"

Emma nodded.

"Good thing for you. Now if yer smart, missy, ye'll know whose side yer on, and ye'll end up plump in the pocket with His Lordship Aubrey and the whore's get, both paying you."

Wallop applied his fork and knife to the pie and lifted a large bite to his mouth. A drop of glistening gravy hit his waistcoat below the napkin and settled in one of its folds. He chewed with slow ponderous working of his large jaw and patted his mouth with dainty taps of the napkin. His shrewd eyes never left Emma's face.

"It's best we come to an understanding, miss. Josiah Wallop is a businessman. His business is dealing with inconveniences. Your highborn gent knows no more than a baby how to deal with inconveniences. So he turns to Wallop." Wallop shook his head. "These are inconvenient times, they are, so business prospers. Wallop puts a half crown in the plate at St. Margaret's every week. Now, girl, you don't want to become an inconvenience, do you?"

Emma shook her head. She kept her face as blank as a wall.

Wallop nodded. "Good lass. Now let's see wot you have for me." Wallop heaved himself out of his chair and unrolled a small scroll of the house plan on the table next to his pot of ale. "Wot can you tell me about where he keeps to and what he does?"

Emma's plan was simple, a mix of truth and lies that would leave Wallop trying to sort the wheat from the chaff.

"He sleeps on the second floor in the north wing." Emma put her finger on the place, and Wallop made a note. "He has a large servant, Adam Digweed, who looks out for him. The household staff includes the butler, who serves as Daventry's valet, four footmen, a housekeeper, five maids, two laundresses, a cook, and three scullery maids. Out of doors there are a groundskeeper, four under-gardeners, a head groom, and two stable boys. When the estate manager comes, he and Daventry drive about the estate with an armed companion. He dines with the boys in the dining room in the southwest corner, ground floor." Again she put her finger on the spot.

"Digweed, eh? A big man, you say?"

"His hands are bigger than my head. His shoulders would touch both jambs of the door, and he'd have to bend down to enter." She did not mention that he was away in London investigating the new tutor.

"The big fellow must sleep sometime. Find out where Digweed's quarters are and when he's not with his master. An accident waiting to happen is wot that whelp is. You know, a blowup, a tumble, a smash."

Emma kept her face still. Let nothing show. Wallop

must think her indifferent to her employer. After a minute, he seemed satisfied, and rolled up the map.

He settled himself in front of his plate and speared a dripping bite of fowl. "What can you tell me about his dogs?"

"Nothing." She hadn't seen any dogs.

"Josie Wallop doesn't like *nothing*, missy. Josie Wallop doesn't take *nothing* for an answer."

"I didn't know I was to spy on the dogs. There are no dogs in the house."

"Well, there are dogs somewhere. So you'd best find 'em. Start with the stables. Find out who feeds 'em and when and how much."

"My place is in the schoolroom with the boys."

"Your place is where I say it is. You'd best get out of that schoolroom when you can. You're the inside man on this job, d'ye see? Josie Wallop is the outside man, the best in the business." He tapped his head. "Up 'ere I've got everything stored about that whelp. I've been watching 'im since 'e were just that whore's fry. I know everything that passes in or out of that house. I know who that maid of yers flirts with in the village. But yer the inside man."

A fit of coughing stopped him, and he took a long pull at his ale pot. "The whelp received a package yesterday delivered by his London visitor. Yer ta go over the house when he's abed and find it. Ye do see 'im at supper, don't ye?"

Emma nodded.

"Well, make sure he sees you, missy." Wallop's eyes narrowed. "And don't go wearing that old rag." He shook his finger at her. "You look like you came straight from the workhouse in that frock. Yer ta wear wot's in that trunk, mind. Has he seen your dairies yet?"

He made himself understood with a leer. Emma shook her head.

"Well, you weren't picked for yer wit, girl. Make sure that he sees 'em. Yer ta get close enough to hand him his bath towel. If you don't, you'll be wearing a hemp necklace."

E MMA picked a seafoam silk gown for supper that had Ruth shaking her head and searching for pins to secure its low bodice.

"Ruth, do the hall people go to the village often?"

"Most of the tradesmen come here, miss."

"I'm sure, but do you or other servants go into the village?"

"On Sundays mostly, miss. Everyone in the big house has family in the village. My aunts is there, and most of us know someone who works in a malting house, malting being the main trade hereabouts."

"Do you have a young man in the village?" Emma watched Ruth in the mirror.

The girl flushed. "Now, miss, a girl like me?"

"I suppose Mrs. Wardlow and Mrs. Creevey know all the tradespeople."

"Of course, miss. How would they get honest service?"

"Are there never strangers about?"

"Only passing through, miss, on their way to Newmarket for the races mostly. Even some fools that ought to know better just can't stay away when there's wagers to be made." Ruth frowned and jabbed a pin in Emma's curls, and Emma thought her maid might have a sweetheart after all, someone to whom she would talk as artlessly and openly as she talked to Emma. If Wallop knew how to ply Ruth's beau, he would have a way of obtaining information about Daventry. He would know if Emma wore the fine silk dresses in her trunk.

"Ruth, do you know anywhere where might I shop, for small things, you know, shoes and shirts?"

"Oh, you'll want to go to Symonds' Emporium on Witt Street."

Nearly twelve feet of linen-draped mahogany, four sets of glowing candelabra, a half dozen serving dishes, and seven active boys separated Emma from Daventry, but she felt his scrutiny nevertheless.

Her *dairies* as Wallop had called them were on display, or at least as much of them as she and Ruth could not contrive to cover. Emma's gown had a bodice of two halves that crossed in a deep vee. Ruth had contrived to pin the halves together, but the tops of Emma's breasts rose in curved white slivers above the narrow bodice.

Wallop's comment made her understand Aubrey's intentions more clearly. He had chosen her to be a lure, a bright thing flashing in the stream to catch Daventry's notice. Aubrey could not guess that she had no experience attracting men. She had not met any men to attract. Tatty simply made it a rule of their prison life to discourage their guards from thinking about them as women. If Emma so much as smiled at one of the new guards, Tatty would scold. *You don't want them looking. If they start looking, they want to touch. If they touch, they want to take. That new one may have a pretty face, but he's just as mean as Fausto.*

The mention of Fausto worked every time. When Fausto was on duty, they went hungry rather than touch the soup. Fausto was the only man who'd ever kissed Emma. She had endured his kisses for an interminable week in order to escape. Fausto's kiss was like taking a dying fish in one's mouth. When Fausto pulled her face to the bars, she already tasted fish and felt her stomach churn. Daventry's gray gaze had quite a different effect on her stomach. Maybe it was the silk dress that made her feel a glad leap of welcome when Daventry's eyes turned her way. Tonight there was the silk dress and no Fausto. Emma's stays seemed less a confinement than a necessary frame to keep her limbs from melting into the liquid flow of the gown.

A footman placed the soup in front of her. Mrs. Wardlow had changed her menu. The soup was a delicious potato and leek. Emma wished she could concentrate on it instead of on her employer, but her breasts felt his glance. They tightened and seemed to swell against her corset, and they sent out strange flashes of sensation to the rest of her body. The thought brought a memory up from the depths.

One of the great finds of their prison life had been a piece of broken mirror scooped up from the path on their way home from chapel one day. She and Tatty had used it to signal Leo across the fortress courtyard on their way to and from chapel. With that mirror they had arranged meetings in the confessionals. The guards never took the sacrament. An old priest had married Tatty and Leo as they knelt on either side of him and spoke through the grate.

Footmen cleared the first course. Emma did not know what the conversation had been. She felt Daventry's cool, aloof look as if it were a hot ray of sunlight that seemed to glance off her breasts and shoot heat deep inside her.

Daventry could look at her, and her stomach seemed to drop away. Femaleness, which had been hiding inside her, a shadow creature, wanted to come out in his presence and stretch and move and show itself in the light.

That was a bad idea. She didn't need one of Tatty's sayings to know it. A mouse didn't need to be told that the hawk was not his friend.

He stopped her at the end of the meal, as the boys hurried off to their hour of games.

"Miss Portland, do you think you can handle them at supper as well as during the day?"

"Handle them?"

"Instruct them in civilized behavior at a meal."

"Of course."

"Good. I have other engagements, so I'll leave you to it then. You'll dine with them from now on."

She nodded. He had his charges and his estate on his mind, not his wards' tutor and her dairies.

Chapter Eight

✤

FIFTY years into her marriage, nothing could daunt Charlotte, Duchess of Wenlocke, certainly not one of the duke's imperious footmen on guard outside her husband's library on a frosty morning. She waved the man away with a flick of her wrist and entered.

Her husband looked up from his chair, a snarl forming on his stern lips. Charlotte merely raised a brow, conscious of an unexpected stab of dismay. Her husband, who had sought all his life to dominate his fellow men rather than conciliate them, sat at his fire, a woolen carriage rug over his knees, his gold-headed black cane at his side, dwarfed by the baroque splendor of his own library.

As she strode toward him she could see that he read no book, no papers. He was brooding. Charlotte had no use for brooding, a self-consuming act. She picked up a copy of the *Morning Chronicle* from his table and dropped it in his lap.

"Go away, wife."

"I've returned safely, you see, so no need for any concern on your part." Charlotte could properly claim to be the only living person who had ever heard Wenlocke laugh. Twenty years had passed since he could laugh.

"I was aware of your return." He brushed the newspaper to the floor.

"Our daughter is well. Our granddaughter Sarah has recovered from the measles." For a time there had been a genuine camaraderie between them when Anne and Granville were children. Wenlocke Castle, for all its cavernous rooms suitable for bivouacking the local militia, its seventeen staircases, its endless frigid passages, had been a home.

"I rejoice in the news." His familiar icy voice lacked spirit.

Charlotte stirred the fire. Age had been kinder to her than youth. At thirteen she had reached her full height just shy of six feet. The fashions of the time on a woman of her stature had given her the appearance throughout her adolescence of a circus figure lurching about on stilts. At seventy, she could use her height to her advantage in her lifelong struggle with her husband.

She came to stand over him, feeling the unreachableness of his isolation, and chose as her weapon the arrows of outrage rather than strokes of kindness. She launched the question on her mind. "What have you done with my Emma?"

He did not pretend to misunderstand her. Annoyance flickered in his gaze as he looked up, momentarily provoked out of his inner retreat. "The little murderess?"

"Nothing of the sort. Emma is the granddaughter of a dear friend of mine." Charlotte chose her next words carefully. She had promised to keep Emma's secret after all. "She's an impecunious gentlewoman of good birth and unfortunate circumstances."

"Not according to the request for her pardon, which you wished me to sign."

"A small matter for a man of your influence."

"You think the law should bend to suit you?"

"We agreed never to meddle in each other's spheres. Emma Portland was under *my* protection. That alone should have guaranteed your signature on the document."

He stared at the fire, his harsh profile frozen. Years earlier Charlotte's mother, assessing Charlotte's dismal prospects on the marriage mart, had simply removed her daughter from London. She had sent Charlotte abroad in the company of her childhood friend Louisa, whose parents had married her to the prince of a minor duchy in the north of Italy. Charlotte had loved Italy, felt herself very much of use to her friend, and returned to England if no shorter, at least very handsome, with a poise and self-mastery equal to the social demands of a London season.

To her great good fortune changing fashions favored her tall, spare figure, and the surprise of her reappearance in society had been enough to draw the attentions of the haughty Duke of Wenlocke, whose height gave Charlotte the agreeable sensation for the first time in her life of being petite and feminine. If he was not as warm in nature as Charlotte would have liked a husband to be, he was as rich and titled as her parents liked.

Now she towered over her husband, huddled in his chair, his power to pass Wenlocke on to his self-appointed heir usurped by the courts. Charlotte was not deceived by his manner. Forgiveness was not in her husband's nature.

"Your murderess has a favor to do for me if she is to earn that pardon."

The words knocked the confidence right out of her. She thought she understood his anger at the woman who had stolen their son, but Wenlocke's enmity had taken a darker turn when he attacked an innocent. A wounded dragon was the most dangerous sort. "Where is she?"

"She is in Aubrey's care. He has a man looking out for her. She won't escape, and if—"

"—Escape? What have you done with her?"

He waved a dismissive hand. "The law has a claim on her, and it shall have her if she crosses me."

"You did not turn her over to the magistrates?"

"I will if she fails me."

Charlotte's mind raced. Word had not yet come from Tatty. If the law got hold of Emma, she would not save herself, and the verdict would go against her. To think of Emma imprisoned again, in danger, sent a surge of anger through Charlotte, propelling her into motion. She spun and strode to her husband's grand desk.

She tore through his papers, scattering them like fallen leaves under her onslaught.

With a roar Wenlocke threw off the carriage rug over his knees and hoisted himself upright, swaying briefly, then seized his cane and leaned heavily upon it. "Madam, you overreach yourself."

"And you overestimate yourself, old man. I have not interfered for four years as you persecuted that boy and his family." Charlotte yanked open drawers and upended files. "This girl, this poor child, has nothing to do with your war on our grandson. I'll not let you destroy her, too. It is a wrong I cannot allow."

Wenlocke reached the desk and grabbed its edge with a gnarled hand, getting his balance. "Wife," he snarled.

Charlotte went on turning over papers, heedless of his presence.

He slammed his cane down. It struck beside Charlotte's

hand, trapping the fluttering papers. "That whore's get has no right to Wenlocke."

Charlotte took a steadying breath. Her hand looked old and shrunken but steady next to the black cane. The diamond her husband had given her on their wedding day was loose on her long lean finger, and the large square-cut center stone had slipped from its upright position, but it still sparkled with cold brilliance. She straightened to her full height and lifted her hand from the desk. She had found the pardon request and held it up triumphantly. "I will find Emma and free her."

She stepped around the desk. From the door she looked back. "Beware of the law, Wenlocke. The law says that boy is my grandson, all that I have left of Granville. I will see him for myself."

"I will destroy him, wife. Make no mistake. Courts, lawyers, they can't take what is mine. Mine—"

Charlotte closed the library door, cutting off his last angry syllable.

Rage carried her to her own distant suite of apartments in the opposite wing of the castle. Then it left her shaken and empty. She sank into her desk chair and let the past have its way with her.

It lay in wait for her these days. In London her daughter had shared with her the papers' accounts of the court case concerning Wenlocke's purported heir. Those troubling accounts rather than her granddaughter's illness had kept her in London. The young man himself remained a mystery.

Such a zest for life her own sweet boy Granville had had. Such treasures he'd brought her from the estate. Even when he'd become a young man on his own in town, he'd written letters to amuse and delight her. She had early understood that he was not going to be cold like Wenlocke. He had such a ready laugh.

When he had fallen scandalously in love with the most notorious courtesan in London, Charlotte knew that he was seeking warmth. Recalling her own mother's wisdom, Charlotte tried to offer a little distraction to turn the boy away from Sophie Rhys-Jones. She reasoned that a young man bursting with energy under the control of a father who gave him nothing to do needed a chance to exercise his powers in the world.

Charlotte insisted they settle upon him one of Wenlocke's lesser properties, Daventry Hall. But while her son had immediately taken charge of the hall, it had not lessened his attachment to that woman. Only when he purchased a commission and sailed for India in the spring of 1803 did the affair end. Relieved, Charlotte had set herself to wait for Granville's eventual return.

Shortly before Christmas in the midst of a killing frost the news reached them that Granville had perished in September at a place called Assaye. A more permanent frost settled on Wenlocke. Haughty and cold as her husband had always been, he then became unreachable.

When the formal rites of mourning had passed, Wenlocke became a house divided. Charlotte thought to visit her friends in Italy for a change of scene and a respite from her husband's austere way of grieving, so unlike her own, but French armies were on the march everywhere, and after one troubling letter, there was no further word from her friend Louisa while the newspapers were filled with the worst accounts of the French in Italy.

So Charlotte remained in England as Napoleon consumed the continent, and Arthur Wellesley, the man under

whom her son had died in India returned to lead the fight
against Bonaparte.

Wenlocke's coldness became legendary. In time Aubrey,
her sister-in-law's strapping son, found some favor from his
grandfather, and Wenlocke was again busy in his world.
Charlotte left her husband alone. Briefly, with the birth of
their daughter Anne's child, Charlotte had hoped for a thaw
in Wenlocke's perpetual wintry aspect, but a girl grand-
child had had no power to move him.

So Charlotte's life remained centered around her position as duchess, caring for the people of Wenlocke. She
saw to the running of two schools, one for the children of
tenants and another for the offspring of her large household
staff and her groundsmen. She maintained correspondence
with a great number of artists and naturalists and supported their work. And she took a direct hand in the naming of vicars to all the livings in her husband's gift.

The startling news three years past that Sophie Rhys-
Jones claimed to have married Granville and borne him a
son had caused Charlotte to weep and collapse as she had
not allowed herself to do at any time in the early years of
her grief. For a fortnight grief and giddy exhilaration had
warred in her, and she had wisely kept to her rooms until
she could behave again with the dignity of a duchess.

Her husband insisted that such a marriage could never
have taken place and that the young man produced by the
Jones family was an imposter with no connection to the
ancient line of Granvilles of Wenlocke. Charlotte's knowledge of her husband suggested otherwise. He continued to
blame Sophie Rhys-Jones for robbing him of Granville. He
could not forgive her for having a living son, and all his
bitter anger had no other object but this youth.

Charlotte had not seen the young man. His family kept

him closely guarded. An appalling story circulated in the press and in the print shops that her husband had arranged for the boy's abduction and captivity. In November after three years and great expenditure, the boy had won. The court had proclaimed him Marquess of Daventry.

The news of it had stiffened the gait and hardened the visage of the duke still further. Charlotte did not know how she felt about the court's ruling. The possibility that she had a living grandson, that a bit of her own dear boy had survived, caused her moments of intense agitation, hope, and caution in a terrible struggle. She wanted to see this youth, to judge for herself whether he had anything of his father in him. That was not to be for the moment.

Her concern at the moment had to be finding Louisa's granddaughter. Charlotte schooled herself to patience yet again. Louisa's granddaughter was an extraordinary gift, something from the storm of the past washed up on Charlotte's shore that she did not mean to lose.

She smoothed the pardon request in her grip. She would take it to the king herself. He might hide at Windsor from his subjects as much as he liked, but he would see the Duchess of Wenlocke.

Her husband could not stop her. For all his power in the world he could not match her power at Wenlocke where every person from the lowliest scullery maid to the exalted eminence of her butler was deeply loyal to her. Charlotte would discover what Wenlocke and Aubrey had done with Emma Portland.

Chapter Nine

༄

A T two on another long afternoon of the boys' resistance, as Emma leaned over to help Robin form the letter *A*, all the slates hit the floor with a bang. Emma jumped, and the boys leapt from their seats and charged from the room. The door banged behind them, and their voices and footsteps echoed down the stairwell, a fading din that told her they were past recalling.

She straightened and looked around the deserted schoolroom. Slates lay on the floor. Chairs, three overturned, faced every direction, like wreckage washed up on a shore. For two days her lessons had gone well. The younger boys might not admit to learning, but she had seen them mouthing words and making letters with their fingers on their slates.

She crossed to the window and saw them burst from the north door, running in a wide broken line down the slope toward the nearest wood. They were not much like the students she had been coming to love in the duchess's school.

Their rude liveliness made for constant banter and restless movement that erupted in sudden brawls. Lark made the most difficulty. Today he had organized a pattern of slate dropping. The startling smack of slates hitting the floor had punctuated her morning math lesson, breaking the concentration whenever the boys seemed on the verge of understanding.

Tatty would call them blockheads, but Emma could not. She was beginning to understand their resistance. They feared that Daventry would send them away as soon as they could read and compute.

She leaned her forehead against the cold glass. She should not care. She should not feel the abandoned schoolroom like a wound. She was not a true tutor but a spy. Teaching might have been her work, an odd thing to think, if she had stayed with the duchess, but that brief life had ended when Aubrey connected her with the murder in Reading.

The duchess had put a Latin saying over the schoolroom door at Wenlocke. *Incipit Vita Nova—Here Begins New Life.* Emma had taken the saying to heart. She had certainly needed a new life that day. Her old one was gone forever. And those students, the duchess's people, seemed to know the secret of how to be happy. Emma had thought she might learn it from them.

A new life was a good thing, becoming someone else, going beyond where you began, but it struck Emma that some students even in the duchess's school found seeking a new life an act of disloyalty.

The thought brought her back to Daventry's wards. Their unwillingness to learn was an unwillingness to let go of the past, of who they once were. Lark reminded them each day of how to speak and think and fight as if they still lived in London's streets. Daventry wanted them to leave that life behind and learn to be new men, but he had to teach them, and now he rarely saw them. He kept to himself by day and left Emma to oversee them at supper.

"You again," Lark had complained.

Emma knew Daventry was avoiding them because of her dairies. Whatever Wallop hoped would come of Emma's shameless display of her person, in fact, her attempt at seduction had driven him from his own dinner table.

The best thing Emma could do for the boys was to keep making her plans. With each trip to the village, she collected and hid something for her journey. She had a sturdy pair of half boots and an extra woolen gown. Once she escaped, Daventry could find his wards a true teacher who would teach them to lead those new lives. If only she knew that Tatty was on board that ship. She felt in her pocket for the small piece of Leo she had left, the medal lying warm against her hip.

Through the window she saw the boys reach the wood. Standing watching others escape suddenly seemed pointless. What she wanted was to be in motion like her reluctant charges, to be moving her limbs and breathing fresh air. She took one last look at the deserted room and turned for the door. Haste did not make her careless. She practiced turning the knob. It didn't make a sound.

The blue skies of her first days at the hall had vanished. A steady west wind brought in low steely clouds. The sharp breeze mingled the smells of fresh-turned earth and river. Emma pulled her thin cloak around her and counted her steps. It would be good to know exactly how far it was to the trees.

Where the path to the wood passed the stables, she paused, remembering Wallop's order to find any dogs Daventry kept at the hall. She did not like to think what Wallop might do to a dog. As she debated, a noise came from within the stable that made it impossible for her to pass by. It was a sound with an irresistible hold on her memory, a pony squeal. Emma froze, listening as the high glad squeal became a long wavering trill descending to a rusty hiccupping bray. In the stable a pony greeted a friend and wanted a treat.

She forgot her step count. Still, she did not move. Once one cracked the lid on the jar of the past, bad memories inevitably escaped with the good, but a second pony answered the first, and Emma gave in to the pull of her childhood. She was no different from her students, easily swayed by the past.

In the stable the head groom turned to greet her, an old black-and-white spaniel at his heels. "Miss?" He doffed his hat and bowed. "Ned Begley."

Emma nodded with a glance at the dog. She decided that Wallop did not need to know that Daventry's groom had an old dog.

"You're not afraid of old Hector, are you now, miss?" The groom gave the dog's head a fond stroke.

Emma shook her head. "Hello. I'm Miss Portland, the boys' new tutor. Did I hear a pony?"

"You did, miss." He beckoned her to a pair of stalls. "Here you go, meet Hiccup and Budge."

A pair of shaggy-maned dark brown faces peeped over stall gates at her. She held her hands out to be sniffed and waited for a sign that she could rub the brown faces and ears.

"Have they been ridden lately?"

"No, miss. Nobody much rides in the big house. Thought the boys might want to learn."

"Not Daventry?"

"Doesn't ride, miss, though he do drive sweetly. The lad was made to hold the reins."

"May I ride Budge?"

Ned gave an embarrassed laugh. "Don't know that we have a proper lady's saddle, miss."

"A bridle will do." Emma unlatched the stall gate and stepped inside to stroke Budge and talk to him about going for a ride. "Do you have a treat for him?"

"That I do, miss." Ned handed Emma a handful of sweet, grassy-smelling hay, still green. She heard Hiccup demand a treat, too.

The pony munched, and Emma closed her eyes and curled her hand in the shaggy mane, whispering in the pony's ear a promise to come with a brush soon. Childhood afternoons rose up around her with Tatty and Leo and their groom Nicolo and ferny woods and little orange mushrooms and icy mountain streams in their last plunge before reaching the sea.

When Ned brought the bridle, Emma stepped up to the pony and went to work. Budge quivered with anticipation. Minutes later Emma opened the stall and led him out and vaulted up onto his back in a move that came to her out of no conscious place. It was just there, like the next note in a familiar song. Her skirts bunched awkwardly, and she paused to tuck them under her while her knees hugged Budge's round flanks, signaling her wishes.

Once beyond the stable, Budge seemed to sense her need for a run, and off they went down the path that split the trees. Her cloak billowed out behind her, and her eyes watered from the cold rush of air. She felt alive.

As they slowed to enter the wood, she could see the boys perched on limbs above her and hear them calling. They were throwing stones at crows but stopped to look down at her, curiosity getting the better of them.

Lark whistled, and the boys began to move. "You can't catch us."

Hah, Lark, try me. She laughed and nudged her pony's sides. The boys might excel at climbing, but she guessed they would be no match for the swift little pony.

They clambered from limb to limb, shouting and pelting Emma with leaves and twigs. Budge gave her a burst of speed whenever she called on him, so she had no trouble keeping up with their agile antics. Turning the tables on them, she led them deeper into the wood, and when they ran out of wood, Emma and Budge burst into a wide field and galloped on. It felt like freedom, like escape, like leaving behind lies and fears and guards and prisons. There was only a brown landscape under a low gray sky and a warm pony.

J AY burst into Dav's library as Matthew Gibbs, his estate manager, rose to leave. Gibbs, a lanky, redheaded ex-army engineer, a friend of Will's, looked at his watch. The man was capable of prodigious efficiency. He was investigating Dav's tenants and neighbors, determining which of them had dangerous loyalty to the duke. One of them at least reported to the duke, and as a result the local bishop was taking Dav to court over an unpaid tithe. Today Gibbs had brought Dav a heavy volume on tithes.

"Grinder's run off, Dav." The boy was breathless.

"Drove her away on the fifth day, did you?" Maybe he had gone too far in leaving her in charge of them. He knew the challenge of keeping them in line. He had only stayed away because of that dress she'd worn to dinner.

"She stole a pony and rode straight off."

Dav gave Jay a sharp look. The boys didn't peach on one another. That was the oldest code of the streets, but here was Jay bursting with a tale to discredit her. "Did she strap her trunk on the pony's back?"

"No."

Gibbs gathered up the papers he'd brought for Dav to sign regarding the tithe problem.

"Likely she's not run off for good. Where did you last see her?"

Jay studied an open book he could not read. "She rode north across the fields."

"She'll come back." It was the wise thing to say even as he wanted to rush off in pursuit.

"You should sack 'er. Can't let 'er steal from you."

Jay's story didn't add up. The one thing Dav's newest employee seemed to want was time. He hadn't forgotten that she was the one to insist on a fortnight and on her freedom to walk to the village every other day.

"How did you happen to see her steal the pony?"

"We were in the wood." The admission caused Jay to take an immediate interest in the carpet. Gibbs frowned. He didn't like any of Dav's people going into the woods without a pistol.

Dav let Jay squirm, waiting for a true picture of events to emerge. "You walked out on her."

Jay's head came up. "We stuck to it for three blinkin' hours. She worked us somethin' terrible."

Gibbs laughed. "Sounds the way any lad feels about school."

There was the problem. With nothing to salvage, or scavenge, or steal, with no one to fight or elude, the boys grew quarrelsome and restless. They could not see how sitting still to read a book could help them make new lives. But they had kept Dav alive for two years. He could not simply step into his new position and riches and abandon them. They needed new lives of their own. They had neither his friends nor his enemies. They only had him. There was only one thing to do—find the grinder and bring her back. If he had to confine them all to the schoolroom, he'd do it.

"Come on then, Jay." He rose. "Let's find her."

"And sack 'er."

"Take a pistol if you leave the grounds," Gibbs advised.

Jay's eyes widened. "Are you going to shoot her?"

"No." Dav looked at Gibbs. "I'll be careful."

H E found her where a ditch marked the edge of a field, hugging the shaggy beast, her faded red cloak the one warm, bright note in the somber landscape. Someone had used a harrow recently, breaking up the clods, so the breeze carried the smell of turned earth. The wind had pinkened her cheeks and freed loose strands of gold to fly about her face. He wished he had seen her gallop. She leaned against the pony, giving and taking comfort, indifferent to wind and cold. She looked up at the sound of his rig approaching, and he noted the turbulent blue of those eyes. Her vulnerability in the mud-flecked cloak maddened him and made him want to pull her up and crush her to him. He tried for civility instead.

"Telling your troubles to Budge, Miss Portland?"

Emma clung to the pony. Daventry read her gesture with uncanny accuracy. She leaned against Budge as if to tell him how lost she was, so far from home that even the dirt had a different smell. Only the pony felt familiar, but ponies were practical beasts, and she could not expect Budge to abandon stall and hay to run away with her. She had nowhere to go, no money with her, and no news of Tatty.

"At least a person can count on a pony's discretion. They never tell secrets."

"You have secrets then?"

"Don't you?"

"Tie the beast to my rig, and I'll take you back to the house."

Emma tied the pony as he ordered. He watched her tether the animal, and under that attentive gaze, she was grateful to rely on old habits that required no thought.

When she looked up at him, the man she was to betray, the red glow of the lowering sun turned his angel hair to gold. Except for that hair, loose about his face, he was the perfect country gentleman in a coat and trousers as somber as the darkening landscape.

His scrutiny made her hesitate again at the side of his rig until he extended a gloved hand to help her up, and she felt how easy it would be to put her hand in his and surrender to his strength.

His horses awaited his command. She put her foot on the wheel and let him pull her up, feeling the easy strength of his arm. Emma was surprised at the warmth of his clasp and the comfort it gave her. The urge to flee had been strong as she and the pony raced across the fields, but she had recognized the exhilaration of the moment as a fleeting thing.

She landed next to him. His hand still held hers, warming it, his thumb sliding over her knuckles. She could not look away from their joined hands. She was used to men with their bars and their keys and their weapons, but Daventry had some other power. She felt her body incline toward his and stiffened.

He released her hand with a careless laugh, though her hand, no longer numb, still felt his. Budge snorted to remind them of the stables and oats.

Her cloak fell against his thigh, and she shifted on the narrow seat, pulling the garment close around her. The knot at her throat gave, and Daventry turned at once. "Will I always be tying your cloak about you, Miss Portland?"

He took charge of her cloak strings as if they should obey him. Emma tilted her face up to give him access. The soft leather of his gloved fingers brushed the under side of her chin. Emma released the breath that she had been holding. His hands stopped their motion. A huff of breath escaped him, a white vapor in the icy air as if they made awkward wordless conversation.

Let me.

Yes.

More.

No.

A sudden flush of warmth stole over her. His fingers finished their work, and he picked up his reins.

He turned his horses toward the towers of Daventry Hall. She and the pony had crossed open fields, but he would take his rig along the river road as dusk approached. Emma wondered whether Wallop had someone watching in the cold of the waning day.

"Do you want to tell me what happened to send you in a mad gallop across the countryside?"

"How did you know I had gone?"

"Jay came to me, claiming you'd stolen a pony and fled."

"I went to find the boys in the wood, but when I heard the ponies, I remembered . . ." She paused briefly as a crowd of memories rushed forward in her mind. "We had ponies, my brother and I. We were free to ride them in the orchards and the hills with our cousin. The three of us rode often."

"So talking to ponies comes naturally to you?"

"It does."

"More naturally than talking to men."

Emma glanced sideways at him. How did he guess these things about her?

"Can you tell me how the boys are getting on?"

"Yes." She seized his offer of the topic. Her wakening memories were leading her to make dangerous revelations. She needed to tell him lies about the vicar's daughter she was supposed to be, not truths about ponies and lost times. "They want to learn to read, you know, but they fear it. It means leaving their old life behind, and they are unsure about that."

"That old life would have ended badly, if we'd stayed in it. I want them to be gentlemen."

"Then you have to be present to show them how."

"At supper, you mean?" Dav turned to her and thought instantly about going back to looking at golden hair and blue eyes and creamy slivers of flesh that he should not touch.

"I can eat elsewhere," she offered as if she'd read his thoughts.

"Now that's a facer."

"A facer?"

"Your brother did not care for prizefighting? He didn't teach you the jargon?"

"No. He fenced. What's a facer?"

"A facer, a leveler, is a direct hit, Miss Portland."

"I do want to be honest with you."

Oddly, he believed her, though he knew she was hardly telling him the truth about her past. He had seen the inner debate darkening her blue gaze, as she hesitated to take his hand.

"You left because of me, didn't you?" she said, turning

toward him. They were approaching the bridge and the turn, and he could scarcely drive and look at her and think of the question she was asking and the matter of that dress.

"Where will you eat?"

"I can eat in the servants hall, can't I?"

His jaw was too tight to answer. It was a rational decision. It removed temptation. He should be grateful to her for her plain speaking. So why didn't he like the idea? He knew why, because it suggested that she had no interest in him, suspicious or otherwise. That was rub.

In the gathering dark that closed in around them, he had touched her and spoken with her and their shoulders had brushed. Agreeing that she could eat elsewhere was not what he wanted next.

H E met the boys as they stood in a sheepish line at the stable door.

"Did we miss tea?" Robin asked. His face was mud-streaked, and a dry brown leaf clung to his straw-colored hair above one ear.

"You know Mrs. Wardlow's rules."

"Because of 'er." Jay blamed Emma.

"Not because of 'er." Swallow elbowed Jay. "See, Lark, she does know something useful." They watched her lead the pony into the stable.

"Wot, riding a pony? A circus trick." Lark could not be persuaded.

"Faster'n walkin'."

Dav walked on, falling in beside Lark. "Have supper with me tonight."

"Not Miss P.?" Lark cast him a suspicious glance.

"Not tonight."

"Supper with Dav tonight, lads," Lark called.

He owed it to them. He had commanded them and sheltered them and depended on them. He could not let them down because of a dress that hinted at a sweetness and softness for which he felt starved.

Chapter Ten

❧

EMMA was suffocating, pinned down. Her limbs strained against the hot smothering weight. Her throat worked, but she could not unlock her jaw to cry out. Wordless moans filled her ears.

A pony screamed, and she woke, tangled in linens, breathing hard, a thin gown clinging to her sweat-dampened body. She saw black, as if the world had been wiped from a slate. A faint high-pitched cry filled her ears, the tantalizing residue of some sound that had just ceased.

She lurched upright, straining to hear, but her heart thumped in her chest and her breathing gusted in her ears. Whatever had wakened her was maddeningly silent. She heard nothing except her body's own fear.

At last a knock came. The plain, homely sound of knuckles on wood gave immediate dimension to the darkness. It was the darkness of a single room not eternity. She pressed her fist to her mouth to stop a sob.

A muffled voice spoke her name, and the doorknob turned. A fall of light split the darkness and spilled across the cream-and-gold carpet. In the open doorway a candle illuminated a man with loose wheaten hair around his shadowed face. *Daventry.*

"You had a nightmare, Miss Portland." His voice broke the spell, and she came back to herself. The present moment connected itself to the long thread of moments that had gone before. She was Emma Portland now, in England, in Daventry Hall. Tatty was gone. The spy was dead. Leo was dead. Beyond that she could not go. A shuddering breath escaped her.

Daventry crossed the room on bare, silent feet and set his candle on the table at her bedside. His open-throated white shirt caught the light and glowed. His solemn lake eyes regarded her, cool as moonlight, but under his gaze she grew conscious of her damp nightgown. She dare not look down at herself. The delicate lace-edged silk clung.

He reached out his hand, and Emma took it and let him draw her onto her knees. He gathered her to him, pulling her head against his chest, and she gave herself up to being held.

His body was heated like her dream, but the contact made her press closer. Her breasts flattened against his chest, and his muscles tightened under her cheek as if their bodies spoke a common tongue. His heart beat an urgent tempo in her ear, but one hand made steady sweeps across her back.

"I heard a scream." She tried to explain herself, but a violent shudder cut off the words.

His chin rested on her head. "You may have heard a peacock cry. We have them on the grounds." One hand cupped the back of her head. The hand on her back went on stroking.

"You're in the blue room," he said. "The color suits you I think. Some lady must have chosen the chintz drapery. There's a tester bed, a gilt chair, and a oval mirror in the corner to flatter you." His voice, low and rough, went on naming ordinary objects as Emma's pulse slowed.

"I'm sorry I disturbed you."

"I was just reading. What do you know about tithes, Miss Portland?"

"Nothing." Her mind was blank. But she felt the change in him, a stiffening that signaled his intent alertness to her words.

"Your father the vicar never spoke of them?"

Oh, another mistake. Emma realized she was supposed to be the daughter of a man who lived on tithes. She shook her head against Daventry's chest, incapable of lies or fictions. Her lips brushed his collar, and he seemed to catch himself. His hold stiffened more as if he could no longer bear to have his arms around her.

He pulled back, and she waited for him to denounce her as a fraud. A damp strand of her hair stuck to his rough cheek. His fingers freed it. At the gentleness of it, she couldn't keep her fists from closing on his shirt to keep him there. Beyond his shoulder the room assumed shadowy dimensions. A wall coalesced around her dressing room door and another appeared around the fireplace.

"I'm just learning about tithes myself."

"What have you learned?" Emma thought that to make him answer would keep him there with one hand in her hair and the other sweeping across her back. Beyond the candle's wavering flame the black corners of the room shifted, as if the dream lay in wait for her.

"Honey is tithable, but salt is not."

He stared down at her, and Emma felt herself yield her

true self, a girl with nothing in the world but nightmares and plans of escape.

He seemed to lose himself in watching her. "Acorns are tithable, but not if the hogs eat them."

Emma pressed closer. His hand stroked to the small of her back, waiting for him to go on.

"Apples are tithable if they fall from the tree, but not if they are stolen." His voice had grown low and almost harsh.

"Wild cherries growing in the hedgerows are tithable." A laugh shook his chest under her ear. "You're safe now, Miss Portland. I should leave."

No. Emma could feel the dream crouching, ready to spring.

"If the nightmare comes again . . ." He was pulling back as he spoke. "Think of a good memory like your ponies."

Emma shook her head. He didn't know how the good and the bad were woven together. As soon as he spoke of the ponies, the cherries in her head vanished from the hedgerows. The bare branches turned brown and full of crows. She clutched his shirt, bunching the fabric in her fists. The dream sprang.

Two crows sat on the fence as a younger Emma and Tatty returned from the village with flour and oil for the farmer's wife. At their approach more crows flapped up in a raucous black whirl of wings and cries from something on the ground. A French soldier laughed from the open farmhouse door. When Emma turned back, she saw the thing on the ground. Her pony's head.

She closed her eyes. Her body began to shake in rough shudders. Daventry gathered her closer, his arms tightening, containing the shudders until they subsided into hiccups, and even those stilled. He lifted her chin.

"Tell me what happened to those ponies you used to ride."

Emma shook her head. She could not speak.

"Look at me." His thumbs brushed tears from her cheeks. "I'm real. I won't let the dream have you. I won't let Budge and Hiccup be hurt."

Dav felt the danger in the moment. Her eyes confessed some horror she could not name. She clung to him as she had to the pony. He had comforted her. He should leave now, offer some polite assurance that he was nearby, and not take anything from the shaken woman in his arms. But in the glow of the candle she was all pink-and-cream flesh. What he saw was a vision conjured out of his own sleepless desire, a warm tousled girl with a crown of golden curls and a filmy garment of ivory silk twisted about her waist, so that the pattern of the lace exposed the rosy peak of one sweet breast. She smelled of lavender and roses, and the heady scent of her filled his head.

She was like him somehow. Whatever lies she told, the dream was true. He did not press her to tell him more. He knew it was a dream of unbearable loss. There was just one comfort left to give. He leaned down then and took her mouth, claimed it with his own, just a touch at first.

Emma took Daventry's kiss. She opened to him, expecting the thrust of his tongue, but it didn't come. He meant the kiss as comfort, but she needed him to want her, so he would stay and keep the dream away. She arched her body up to his, and his hands swept down her back to gather her closer.

I need.

What?

I don't know.

Let me show you.

Dav slid the silk off her shoulder, freeing her breast. He let himself cup the softness of it in his rough palm and close his thumb over the peak as he had wanted to do the first day. His touch drew little whimpers from her and more arching of her pliant body. It made him dizzy with wanting to put all of his aching self into her warmth. He reached down and cupped her bottom to pull her against his straining cock. Her startled gasp stopped him. He opened his eyes to meet her wide gaze, realization plain in her eyes of where such caresses might lead.

"I think I've put the nightmare out of your mind," he said. He pulled the silk gown back over her pale breast.

She nodded, and he took a deep breath and made himself step back.

EMMA watched him. He stood in the doorway almost beyond the candle's reach, the white of his shirt and the dark depths of his eyes distinct in the shadows. "If the dream comes again, call me."

She nodded. She wouldn't though.

When the door closed behind him, she made herself get out of the bed and put her feet on the ground. The chill of the room cooled her at once, puckered her flesh and set her teeth chattering. On shaking legs she went to her dressing room for a shawl. She wrapped herself in soft wool and sat in the big bed to think.

She had come into her womanhood in prison. Tatty had shown her what to do, but Tatty had not prepared her for this.

She must not like him. She must not find him warm or good or funny or kind. Above all not kind. She must think of him as a wall, an obstacle, a problem to solve.

He would remain after her escape with his house, his boys, and his wealth.

She would walk across England. It was not a big place, not so vast as the continent she and Tatty had already crossed. England was a mere island. An island could not be so very big.

She laughed at herself. She couldn't help it, but she knew that it was not good to laugh in an escape. The time to laugh would be after her escape when she had reached Bristol and found a ship bound for America. She could go as a servant. Servants did not have guards or fish soup.

Daventry was not the man that the duke and Aubrey had led her to expect. They thought the greatest danger to their plan would be to have her exposed as a spy. True, Daventry saw too much, understood too much. He must see now what he'd suspected earlier—that her careful papers were a lie. She knew nothing of tithes. She woke from dreams no vicar's daughter with her nose in her books could ever have.

But that was a danger Emma could handle. The real danger was that Emma liked Daventry's kisses. The real danger was that she, like his boys, would want to stay with him, that she would cling and delay her escape until the law caught her.

She had to find a way to resist him. She lay back and pulled the covers up over her. The linen slid over her breasts, made sensitive now by Daventry's embrace, and sparked an instant recollection of his kiss.

He was the second man to kiss her, as different from her first as honey from gall. Fausto had been the first. He had been the youngest of their guards, but not the kindest. Kissing him had been part of the escape plan, the distraction part. Each time Fausto shoved his fishy tongue in Emma's mouth, Tatty had stood by, testing the keys at Fausto's waist in the lock of their cell.

Emma shuddered. She was here to buy her life and Tatty's with information. The sweet, sweet comfort of Daventry's embrace would not keep her from the crows. Only the duke's paper could do that. She could only get the paper by spying.

Then she realized that she had discovered one thing about him, after all, without spying. He was a man who understood nightmares. Things had happened to him that gave him an intimate knowledge of pain and fear. If she let Daventry want her, she would betray him more than she ever intended. He was a man who would not take betrayal well.

D AV leaned against the wall that separated her from him, his body hot and hard and throbbing with frustrated desire. He didn't like walls, but he was grateful for this one, the only thing keeping him from giving in to his most inconvenient discovery of the effects of lust.

He held himself perfectly still. He understood himself too well. He had given her the room next to his and sent Adam away not to investigate her lies but to lie with her. Only the girl's eyes, so wide with terror they'd gone black, had held him in check. His mind had recognized her fragile waking state, still so deep in the dream that only the thinnest rim of blue remained around the pupils of her eyes.

He knew himself to be a most fortunate man. Kidnapped at thirteen, held in captivity by a stranger for two years, he had escaped and made a life for himself on the streets. He was even more fortunate in his family, who had not given up the search for him in spite of the danger to themselves from his great enemy and his enemy's hirelings. When his family had found him, they'd shown him how to come back to them and to the life he had thought he'd lost forever.

His brothers had gone a step further, understanding that the man who'd taken him at such a young age might have damaged his sensual appetite. Xander and Will had found a way to have what seemed an impossible conversation and had helped him understand that Harris's actions did not change who Dav was. There were ugly names for men like Harris and even for men for whom love of their fellows was as natural as breathing. But Harris had been largely impotent. There, Dav had been lucky, too. Impotence had made Harris more likely to use his fists, but it had saved Dav's person from irreparable damage.

In time his brothers had arranged for him to meet a matter-of-fact young tart from a thriving establishment run by a group of women who could afford to be selective in their clients. One memorable night with her had done a great deal to complete his release from Harris.

She had pressed him with surprising frankness for the details of his sexual experience with his captor and showed him how his body was meant to work, all the while instructing him in the mysteries of the female body—its workings and its pleasures. He had not minded the lessons.

"Ever cast up your accounts?" she'd asked him.

He had had to admit that he had.

"Well, did you eat again?"

He laughed. "I did."

"Well," she said. "Ye've got to cast up 'arris, like 'e was somethin' bad that you ate. Your mind can get it all twisted, but the body is honest. It shivers and sneezes and sleeps. The belly grumbles and aches and gets rid of bad food. Listen to your body."

And he had. He wasn't fool enough to think he'd impressed her, but he didn't disappoint. She frankly admired his body and told him ladies would like it. For weeks afterward, he'd suffered a plague of cockstands, reassuring if inconvenient proof that he would mend.

Now that he had no doubt of the direction of his desires, he must not give in to them. He had been aroused. Emma Portland had been frightened. Her inexperience had thrown him off. She clearly knew enough of kisses to take his with a greedy hunger for it, but she had no knowledge of how to kiss back. He had tried to slow them down.

Neither truly knew who the other was. She was no vicar's daughter, but she was strangely innocent. She didn't know how to kiss him back, but she had received his kisses with an insistent need that told him she had been as powerfully affected as he had. Still he had the power in the situation. That alone should keep him from touching her.

He took up his book again, *A Practical Treatise on the Law of Tithes*. It should make a fitting penance for his advances on Emma Portland. The language of tithing laws had a biblical ring, and every page of the large volume in front of him rang with the voices of stern rectors and bishops claiming their rights.

The trouble was that tithes now made him think of Emma Portland. She tasted of honey and salt. The kisses he stole from her were like the sweetest apples. If he thought about cherries, he would make himself crazy with desire. If he were the gentleman his family tried to make him, he would apologize for his advances. But he didn't regret them. Given a chance he was more likely to repeat the offense than apologize for it. If Adam didn't return soon, the girl had no chance.

Chapter Eleven

❧

IN the morning Emma was no match for her charges. Their thoughts were on the afternoon's promised boxing lesson. Hers were on Daventry's kiss. Her math lesson went nowhere, and when Lark began throwing a beanbag about the room, she admitted defeat. To save the room from utter destruction, she stepped in the middle between Lark and Rook, and when she had order restored, she dismissed them.

Adam Digweed still had not returned from his investigation. She had an hour to spy before it was time to walk to the village and face Wallop. He would press her about the package Daventry had received. She had to take a chance while Daventry visited tenants with his estate manager. Emma decided to try his library, the likeliest place for any sort of document.

One oddity of her employer that she hardly knew what to make of was his habit of leaving doors open. From the corridor she could see that the library was empty as she'd expected.

His cozy library was nothing like the duke's grand library at Wenlocke. His library was a working place. While his wards resisted learning one new thing, he seemed to want to learn everything there was to know. She wondered what he searched for in all those open books.

Recalling her first visit to the library with the boys, she looked for what might have altered in the room. It was easy to dismiss the books on the floor or on the chairs. They lay flat, untouched recently. Some had scraps of paper tucked in the fold covered with writing in a bold flowing hand. On the desk itself was a small clear working space and a tray of the usual writing implements, pens, mending knife, sand, and an inkwell. A stack of three closed volumes filled the upper right corner. An open book lay facedown next to the stack. The rest of the desk was covered in closely written sheets, lying as if a wind had rustled them into a drift of paper.

Emma took a breath and crossed to the desk, conscious of invading his territory. The volume facing down was a treatise on tithes. It instantly brought back the night. She leaned to look at the stacked books and read their titles, all on the law. She turned to the papers. She dared not disturb them. On one was a long list of names under the heading "Contributions to the Reverend Bertram Bredsell's School for Boys." Emma ran her finger down the list of names— Dorward, Lambert, Palgrave, Ruddock, Wenlocke. She fixed her gaze and read more carefully. The Duke of Wenlocke had contributed a thousand pounds to the school.

Emma could not imagine the icy duke acting out of compassion for boys. She lifted the top page of the pile and peeked at the next page, looking for Wenlocke's name again, and there it was in a curious sentence like a journal entry.

*7 August, 1816: Offered Wenlocke proof of his son's
legitimate living issue.*

She slipped her finger under another loose sheet of paper
to lift it when she heard voices in the corridor. She dropped
the page and turned to face the open library door. Daventry
strode in, and came to an abrupt halt.

Their eyes met, and in his a quick flash of warmth
instantly cooled. "Finished your lessons this morning?"

"Your afternoon boxing plans distracted the boys. I let
them go early."

He came to stand beside her with a glance at his desk.
"Were you looking for me?"

"To apologize. I regret that my nightmare disturbed you
last night."

"Your presence in the house disturbs me, Miss Portland."

"Will you send me away then?"

Dav knew he should. To find her in his library standing
over the pages of Norwood's report roused the worst suspi-
cions. "The lessons going that badly, are they?"

"As well as the study of tithes, I suspect."

Dav didn't trust himself to speak for a moment. The
word hung in the air between them. It brought back the heat
and closeness of the night. He needed distraction, but the
only thought he could summon came from the thick tome
he'd been reading when he'd heard her cry out. He had spent
hours in the room next to hers, not trusting himself to
undress, working his way through great and small tithes,
predial and personal tithes. In Adam's absence awareness
of Emma Portland had dominated his consciousness.

She made a little distracted motion as if reaching for
something in her pocket and discovering it wasn't there. He
remembered her touching that pocket on her first day.

"Tithes can be troubling." He thought that sounded safe. Instead of something like, *Kiss me, let me touch you.*

"And do you have a problem with tithes now?" Her empty pocket plainly bothered her.

"I do. Some fellows cut oak wood for a portion of the estate, and the bishop claims the wood is subject to a tithe that wasn't paid. His suit goes before the Court of Exchequer. The question is was the new wood grown from old stumps or from acorns?"

"Have you put the problem to the boys?"

"You think it might make a lesson for them?" She hadn't come to his library to speak of tithes or his wards.

"I think you might show them how much reading helps you in your position." Again she made the distracted gesture.

"Miss Portland, you touch your pocket repeatedly. Did you lose something?"

She nodded. The blue of her eyes vanished in a bleak gray like the color of loss.

"Something valuable?"

"It was my brother's. I must have misplaced it. I will look again."

He was aware that in her distraction, she was speaking a truth.

"I'll ask again then. To be sure that you find it."

She nodded. "If you'll excuse me, it's my afternoon for a walk to the village."

THE boys huddled in the chapel. Lark held the prize in his open palm for all of them to see. Taking it from her had been easy. What to do with it was the question.

"What is it? Looks like a moon." Robin leaned over Lark's hand for a closer look.

Jay pushed Robin back. "Some kind of medal."

"Is it gold?" Swallow asked.

"It is." Lark had seen enough gold in Daventry's house to know the real stuff.

"We should give it back," Robin said.

"Ah, Robin's sweet on her," Raven sneered.

"Am not." Robin gave Raven a shove.

Raven, bigger and tougher, shoved back. "Are so."

"What are the words?" Finch wanted to know.

"Doesn't matter." Lark didn't want them trying to read the blinking thing. As if they could.

"What does it mean?" Swallow asked.

That Lark could answer. He had known from the moment he'd palmed it. "It means she's not who she says she is."

"So we take it to Dav, right?" Finch, always wanting to do the safe thing.

"We give it back?" Robin really was sweet on the grinder.

"No, not yet. It stays with me. I say what we do with it and when. Not a word now." He made them put their fists together. "Swear it, all of you."

To the roof, lads," Dav ordered after lunch. Whatever Emma Portland was missing, he had a suspicion his band knew something about it.

A stiff breeze blew and leaden clouds gathered, but they shed jackets and shoes and neckcloths, and he let them enjoy the freedom of the place, sliding on tiles and walking precarious edges. Jay hand-walked the length of the highest peak. Finch did his bent-kneed slide down almost-vertical surfaces, arms spread. Even Robin had grown into the kind of balance needed for navigating the place, though he still couldn't leap far.

They collapsed around him after their burst of energy against sun-warmed slate in a lee of the wind, a reminder of their old habits. It didn't smell like London, but it felt like London to lie against stone with the wind whipping over them and the sky above.

"It's like old times."

"Except Daventry'll dirty his fine clothes," Swallow warned.

"That's why he has a valet," Lark said.

"And a butler and footmen," added Finch.

"And laundresses and cooks and maids," shouted Swallow.

"And grooms and gardeners." Jay punched a fist into the air.

It made them all laugh, the unreality of it, living in a palace instead of on the rooftops of London with only the elements to warm or cool them, and their own luck and skill to keep them alive and ahead of landlords, police, and worse.

"A marquess has everything," Robin said solemnly.

"Don't forget the problems," Dav reminded them.

Lark was instantly alert and scornful. "What problems does a marquess have?"

"Is your grandfather up to more deviltry?" Jay asked.

"Just another lawsuit. This one's to get money for some trees that were cut." No tithes had been paid from the moment his brothers brought the lawsuit on his behalf, and trust his grandfather to know to the penny the sum of those unpaid tithes. Dav had not been marquess a week before the local bishop had brought a suit in the Court of Exchequer for arrears of tithes. There was no question but that his grandfather was behind the suit.

"He'll bleed you dry."

"Not if my lawyer's smarter than his lawyer. Let me tell you the problem and get your opinion." Dav explained the tithe problem. They all had opinions.

"Fighting in court is not real fighting, is it, Dav?"

"It's not like a mill, where the other fellow is right there, and you can knock each other down until one cries enough." Dav had to agree. He would prefer a good mill with his grandfather rather than a war of shadows.

"You'll never give in, will you, Dav?"

"Do we stay here forever then? Or can we go back?"

"Do you want to go back?"

"Sometimes." Robin was honest at least.

"We can't go back if we forget how to prig. We'll end in Coldbath Prison or worse."

"We'll be transported."

"No, you won't. You'll go back when you're ready with money enough in your pockets so that you never have to prig again." It was hard to say, but true. He would let them go. He wanted them to be ready to go, but he supposed that even that wouldn't be in his power.

"How much money is that?"

"Good question, Finch."

"If I have five quid, will I never have to prig again?"

"If you had five hundred quid," Lark scoffed.

Raven gave long whistle at the sum. "Five hundred quid? 'Oo has that kind of blunt?"

"I bet Dav does," Robin said loyally.

Lark sprang to his feet and stood over them, facing Dav. "What are we doing up here? We're dreaming, aren't we? She narked on us, didn't she?"

Dav didn't move. He looked up at his defiant second in command, whose troubled eyes gave away his guilt. "About what?"

Suddenly none of them could meet his gaze. He waited a long, sinking moment.

Lark looked out over the greening landscape before he turned back to Dav. "Nothing. You believe her, not us, that's all. I saw her go to your library."

"She did come to the library. She recommended I share some of the estate matters with you."

Dav could see that Lark didn't believe him. The others had the grace to look ashamed, but no one would admit to taking anything. He'd taught them that himself.

Swallow spoke up at last. "We'll thank miss for the idea, but we can't solve your problems today, Dav. Today's a training day."

E MMA concentrated on the road to Somerton. It was possibly the worst road in England because it had Wallop at one end and Daventry at the other. Daventry would make her forget her purpose. Just a few minutes with him in the library, and she'd forgotten what she was searching for there.

She looked at the road. She needed to know its dips and turns and ruts so she could pass along it at night. She picked out landmarks and noted the threads that marked her hiding places. Her supply line was almost complete. There was a sharp bend after the bridge at the end of the hall drive, a long flat stretch, then a boggy patch where lumbering wagons had sunk deep before the last rise into the village. She balanced precariously on the narrow dead grass margin. Still her petticoats were six-inches deep in mud when she reached the village.

She was late, and she had lost Leo's pin. Her empty pocket where she had kept it for so long lay flat against her hip. Leo had worn his uniform so proudly before the French came and ended their old life. His coat had been deep blue with a red collar and cuffs, cut to show off his fine physique with a double row of gold buttons down the front and bright gold epaulets on his shoulders. A light blue sash crossed his chest, and at the top of the sash were pinned his honors, a row of overlapping ribbons with his medals dangling from them. When they'd had to leave home for good, she and Tatty had sewn the medals into the hems of their gowns. The gowns had fallen to tatters in their cell, and on the long journey to England they had sold the medals one by one. Emma had had just the one left, a crowned half moon, a little bigger than her thumb.

She banished the image and tried to recall whether she had tucked her talisman in her pocket as usual. She thought she had.

This morning the dream and Daventry's kisses had left her weary and not at all clearheaded. She had not taken proper charge of the boys, and they had been quick to take advantage. The boys were on their feet for the morning counting lesson when Lark had begun a game of tossing a small bag of beans about. She understood that boys would toss any loose object within their reach, but this time the game led to chairs being overturned. They had abandoned her lesson, laughing and shouting.

The moment came back to her then: when she had been watching Lark, and Rook had bumped into her and steadied her on her feet. She stopped in the road. They had orchestrated it. Rook had been so contrite. Their bumping her had ended the little game, and the boys had gone back to their desks and behaved well for ten whole minutes. She had been thoroughly gulled. Once released, they had run off.

Standing before Daventry in his library, reaching for the pin's comfort and courage, she'd realized it was missing. She could blame no one but herself. She had ridden the pony. She had had the nightmare. She had accepted comfort from Daventry in the night that had left her with the intelligence of a flea.

She sank down in the dry grass. A coach rattled past headed for the inn. Wallop was waiting. Wallop first, then her pin.

Josiah Wallop was eating a mutton chop when she entered the inn's private room, a large napkin tucked under his chin. Grease from the chop gleamed in his black side whiskers. He greeted her with avuncular heartiness for the innkeeper's notice, but when that worthy left them, he eyed her coldly.

"Yer late, missy. And 'Is Lordship is not pleased with you. Got ta bring you up to snuff, squeeze more out of you, 'e says. Do you want Josiah Wallop to squeeze you, girl?"

Emma wisely did not answer. Wallop washed down a large bite of mutton with a draft of ale.

"Did you find out when that whore's whelp plans to leave the hall?"

Emma shook her head. "He has not mentioned his plans."

"Well, you'd best get 'im to mention 'em. We know he's going to go to London. His mamma begs him not to come in every letter. We steam her letters, you know, every one."

Emma kept her face blank. It was what spies and secret police did everywhere. They steamed letters and rummaged papers and lurked in banks, cafes, and restaurants. They bribed footmen and housemaids, and they could find you a thousand miles from home. She was supposed to be one of them.

Wallop wagged a fat finger at her. "He's a cagey one. He sends nothing through the post. What did you find out about the package he received?"

"Was it a wrapped package?"

"Don't be smart with me, missy."

"If it was wrapped, it must have been unwrapped. If it is a common object like a book or a . . ."

"Have you looked?"

She nodded.

"Where?"

"His library."

"Not his bedroom?"

"On his desk he has a pile of papers full of the duke's name."

"Are you trying to tell me 'e got a package of papers?"

Emma nodded.

"You read those papers?"

"As much as I could."

"Well, what did you see?"

"A list of names of contributors to Reverend Bertram Bredsell's School for Boys. The Duke of Wenlocke was listed there."

Wallop harrumphed. "Don't 'ave to tell me wot I know, missy. You watch yourself. I'm onto your game. You don't want me to have to tell 'Is Mighty Lordship Aubrey that you aren't doing your job. Josie Wallop does 'is job. Never had a customer from Newmarket to London dissatisfied with my work. When Josie Wallop plans a lay, it's a good 'un."

He attacked the meat clinging to the chop bone with fork and knife. "Wot's in your basket?"

"Purchases from the village store to excuse my errand."

"Show me."

"It's nothing."

"Show me." Wallop dropped his cutlery and grabbed the edge of her basket with a greasy hand. Emma twisted away. He heaved up out of his chair and lunged for her. Emma staggered back, but he had hold of the basket and tipped her parcel onto the floor. Sinking back into his chair, he scooped up the package and ripped it open, spilling white linen onto the table. "What's this? Shirts! So you can cover up your dairies, eh." Wallop took a delicate shirt in his fists and tore a sleeve off.

"Stop." Emma hated to plead with him. Tatty would say it was always a mistake to plead with a bad guard. It brought out the worst in them. "I'll tell you something."

He held the shirt.

"Daventry plans to enter a prizefight."

"Oh ho, now that's good. That's a rich one. Could be better'n London. What do you know? When and where?"

"Give me my shirts."

Wallop's face grew sly. "You need to bring me something from his closet, miss, to get these shirts back."

"He trains every week when his brother comes."

Wallop tossed the shirts behind him on the floor. "Well now, you can help yourself, girl. See that you find out which match he's aiming for. Open your legs if you have to, if you haven't already."

Emma retrieved her basket. She was right. Wallop was the kind of guard who spit in the soup. At least he had not found the shoes in the bottom of her basket.

"Remember, you weren't picked for your wit, a dolly

mop like you. Next time bring me a box from his closet, mind."

"Any box?"

Wallop appeared to think. "A man's leather box for his fobs and gewgaws."

Chapter Twelve

❧

Emma went directly to the schoolroom. The boys would be at Daventry's training ground wherever that was. Perhaps they had hidden the pin in the schoolroom. She searched for half an hour and found nothing except a slate on which someone had written *NO MORE LESONS—MIS E PORLAN*.

Emma tossed it aside. One of them at least knew more of reading and writing than he was letting on. She followed the hall to the three rooms they occupied at the end of the north wing of the house. Fate could not ask her to leave the last piece of Leo here. She found their rooms neat and spare, the beds carefully made, a row of hooks for their clothes, a long stand of pitchers and basins to wash in, and towels hanging neatly on racks. Someone had lined the windowsill with a collection stones. There was a bird's nest on an empty shelf.

Emma undid each small, firm bed. Nothing. She felt in

all the pockets she could find. Nothing. She had to stop. Their bare, unfurnished new lives drew too much sympathy. If they had snatched the gold pin from her pocket and kept it, she should not blame them. They could not know its true value.

It was Daventry's room she should search, and she realized she'd been handed an opportunity to do it. The prizefighting practice was going on somewhere on the grounds. They would all be there, even the footmen and Mr. Creevey. She could find the box that Wallop wanted.

The knob of his door turned as hers did, and her practice with that mechanism made her perfect in silent opening. Inside she paused. His dressing room door stood open, but she heard no sound within. She studied the sober furnishings. The room was recognizably his, the colors muted browns and grays with strands of gold and wheat woven in. A grand bed stood against the far wall under a canopy of heavy chocolate velvet. A low upholstered chair in a golden hue sat by the corner hearth. She smiled at the table beside the bed stacked with books, a sign that he slept, or lay awake, on the left side of his bed. The brass candlestick he'd brought with him to her room had been returned. Emma looked away from the bed. It made her insides go odd to think of him lying there.

Under the window stood a handsome mahogany desk and an elegant carved-back armchair with a red leather seat. More open books lay stacked precariously in one corner. A tray held writing implements, and a pen lay across a page covered in his bold hand.

The leather box Wallop described was not visible on any table or surface of the room, but Emma could see that he had been writing at the desk. She read the words in his own hand, but they meant nothing to her, a list of names with whom he agreed about some bill in Parliament. Her gaze shifted to the open volume on the right, and her hand on the book began to shake as she read an account of the hanging of two sisters, aged eight and eleven, at a place called Lynn in 1808. Tatty would say it was a bad luck sign.

Emma steadied her shaking hand. He was not a hangman. Wallop and Aubrey and the old duke wished her to hang, not Daventry. And with her plan she would not hang. She entered his dressing room. Dark masculine furnishings lined the far wall, an imposing wardrobe, a boot rack of gleaming boots, a set of open shelves for hats, and a low closed cabinet. Under the high windows to her right stood a large porcelain-lined hipbath next to a long bench, a tall chest of drawers, and a commode with shaving implements. The room smelled of woods and citrus and polished leather as if Mr. Creevey had been at work there.

If Daventry kept his leather box here, he did not keep it openly. She turned to the wardrobe as the likely place for his secrets. She opened it and drew a breath of him. But the neat rows of coats and trousers hanging there, the white linen shirts, and the pewter gleam of a silken dressing gown were the clothes of his aloof gentlemanly guise. Some other scent buried in the folds of proper gentlemanly attire hinted at that other self she saw at times.

She brushed her hand along the hanging garments, stirring them and releasing more of the scent of him until her fingers caught on a long coat of black velvet. Different from the other clothes, it smelled of soot and stone. She pushed aside the coats around it and pulled it from its place. Threadbare cuffs and a frayed hem spoke of long use. Black as night and theatrical in cut with wide shoulders and a narrow waist, it had long skirts like a magician's cape, free to swirl around the wearer's calves as he moved.

She pressed a tattered sleeve to her face and knew it was more completely his than anything else in his closet.

As she stood breathing him in, she saw under the lifted folds of the coat a tan leather box. She dropped the coat back in place and sat and pulled the box into her lap. A simple clasp held it closed. She turned the clasp and lifted the lid. A stack of letters filled the box. She did not have to touch them to read the first.

Assaye, 1 September, 1803

My dear son,

I must write without knowing your name, but I trust your doting mamma to give you just such a name as will suit you. My own name I will add to her choice when I return from the Indies and we begin our life together.

This place, I must tell you, is a place of heat and color. All the animals you could ever wish to see roam quite freely, unconfined by bars and cages. When you are older, I will take you to the Menagerie, and perhaps I may bring home with me such a pet as will properly shock your mother.

Emma closed the lid and returned the box to its hiding place. For a moment she saw nothing around her. They were two of a kind. She would not give Wallop even one letter from the box. She would deny its existence. She had begun the afternoon searching for Leo's pin and had found instead words that Daventry kept of the father who had been lost to him. She did not want to know that he kept his dead father's letters hidden away with the old coat that she knew must come from his life in London.

The past was a determined enemy. It dogged your footsteps and when it found you, it tugged you back like a receding tide that would drown you in memories and nightmares. You had to resist its pull with all your strength and put one step in front of the other into the bare, unfurnished future. He had put his past in a closet. She would be wise to learn from him and let hers go as well.

She got to her feet, restored his clothes to their neat, concealing order, and closed the wardrobe doors. Her past would consume her, eat her for breakfast with toast and jam like an ogre, if she didn't escape them all.

No one noticed her leave the house with her basket. The sky was filling with dark clouds, and the wind plastered her cloak to her. Still she made her way to a place in the thick hedge on the path to the bridge where she could hide a tin of bread and cheese.

It was on her way back that she heard the shouts and turned to follow them. On a stretch of dead grass between a great hedge and a stand of tall dark trees, a measured square had been marked off with ropes, like a pen for animals to be sold at a fair. The boys clung to the ropes around the square, bouncing on their toes and shouting.

"Trim 'im, Daventry."

"Go fer 'is peepers."

"Go fer 'is ivories."

In the center of the ring, stripped of their shirts, torsos sleeked with sweat, two men danced and feinted and jabbed at each other with powerful quick flashes of strength. They appeared evenly matched in the weaving dance. She stopped, concealed by the shadow of a yew, to watch her first prizefight.

She had not been used to thinking living men handsome or to imagining that she might want to look at them in motion. Angels and saints, flesh of paint and marble, were handsome, not men.

The dark-haired man with the scarred ribs grinned and defended himself with careless grace. Daventry had narrowed his attention to his grinning opponent. He held his fists in padded gloves close to his face, moving in a light sideways dance of his feet. She flinched when his left fist shot straight from his shoulder, so fast she could hardly catch the movement.

The other man countered with a deft twist of his body, laughing. "Hey, I'm your brother, Dav. My wife won't like it if you rearrange my face."

"Draw 'is claret, Dav," Lark yelled.

With a sudden shift of intensity, the men exchanged a flurry of blows, bodies bending and shifting. The dull smack of fist against flesh and the harsh huff of expelled breath mingled with the boys' giddy shouts. Daventry seemed neither to hear nor to see anything beyond his adversary. He did little to defend himself from his brother's blows, but rather seemed to welcome them.

The men broke off the exchange, returning to their wary dance of seeking advantage. Daventry was fiercely beautiful and dangerous in the play of muscle under smooth skin. She recognized this other, elemental side of him, as she had seen it in him the first day when he rose from the stones of the chapel. Aubrey had said he was a hard man to kill. She understood that he would be a hard man to defeat in the fight because he was made for it, like a living weapon that finds its purpose in battle.

"Hey, Miss Portland." Swallow called. They all turned to look at her, except the dark-haired man. Daventry merely glanced, his startled gaze meeting hers, a glad admission in his gray eyes, and the dark-haired man's fist connected with his jaw, and down he went. Emma had stepped toward him before he even hit the grass. The dark-haired man's knowing gaze caught her look before she had a chance to control it. She halted at the ring's edge, clutching her empty basket.

"A facer," shouted Raven.

"Foul, Will Jones, ye shouldn't hit a man when 'e's distracted." Lark complained with a fierce glare at Emma.

The dark-haired man shed his padded gloves and extended a hand to Daventry to pull him up from the grass. He strolled to the edge of the ring and picked a towel up off of a stool and applied it to his chest and shoulders. "Is this your grinder, Dav?" he asked. "You ought to introduce us."

Daventry shook his head and grabbed a second towel. Emma dropped her gaze, her heart pounding. In a flash Will Jones had seen too much. He had investigated her, and she had no idea what he'd found. Emma felt the cold wind through her cloak.

Robin came and tugged her arm. "Are ye goin' to stay to watch us, miss? I'm goin' to draw Finch's cork for 'im."

Too late, Emma looked away from Daventry. She smiled at Robin. "I'm on my way to picnic." She held up her empty basket and hoped no one would look inside. "I'll leave you to your exercise."

When she looked again, Daventry had charge of himself. He cast aside his towel and pulled a loose linen shirt over his head. "Miss Portland, meet my brother, Will Jones, ex-Runner, ex-spy. Will, Miss Emma Portland, grinder to these louts."

"With all those exes, Miss Portland, Dav will make you think I'm dead and in the history books. Instead of merely his much wiser, somewhat older brother."

Daventry actually grinned at his brother. "What should I say then—Will Jones, besotted husband, doting father, respectable officer of the law?"

Will gave Emma his hand and a narrow look. "Actually, Miss Portland, I'm at work on the reform of the London police with Peel. Give us a year, and Parliament three or four, and we'll have an effective force in place."

Robin tugged at Daventry's shirt, and Daventry turned to the boys and urged them into the ring. "Your turn, lads." They scrambled through the ropes, and Lark opened a sack and began tossing gloves at his companions. They began promising to damage each other's noses, teeth, and eyes.

Will Jones's dark lazy gaze was on Emma. He was not a man to be easily fooled. She could see that he understood at once how it was between herself and Daventry. Tatty would say the candlestick needed the candle. "Do you like Suffolk better than you liked Grimsby, Miss Portland?"

"The hall is beautiful."

"Dav tells me you're not fond of fish. The fish stink must have made Grimsby unpleasant."

He was testing her. She gave him a bright smile. His testing meant he did not know everything. "My concern, of course, was my students, and not my supper."

Her smile had no effect on Will Jones with his sharp, suspicious gaze. He knew something and had come to tell Daventry what he'd found.

Daventry turned back to them. "Tell Xan I'm ready for that match whenever, wherever," he said to his brother. "I want it."

One of the black brows lifted in a way that made the resemblance between the brothers plain. "You may be a bleeding marquess, but you don't tell Xan when you're ready for a match. He decides. Even an amateur bout can be brutal."

Daventry's face changed slightly, taking on that look of command that got obedience from all his people. "You'll both be invited to my first match."

"Show Xan your moves when he comes then, but don't tell him I knocked you down." Will Jones turned to Emma. "The family comes here, Miss Portland, but don't be deceived, it's not a visit. It's a bleeding invasion. The parade of carriages will stretch from the house to the bridge. Our mother insists on traveling in style. And safety."

S HE's lying to you, you know. The Grimsby School for Foundlings is a fiction." The brothers sprawled in easy comfort before a fire in the ancient hall with mugs of dark porter and Mrs. Wardlow's sandwiches at hand.

"That part I'd figured out."

"But I suppose it doesn't matter, if you want her in your bed."

Dav knew that his response to Emma Portland would not go unnoticed by his most observant brother. Will had perfected a mask of idle indifference that hid the quick workings of his mind. "It must relieve your fears to know that all my parts are working. I am not irreparably damaged."

Will swore, but he lifted his ale pot in a toast. "To working parts! At least the two maggots who stole your boyhood didn't take that joy away from you, too. You're sure you want her in your bed?"

"I'm sure."

"You sent me her papers because you doubt her honesty."

"Did you find out anything?"

"She has an accomplice."

"Accomplice?" The word had a nasty sound, and the

idea didn't fit with anything Dav sensed in Emma. She might be lying about her past, but she seemed like him, alone in the world. To see her lean against one of the shaggy ponies for comfort, he could not imagine she had a friend in the world, let alone a partner.

"Someone on the outside is either helping or directing her. There is no Grimsby School for Foundlings. Adam confirmed that. But when I wrote to the address in her papers, I got an effusive letter praising Miss Portland's virtues. She or her partner anticipated an investigation. And if that maw worm who had you kidnapped wasn't already dead, I'd suspect him or Bredsell."

Dav ignored his brother's reference to the men who'd done so much harm to all of them, two of them dead, one in prison. Still those men had acted to please his grandfather, who was very much alive and as determined to ruin them as ever. Norwood's report of the duke's actions against the family proved that the Duke of Wenlocke didn't take well to losing. "What does that make her, do you think? A fortune hunter?"

Will appeared to entertain the idea. His capacity for analysis was as sharp and quick as his tongue. "She appears to be gently bred . . . a maiden?"

"Maiden." Dav had no doubt of that. Those inexpert kisses of hers were proof.

Will took a long pull on his ale. "So, possibly, some encroaching mamma, who's been following the account in the papers of your sensational rise in fortune, thinks to put her impoverished daughter in your path before we fire you off in society and a queue of applicants lines up from here to Bath to bag a marquess."

Dav shrugged. In his mother's dreams Dav would wed

some paragon of virtue from the highest rank of society. He knew his brother did not believe that women of rank would be lining up to receive Dav's addresses.

Will sat up, leaning forward. "As flattering as that fantasy might be, it's unlikely. A fortune hunter takes care to disguise her own lack of fortune until she's hooked her man, but this girl frankly admits she's penniless, right?"

Dav nodded.

"No one else answered your notice, did they?"

"No."

"I don't like it. Do you see anything suspicious in her actions here?"

She has nightmares, silk dresses, and a need to hug shaggy ponies, as if the poor beasts could comfort her for some terrible loss. He didn't voice those puzzling observations. None of them fit her paper account of her life or his brother's sense that she was acting out of some calculation. "She does know teaching. Some part of her story must be true."

"You think she taught in an actual school somewhere. So why invent the Grimsby School and the false references?"

Dav shrugged. The lie puzzled him, too. When she talked about her former students, he could swear that she spoke of real boys. She knew more about teaching than lovemaking, of that he was sure. "She wanted this position."

"Even more suspicious."

"She had no idea who I was." He remembered the moment in which neither of them had been what the other expected.

The idea caught Will by surprise. "She came here in answer to the notice, right? To be hired by the Marquess of Daventry, didn't she?"

"Yes, but she didn't know that person was me."

"That means she's no fortune hunter." Will sat up, his countenance dead serious.

"Maybe it means she's an honest woman."

Will's raised brow expressed his full contempt of that possibility. "Even if she's honest, she's not what our dear mamma wants for you. Sophie wants nothing denied you because of birth or history. She has her heart set on welcoming you home from West End ballrooms where you left blue-blooded maidens in a swoon over you. Oh, and she wants to attend your grand wedding at St. George's."

"You and Xan have that covered. You each married into remarkable respectability."

"A bleeding miracle in my case. The poor bishop turns apoplectic every time he thinks of where his daughter sleeps at night."

Dav smiled. Will had a sumptuous apartment with a bed fit for a sultan hidden in the depths of one of London's worst rookeries. It was satisfying to contemplate his sister-in-law Helen's pompous father, the Bishop of Farnham, dealing with that fact. The bishop had made a name for himself with his books of sermons on the subservient role of women before his daughter Helen had defied all his ideas with her courage and her love for Will.

"I don't like you having this woman sleep inside the house, Dav. Where have you got her sleeping?"

Dav lifted his ale to his lips without answering for a minute. "Not in the barn."

Will swore again, thoroughly.

"I'm not defenseless. I've got Adam Digweed, and you and Xan can vouch for the staff. You hired them all."

"Adam has been away for days."

"She hasn't murdered me in my bed if that was her plan."

"Has she any money?"

"Some, I think. She's made purchases in the village."

"Anything of note?"

"I haven't examined her packages."

"You might give her a week's wage, and see what she does with it."

"You think she'll leave. Am I free to follow her?"

"Of course you're free. You're a bleeding marquess."

Dav didn't say anything, letting his brother think about the meaning of those words.

"I'm not thirteen or even sixteen any longer." The real problem was to get Xan and Will and even Mamma to recognize him as he was. For three years he had been that lost boy for whom they searched. Now he did not think they could see the person in front of them.

"I know, but as long as Wenlocke lives, he's your enemy." The statement was as close as Will could come to a plea.

"You think if I leave this gilded prison, he'll strike." Everything about the ancient room in which they sat proclaimed his grandfather's ambition and power through the centuries, power he'd meant to pass on to a proper heir, not a courtesan's son like Dav. Family crests adorned the ceiling panels above them. Fine ancient weapons decorated the oak walls. The Jones brothers had wrested this ancient power from the duke in the courts. In spite of everything Wenlocke had done for seven years from the moment he'd prompted Archibald March to arrange Kit Jones's kidnapping, Kit was Marquess of Daventry. He was Dav, or at least he was learning to be him.

"I've no doubt of it. It will take me a few days more to find out where that letter really came from and to trace Miss Portland's journey here, if I can. In the meantime, watch her."

"You can count on that."

"I can see that she has qualifications that Hodge lacked."

Will rose to leave. "Don't bed her," he advised. At the door he stopped and looked back over his shoulder as if a thought struck him. "You haven't, have you?"

"Not your affair, Brother."

"Well, you can bleeding wait, at least until after the family comes. And let them judge her."

"Go before the rain closes in."

Chapter Thirteen

‰

Dav saw his brother off for London with no further warnings about Emma Portland. Will had said enough to remind Dav of the choice he faced. He sought the roof. The boys were at their tea. The late afternoon clouds had thickened and grown darker, and the wind blew stiff and chill out of the west. He heard the low rumble of distant thunder. He needed the roof. On the roof he might even solve the puzzle of who he was.

In the hall he could put on the clothes of a marquess and inhabit the rooms of a marquess. He could look at the papers his father had carefully hidden to protect him and read his dead father's letters, full of hope for their future together. He could meet with his estate manager and read about tithes in his library, but on the roof he could not be dishonest with himself. The things he had done to survive marked him as indelibly as the white puckers of skin around his wrists and ankles marked him with the shackles of his two-year captivity.

The roof of his magnificent hall covered near an acre, but he could go nowhere from that roof. In London when he'd climbed free of Timothy Harris, the huge man who'd kept him for two years, the city had stretched out before him. He had learned to leap and scramble almost anywhere in London by rooftop paths over the slates among the chimney pots. Here, where he could see for miles across acres that legally were his possession, he could go nowhere, except down through the house. He could go forward by choosing fully and completely the new identity his family wanted for him.

The title did not see to fit him, but even without it he could not be sure exactly who he was. His bastard brothers had been the heroes of his youth, not the figures in books. He had wanted to be like them, quick with his fists, indifferent to society's slanders, and self-sufficient. Xander was the careful one. Will was the rebel. Dav did not know who he was meant to be.

To choose his title was to choose a certain kind of power, a thing of paper and words, unlike the power of his fists and wits which he could trust. Choosing to be the Marquess of Daventry would not make him as free as he had been in that astonishing moment of his liberation from his kidnapper, when at fifteen he had stood shivering, near naked and half-starved on that roof above Bread Street, and chosen his own path.

Still, he could not deny that choosing to be the marquess meant he could do things for his family. He could establish the boys in trades or professions of their choosing. He could free his mother and brothers from Wenlocke's hatred.

He could reform the law itself that fell so heavily on poor boys. He wanted these things. He had been working steadily and earnestly to achieve them.

The trouble was he could not be both. To be the Marquess of Daventry, he must deny that other self. He tried to picture himself dancing smoothly in a ballroom, holding polite conversation with a demure miss or marrying one. But the only girl his mind could conjure had golden curls and blue eyes, and he wanted to hold her closer than even the most licentious waltz would permit.

Wanting Emma Portland was at odds with all those careful, noble, rational desires of his. Wanting Emma Portland was a different sort of wanting, immediate and insistent. It consumed him. He wanted Emma Portland in the way he had once wanted freedom, the way he wanted to defeat his grandfather.

He had only to hear her name mentioned, and other thoughts fled. He worked his jaw, which still felt the ache of Will's blow. Turning toward her had been inevitable even in the ring where he had learned to block out every competing awareness except his opponent. All his training against his tough brothers had deserted him at the sound of her name.

Will's blow, a mere tap from his brother, was meant as a warning to Dav not to take his eyes off the danger they all faced. He should stay on the path he had chosen and conquer the longing she stirred in him. He owed it to his brothers. They had suffered the full weight of bastardy. As the Sons of Sin, neither Xan nor Will would ever be accepted in polite aristocratic society no matter what service they did the nation. Ironically, each had married a woman of impeccable lineage, while Dav, his mother's son born of her secret marriage to a lord, and now recognized legally

as his father's heir, picked a nameless girl of doubtful ori-
gin who told him two lies for every truth.

The thunder rumbled closer, and a flash of lightning lit
up the sagging belly of leaden clouds. A sudden gust pelted
him with raindrops as big as finch eggs and cold as ice. In
minutes he was soaked to the skin. He stayed longer, letting the elements blast him until a reeking bolt split the
gloom in front of him.

He ran lightly over the slick tiles and slipped inside the
bare little room next to schoolroom. The wind slammed
the door behind him.

There was no fire in the black grate, but he pulled his
soaked shirt off over his head and shook his wet hair back
from his face. When he looked up, Emma Portland stood in
the doorway with a slate in her hand.

O H, it's you." She hugged the slate to her chest. She
wore a white lawn shirt under a deep blue velvet gown
that echoed the vivid hue of her eyes. "I was in the schoolroom. I heard the door."

A mad laugh bubbled up inside him. One look from her,
and his resolve to forget her, to mistrust her, dissolved. He
tossed his wet shirt on an old wooden chair. In the dingy
room in the gloom of the storm her bright hair glowed.

He saw her quick intake of breath and the way her fingers tightened around the slate as if she could hold back the
look in her eyes. Too late. He'd seen the admission in her
eyes in the second before Will hit him.

He reached her and took away the slate, capturing her
hands, holding them tight. "You can't look at me like that.
At least not when my brother might knock me to Jericho."

He lifted her warm hands in his cold ones and kissed her

fisted knuckles. He must have touched her hands ten times by now, and still the contact had the power to shake him.

"You must sack me. It is what your brother advises." He could see that she had worked it out in her mind.

"Not what I want." He leaned down to press a kiss against the side of her throat above the lawn collar, inhaling the sweetness of her.

"Is your jaw very sore?" She freed one hand and reached up to touch his face. He pulled her up against him. She lowered her gaze, and her hand slid to his collarbone.

"I can't not look when you . . . not when you are like this. It's the candlestick wanting the candle."

She made no sense. What was between them was nothing as tame as a candle flame. He thought it was a conflagration, one of Xander's blazing gas furnaces at the very least. A cold drop of rain ran down his neck. She leaned to him and caught it with her lips. A violent shudder of longing coursed through him. In the cold bare room with its dusty floor and fireless hearth amid the homey smells of rain and damp wool, he looked for a place to lay her down and crush her under him.

He nudged her back until her shoulder blades collided with the wall, and he pressed his whole aching self to her length, lifting her chin, taking her mouth, and losing himself in the taste and feel of her. The first moments were a frantic making up for all the kisses and touches denied in the days since her nightmare had joined them. He kissed her brows, her ear, her neck. Her sweet hot mouth opened to him, and this time, he plunged in.

The part of him that his brothers feared no longer worked was up and proud and nudging at Emma's skirts.

Emma welcomed the fierce pressure of Daventry's kisses. Almost it was as if they fought, as if she wrestled with the angel warrior, a sensual fighting, a struggle not of blows but to see who could give most. Everywhere against her body she could feel the lean sinewy strength of him. His kisses loosed the desperate tension of her limbs, made her float free of the trap, like the embers going up the flue. She clung to his smooth, strong back, feeling the cool skin heat under her touch.

A raucous noise penetrated Dav's sensual haze. Emma tugged his hair and twisted away. The boys were coming up the stairs. The sound became their feet pounding, their shouts and bursts of laughter. He could hear Adam's deeper voice trying to quell their uproar. He released Emma, her lips ripe and swollen. He had loosed the golden strands of her hair, and her blue dress bore the dark imprint of his rain-soaked body. Her eyes said she wanted to avoid discovery.

He grabbed her by the arm and hustled her to a closet, tucking her inside with one last searing kiss. "Wait, I'll lead them away." He turned back, snatched up his damp shirt and pulled it over his head. The garment felt like ice. His whole warm, throbbing body, protested, the shift from Emma's warmth to cold reality.

In the closet Emma kept her jaw clamped shut on her chattering teeth as Daventry directed the boys away from the little room. They had come looking for Emma, and Daventry sounded easy and indifferent as if he not the moment before been pressing his body to hers. For a moment Emma thought she had dreamed their heated encounter. But the chill of the closet and of her damp skirts was real.

Her breasts felt aching and swollen against her stays. Between her thighs she felt heat and dampness and a throbbing ache.

She could not deny what was happening between them. But it was very bad luck, like getting a thousand evil eyes, or having Fausto on guard duty every day. It was the worst luck imaginable to find in an enemy's kisses a sweetness she had never tasted.

It was bad luck for both of them. It was what Aubrey and Wallop wanted. They wanted Daventry to be careless around her, blinded by desire, unable to see the threads that connected her to his enemy. But Adam had returned, and Daventry's brother plainly knew that Emma Portland was a lie.

She recovered her senses. Daventry had a divided nature. He had come to her from the roof, from the storm itself and given in to his desire for her. But the boys had reminded him of his other self and its cares and duties. He had easily assumed them and left her in a closet.

She slipped out into the dim room. The last light of day made faint gray squares of the windows. She pressed her face against the glass. Rain drummed on the roof and slid down the other side of the cold panes. She would not escape tonight, and when she did, she would leave all thought of him behind. He was not a father, a mother, a grandmother, a brother, a cousin, a home, a name. She would take nothing except what she needed for the journey. She had not betrayed him yet. Nothing she had told Wallop would help in the duke's war against Daventry. If the rain ended soon, she would get away before she did Daventry any real harm. And in her catalogue of losses, the loss of him need not overshadow the others.

She told herself a few more lies as she stood there, letting the cold take over her body. Memories were light, she told herself. One could carry a sack of a thousand of them and not feel weighed down for a journey. And if the memory of a few kisses seemed a burden, why, then she'd just toss them out of her pack.

* * *

Rain delayed Will's return to London past his appointed hour. His twins were asleep, but his wife was awake, leaning up against the chocolate silk pillows in their great bed, her long tawny gold hair in a loose braid hanging down between her lovely breasts. She was scribbling something with one of his pencils in a moleskin notebook resting against her bent knees.

Undressing for her appreciative gaze was one of the pleasures of married life he liked to indulge, and though he was weary of the journey and worried about Dav, Helen's smile invited him back into their secret world.

He shed his outer garments and boots and stood beside their bed to undress. A fire still warmed the room, and his thoughtful wife had placed his favorite French brandy on the table by the bed.

A counterfeiting case he'd worked on when he'd first become a Runner had uncovered this secret warren of linked apartments north of the Strand. Once the crooks had been routed, Will had refitted the place to suit his work. The main room retained the original oak wall panels, door pediments, and wide plank flooring of a time when the neighborhood had been the most fashionable in London. A friend in the trade, leaving her profession to marry, had offered Will her grand sultan's bed with its tangerine damask hangings and posts like young palm trees.

In time when his work with Peel was done, Will planned to move his family to a respectable West End square, but for now he preferred to remain close to the work he was doing, and Helen didn't mind. She had taken over the role of running the boys' school at the top of Bread Street, where she and Will's assistant Nate Wilde and Dav's boy Robin had once faced a terrible enemy.

"Coming to bed?"

"I need to think."

"Then you must not stand before your wife in all your glory."

He paused with his hands on hips about to shed his smalls. He had been undressing absently, and now Helen's gaze turned his thoughts. "Would it help if I got under the covers, madam?"

She laughed. "Likely not. But tell me, did you send the false tutor packing?"

Will shook his head. He had explained before the trip what he'd discovered about the tutor his brother had hired without consulting any of them. Helen, who had been there the night they'd recovered Dav from his kidnappers, knew the danger of the family's enemies as well as anyone.

He lifted the covers and slid naked into bed beside his wife. He kissed her slowly, pressing his body to hers, savoring all the places where her softness yielded to his weight. For a moment there was a danger of forgetting everything except Helen, but she broke the kiss.

Her deep brown eyes searched his. "I think you need to talk first."

Will shifted up against the pillows and took up his brandy. Beside him Helen settled herself on her side, facing him, her fingers drifting over his ribs, her way of letting him know that she was there, waiting. He supposed he was no different from other husbands in that before he married he had not imagined the intelligent companionship of a wife would be so helpful. He knew it now. Thinking about a problem with Helen beside him, whether he asked for her opinion or not, meant he had better ideas.

Now the problem was his youngest brother. Neither Will nor Xander, their eldest brother, believed that Wenlocke's threat to Dav had ended. But Will saw what he believed Xan missed—Dav's impatience with the constraints they'd imposed on him for his own safety.

"Dav wants to fight in an open mill."

"You have been training him for months."

"It's just restlessness. He's not content with a court victory. What he really wants is a bleeding battle with the duke."

"Are you afraid? Wenlocke's near ninety."

"But still dangerous as ever, and there's Aubrey, the nephew. They'll strike at Dav the minute he leaves that house. If we let him go to that mill in East Thorndon or we let him take his seat in the Lords, Wenlocke and Aubrey will attack him."

"You don't think the tutor comes from them, do you?"

"There's no link yet, but I don't like the lies."

"I never told you who I was." Her hand on his ribs sent distracting sensations coursing through him.

"But I could handle you."

She flashed a smile of dispute. "You think your brother can't handle this woman?"

"He has little experience of women."

"But a great deal of experience of the falseness of the world. If she's lying to him, he probably knows it."

Will realized she was right. There was little around him that Dav did not notice. Dav was no fool, and he was capable of cold-blooded action. But Dav had never been in love. In the three years of Will's marriage to Helen of Troy— Will could never think of her as Marianne Rossdale, the bishop's daughter—Helen had taught him that Aphrodite, the goddess of love, was not to be evaded. When the goddess summoned, the poor helpless sod obeyed.

Will recognized that summons now in his wife's gaze, but he wanted to get his brother out of his head first. He put down the brandy.

"What have you been writing?"

"Helen of Troy's advice to women. My father has published another collection of sermons on the duty of women to submit to men. Someone's got to offer women an alternative to submission." She moved to lie on top of him.

"There are times when you enjoy submission." He looked up at her thinking of the first time he had tied her to his bed. She smiled as if her thoughts followed his and dropped a lingering kiss on his mouth.

"Actually, I wrote an impassioned letter telling women how to free themselves from the tyranny of the male sex, but I scratched it out." With an intriguingly bare arm, she showed him the pages of the little notebook with long slashes through the lines of writing. She tossed it aside and pressed against him, her lips hovering near his.

"I've come up with a new plan. I'm going to teach women to read. There is no reason that the Bread Street School should not admit girls. A little carpentry work, and we'll have a girls wing."

"Teach girls to read? Your father's sermons?"

"Novels. And I'm going to write one."

"You're going to write a novel?"

She pressed her lips to his ear. "*The Further Adventures of Helen of Troy.* What do you think?"

"I'm all for women having adventures." He drew his hands down her spine and pulled her closer against him.

She drew back briefly on raised arms that lifted her breasts away from his chest. "But teaching women to read comes first. Helen could read. She's the only character in Homer's whole grand epic who could. They say she learned the skill from priests in Egypt. That's what empowered her, you know, and made her so fearless and determined to be herself."

"Is it? I thought it was her bleeding capacity for turning a man into a besotted idiot over her."

Much later Will held his wife's lax warm body in his arms and knew what to do about Dav. He brushed Helen's hair away from her brow.

"I'm going to send Harding to investigate Emma Portland's references further. Can you spare him for a few days?"

"I can."

"And you'd best prepare to visit Daventry Hall."

"You're going to bring the whole family down on him?"

"Not me. Our dear mamma has hatched a plan to introduce him to some of the eligible young ladies in the neighborhood."

Chapter Fourteen

❧

SOMETIME during the night the rain turned to snow. It snowed for two days until the hedges wore white robes on thin black branches and the paths were buried.

Emma thought of her bread and cheese in the tin in the yew hedge. She would have to begin again, but while the ground lay covered, she mounted a campaign to get her pin back. She announced an end to math and counting lessons. Every hour in the schoolroom was about the words they needed to know to finish the story. She worked them hard, but she put her hand to the empty place in her pocket a dozen times an hour, slumping and falling silent each time she touched the empty spot.

On the second day she made a paper medal for each boy for service to his mates above and beyond duty, and pinned them on the boys' shoulders with great ceremony. And she watched, for signs that anyone felt the least unease, the least remorse. Swallow and Robin and Finch cast questioning looks at Lark, but he gave no sign that he felt anything.

"Don't you need your day off to go to the village?" Lark asked on the second afternoon.

Emma whirled on him. "I do, but at the moment, Finch is on my mind. He's on the edge of a breakthrough, you see, and no one goes anywhere until he gets his chance. Finch?" She turned to the slight boy whose hand usually hid his mouth. She now understood why. He had a chaotic mouth of teeth that crossed over one another and pointed in odd directions. She watched his lips form the word on the slate, and nodded to him to speak.

His hand went up to cover his mouth, and he glanced around at his mates. When his uncertain gaze came back to Emma, she nodded again. "You've got it, Finch."

He dropped his hand and traced the letters with his pencil as he read, "Courage."

Emma let herself smile, and a broad grin split Finch's face before he remembered to bring his hand up again. The other boys crowded around him to look at his slate, and punch his arms and ruffle his hair, and pound him on the back.

"Is anyone else ready?"

Lark's glance quelled any volunteers, and Finch shrank in his seat, looking guilty for his triumph.

B Y evening of the third day the skies had cleared. As Emma dressed for supper Ruth was full of excitement over the imminent arrival of Daventry's family. She told Emma of the intense preparations Mrs. Wardlow and her staff were making. Extra girls had been recruited from the village to prepare an elegant supper for a select group of Daventry's neighbors. One of his sisters-in-law, Lady Cleo Jones, had arranged the party.

"Why, we've not had a party here since I've come. I suppose it's not a proper ball, but it's ever so romantic. Girls from the neighborhood, coming to dance with His Lordship. I think they all want to catch his eye, his being such an eligible young man for a lady."

"Yes, I imagine they're quite curious about him in the neighborhood." Emma had not seen him since he had put her in the closet. She ate with the servants. No one noticed if she skipped the fish at the servants' table. Her silks hung in the wardrobe, and Adam stood guard in the hall at night.

"Are you fond of dancing, miss?"

"No, I don't care for it," Emma lied.

"You should spy, miss."

"Spy?"

"We're all going to take a peek. No harm in it. They'll be in the great hall, and well, we can look down on them from the chapel vestibule through the screen."

"Does Daventry dance?"

"Why wouldn't he?"

Emma shrugged. "Didn't you tell me that he did not live a gentleman's life when he was young?"

Ruth frowned and paused. "Yer right, miss, I forgot." She tried to puzzle it out. "He must have learned since."

"Who are the musicians? Strangers?"

"Oh no, miss. We'll have the usual fiddlers the quality hereabouts have always had for assemblies and such. And Adam will look out for Daventry."

Emma tried to tell herself that the party was no danger to him. His family had planned it. They would be present. The guests would be neighbors, known to each other. The musicians troubled her. She didn't like the idea of carriages coming and going with a noise and bustle that was bound to create confusion. Anyone could slip into the hall unnoticed amid the comings and goings. She told herself it was a foolish thought. The fiddlers would fiddle and the guests would dance.

Emma headed for the stables on the afternoon of the family's arrival. The grooms were busy attending to the arriving carriages with their horses that needed tending and stabling.

Ned Begley, the head groom, touched his hat to her. "Off for a walk, miss?"

Emma nodded.

"Keep an eye out for that black spaniel of mine, Hector, will you? He's gone missing."

Emma said she would, but the request sent a shiver down her spine. She had not visited the ponies since the snow. Her feet felt suddenly heavy, and she moved like an old woman until she heard Budge whicker. From the open door she could see the ponies leaning their heads over their stall gates. They gave her their usual greetings and demanded petting and a treat. She checked their feed and found nothing suspicious in its look or smell. She stroked Budge's forehead and rubbed behind his ears. She suspected that Wallop had done some evil thing to Ned's dog, but he had left the ponies alone.

She peeked from the stable doors at the hive of activity in the drive. As his brother Will had predicted, Daventry's family arrived in a parade of carriages with luggage strapped above and behind and outriders and servants and children. Emma watched them pull up before the front entry porches, where the staff was lined up and where the boys, groomed and impatient, broke rank to greet each new arrival.

Mrs. Creevey and her cheerful husband supervised grooms and footmen and maids handling horses and baskets and luggage.

Daventry emerged from the shadows to shake his brothers' hands and submit to kisses from his sisters-in-law and his mother. Again Emma's understanding of him shifted. He was not the angel warrior or the aloof lord, but a man connected to a large and loving family. She saw duty and responsibility in the way he noticed everyone and listened and gave orders. But detachment, too.

S OPHIE held her major's note as she looked out over the grounds of the hall. *Marry me.* It began. *Now or never.* He wanted an answer tomorrow. And deserved one. It had never been her intention to make a good man suffer. He was the most exasperatingly understanding and forgiving lover. She had never had a lover like him, not even Granville.

From the moment they'd met in Paris when she had stood below the great church on the banks of the Seine contemplating the thickness of the ice and the darkness of the water beneath it and wondering how swiftly the river would carry her away he had understood her. They called the church Notre Dame, our mother, the pure, good mother, while she, Sophie, had failed as a mother, had lost her sons or turned them against her and hampered them in their lives in spite of all her care.

Mademoiselle, he'd called her, sharply but with shameless flattery. That had made her laugh, and he'd coaxed her away from the river's edge to a cafe and then coaxed her to laugh and to live again.

Within days she had begun writing to Xander, encouraging him, pouring out her own faith in Kit's survival, on pink pressed paper. Later when the ice on the Seine broke up, they strolled for hours on its banks or sat in the parks.

The first time he'd asked her to marry him had been a lovely spring day, the first of May, with flower girls on every street corner in Paris, selling their sweet bunches of *muguet*, lilies of the valley. She had explained that she could not marry him until she knew her youngest son's fate. And he'd understood and waited. And then such hopes they'd both had in the giddy days after Kit's recovery. He had come with her from Paris at the news that Xander had found Kit alive.

And when Kit had come home at last, she had filled her London house with his urchins and laughed every day, and her major had waited for her to look at him and say the word.

But Henry Norwood, their solicitor, had warned them with a sober face under his kindly white brows that the court case against Wenlocke meant that all her past would be raked up, all her follies and errors. Not only Candover who'd seduced her at fifteen and Oxley whom she'd pursued to avenge herself on Candover, but every man who'd courted her or dangled for her, even those whom she had rejected. Every indiscretion, every tempestuous outburst in an open carriage or a theater box, every extravagance would be a weapon in the duke's hands to use against her son. Henry did not say it, nor did he have to, that for Sophie to have a new lover would jeopardize her son's case.

Privately, she supposed that Luc himself would turn against her when her whole scandalous past lay exposed. He was a gentleman above reproach, and her past was like the wretched furnishings of some tenement where the people had been turned out, everything ugly and cheap heaped in a cart and dragged through the streets. She could not bear to see his love fade, so she had sent him back to France.

She had never expected to see him again. One really could not refuse a man more than once. But just last week he had come to the house on Hill Street, her last remaining property, so much had been sold in the fight against Wenlocke. Luc had burst in, really, and declared his love and told her to put an end to his long wait. He wanted to grow old with her. They could live wherever she wished.

When she began to protest that he could not be serious, he did not know what he was asking, he did not know who she was, he had taken her in his arms and kissed her in that way he had, a man who knew his own mind. And she'd responded, come alive in his embrace like the wanton she had always been.

She was fifty, a grandmother. Really one was supposed to be over such desires and not to feel in one's breasts and one's belly the warm, rude stirrings of life. She had almost come to believe in her own respectability during the long battle with Wenlocke. She had lived a sober, discreet life for three long years, conscious that she hardly deserved the blessing of Kit's return and that she must do everything in her power to show that she was grateful, grateful, grateful to have him back. She was no longer wealthy. Though she did not think her sons would let her sink into poverty, she felt awkwardly dependent in relation to her major. He had vineyards and a chateau. A crumbling ruin, he claimed.

Her sons, the Sons of Sin, the papers called them, had triumphed over all her flaws and errors. They had become the men they were meant to be. She could not even regret her lovers, Candover and Oxley, because they had given her such sons. Xander, who should not have forgiven her, but had. Will, for whom in some way she had feared the most, and Kit, who remained a mystery to all of them, but who now as Daventry—she must remember to think of him as Dav—was more like his father than he would ever know.

And his dear sweet father. He had loved Sophie so differently from Candover or Oxley. She knew what her major wanted of her. He wanted her to put Granville in the past, too, the gallant young husband she had loved and sent off to India. Granville had seized love. They both had. But he had seized something more, the chance to be active in the world, as if his father had held him back for so long that once freed, he had to fill every moment with the chances longed denied him.

Her son could not know that the room he gave her for this visit was the very one in which she had spent her wedding night. She sank under the weight of her own past down on the silk-covered bench at the foot of the bed.

Granville's family had buried him at Wenlocke with little ceremony according to the papers. She had scoured them for an account of it and found only a few lines. At the time their marriage remained a secret, so she had received nothing of his, only the news that he was no more.

The house brought it all back. Rolling up that drive in Granville's carriage with his ring on her finger and his babe in her belly and the sun on the golden stones of his house, her future had seemed assured, her sorrows banished. On her long ago wedding day she believed she had sailed into a calm harbor. His people had welcomed her, and together they had visited his ancient nurse and left the treasured records of their marriage in her safekeeping.

Even now after twenty years it seemed a terrible injustice to cease to mourn him, to accept this new love that had come to her, to have her life filled with sons and grandsons. Someone ought to go on loving Granville as he deserved.

Tomorrow, her major said. Tomorrow. The little note ended. *Meet me in the stables at ten.* Tomorrow she would decide.

She rose and slipped the note into the bodice of her plum silk gown. She knew that it showed her fair skin and dark hair to advantage. She checked her mirror for gray. Finding only one strand, she tucked it under its darker fellows.

Chapter Fifteen

༄

THEY were all at dinner. Below stairs and behind green baize doors, the staff rushed about, busied with dozens of serving tasks for the large party in the dining room and the guests to come for the evening's dancing.

The unfamiliar faces of extra maids and footmen made Emma uneasy, but Mr. and Mrs. Creevey seemed to have everything in hand. Emma herself passed unnoticed amid the bustle.

She returned to the schoolroom, and wrote again on each slate the words she had chosen for the boys. Her new plan, the best one so far, was to slip away at the exact moment Daventry's family left. Wallop and his men would watch the family's progress through the town. Emma would circle the other way and be a day, a night, and another morning on her journey before Wallop missed her and began to search for her. It was a sensible plan, but Tatty would say don't cry fresh fish before you've cast your net. Emma was not yet on her way.

The schoolroom door opened and closed behind her. Before she could turn, a pair of strong arms captured her and pulled her into a tight embrace. *Daventry.*

"Meet me on the roof tonight." He kissed her under her ear.

"But your family, your guests."

He loosened his hold just enough to let her twist to face him. "Don't let my family daunt you."

"Mrs. Creevey advised me to stay out of sight, you know."

"When everyone retires. You know the door. Wear something warm."

She opened her mouth to protest, but he stopped her words with a brief ardent kiss. "Be there."

Then he was gone.

Emma put down the slate she still held. She should not meet him. She should sleep as soundly as she could in the last bed she was likely to sleep in for weeks. She should not let him think her a willing partner in madness. He should know that she at least was sensible. She should put the idea out of her mind and not think of her old cloak that Daventry had tied beneath her chin with his warm touch.

D AV lifted his glass and looked at his family. They had gathered in the drawing room for some time together. In half an hour Dav's guests would arrive, four local families, whose curiosity at least overcame their skepticism about his origins. Apparently his title made them willing to overlook his own dubious past but not his mother's. His neighbors would come to dance with the new marquess but would not dine with his scandalous parent. The thought of the snub to Sophie tightened his jaw.

Below in the hall the hired musicians tuned their instruments. Two or three of the rooms in his mother's town house would easily fit in his drawing room. But his brother's growing families and his own boys peopled it quite nicely.

On a gold sofa his mother had Will's drowsy twins on either side of her looking at a picture book. Her major was playing chess simultaneously with Lark and Swallow. It occurred to Dav briefly that his mother was avoiding her admirer, who had just returned to England.

Nate Wilde, Will's reformed thief, who outdid them all in sartorial dash, was teaching the other boys and Xan's oldest the finer points of lottery tickets amid much nudging and some shouting. The smallest babe was in bed, and Dav knew that his sister-in-law Cleo would leave soon to check on him. His grand house made her uneasy at times to be so distant from her offspring. But at the moment what he could feel was the awareness vibrating in the air between Helen and Will and Cleo and Xander. The four of them were listening to a story a rather sheepish Charlie Spencer was telling. But that pull between his brothers and their wives felt to Dav like a palpable thing, reminding him of the one person absent from the room. The thought that he'd kept at the edge of his mind, refusing to acknowledge it, shoved its way to the center. *Where could he make love to Emma?*

The trouble with entertaining his married brothers, he realized, was that it reminded him of his solitary state and his empty bed. Everyone else had a room, except his mother and her major, an extraordinarily honorable fellow. His mother's sons possessed her passionate nature.

Xan's gaze caught his, and Dav roused himself to attend to Charlie's story. Constables had arrested the boy for distributing Plaice's leaflets on contraception to workingwomen on Bread Street. At seventeen his young brother-in-law was eager to transform the world. He idolized both his sister, Cleo, who now served on the board of Evershot's bank, and who had become quite a financial expert through the bullion crisis, and Xan, who continued to push for more light and more clean water for London.

Charlie shoved his hands in his pockets. "Well, I'd do it again. Besides, it's not uncommon to be arrested in our family. Xan's been arrested, after all."

"Maybe there's a better way," Xan suggested.

"The rights of women will be the subject of my first speech in Lords, you may be sure," Charlie proclaimed.

"Bravo, Charlie." Helen Jones raised her glass to him.

"Let's get you through university, first, before you take your place in Lords," Cleo advised her younger brother.

The gold clocks on the mantel chimed the hour, and the family party broke up. Will clapped a hand on Dav's shoulder and told him, "The first applicants for your hand are at the door. Do the family proud, brother."

Dav thought of the roof and Emma.

D AVENTRY did dance. Emma stood behind three maids watching the elegant couples below.

The men wore black evening dress. The women's gowns shimmered in pale colors, and light flashed on pearls around white throats and jeweled combs in dark hair. It was a scene such as Tatty had described long ago when they had practiced dancing in their cell.

Below the gawking maids was one avid watcher of the

scene, her dark head bent to take it in, a gentleman at her side.

In a moment the woman turned her face up to the gentleman, and Emma saw her dark expressive eyes full of intense pleasure. His mother had wanted to see him dance. She grasped her companion's hand and bright tears sparked in her eyes and trembled down her cheeks, and she laughed and dashed them away and laid her head against her companion's side. Emma thought she had never seen such perfect joy. It wounded her to see his mother's yearning for Daventry's happiness.

Three hours later the house was quiet again. Emma took no light. She could count her way to every door and stair in the north wing. In the little room, she reached for the door, opened it, and stepped out into a night so cold under a bottomless indigo sky that she reeled a little and felt the roof slope under her and her body tilt alarmingly when a strong grip caught her and pulled her back to a level surface.

"Steady, love. The roof slopes there."

He was nearly invisible, as dark as the night itself. "What are you wearing?"

"An old coat of mine."

He pulled her into an embrace, and she felt the velvet of it as he pressed her head against his shoulder. She recognized the scent of cold fires and stone from the day she had searched his closet. She knew what it meant. He had sipped a taste of his future tonight when he danced with his eligible young neighbors. Now the ragged coat and open roof pulled him back into the grip of the past.

He broke their embrace, but Emma held his arm for steadiness. "My legs are shaking."

He kissed the top of her head. "Come just a few steps. We'll sit and look up at the stars."

He took her hand and extended it to where she could touch the wall and led her from the shadows to the open roof. He lowered himself to sit, leaning his back against the upper wall and pulled her down to nest against him between his legs. He pulled his old coat up around them and leaned her head back against his shoulder. "Now you can look at the dizzying stars and not fall down."

He was right. With his body around her and his warmth at her back, Emma felt anchored even if the stars seemed to swirl in the blue black depths above them. The illusion was of falling backward, but he was there to catch her, heat at her back.

Emma did not remember ever looking across such a distance. She counted steps and measured a path from one thread-marked doorknob to the next while he gazed from his towering roof into infinite distances.

"You can find your way anywhere by the stars," he said.

You *can,* she thought.

His hands moved on her hips, settling her more deeply against him. His warm palm flat against her empty pocket paused.

"You didn't find your brother's keepsake?"

She swallowed the lump in throat. She hadn't found it or shamed the boys into returning it. "No."

"You have nothing else that's really yours, do you?"

He saw through her disguise. She should not be surprised at it. He had from the first. He stripped away all the false layers with which the duke and Aubrey and Wallop sought to disguise her. *I have myself,* she thought. *I belong to myself,* but his arms came around her in a fierce possession as if she belonged not to herself but to him, and time contracted while the stars danced and Daventry's heart beat at her back.

No one had taught Dav about wanting and not having. His experience had been with a professional, who openly enticed and readily offered. She had been barely clothed from the beginning of their encounter, not cased in stays and skirts as Emma was. He had not yet had to deal with a woman's trappings.

It took some doing to shift Emma in his hold so that he could reach up under her cloak to feel her ribs and run his fingertips across the soft swell of her breasts above her stays.

At his touch she pressed more deeply against him. Emma's sweet, round bottom now nestled snuggly against his hot, stiff cock. With every shift of her backside against his yard, crazy images flashed in his mind.

He buried his face in the curls at the back of her neck and shifted his hand to nestle between her thighs. To touch her there filled him with a mad combination of triumph and need. Her body answered with a restless novice stirring and a quickening of her breath and pulse.

It made the mystery of her plain. Will believed she was acting out of some careful calculation or in obedience to an accomplice's plan. Sensually, she was an innocent even if she was not a vicar's daughter as she claimed, not a woman with a safe, well-ordered past of study and duty, but a constrained spirit longing to escape.

The wind moaned against the chimney stacks, and he tipped his head back against the stones. A roof was a crazy place to take a woman when you wanted to be naked with her. Need for Emma was doing strange things to him. He was a poor specimen of a marquess to give great state bedrooms to his brothers and their warm wives and take his own lover to the roof as if they were a pair of London strays.

"Emma, I want to touch you, to make love to you, but the roof is not the place. I've got to stop." He looked up into the fathomless sky, letting his pounding heart slow its mad rhythm.

"I don't mind the roof. I like being here with you."

"Then we'll stay, but let's go higher to look at the whole sky."

"Higher? You'll scare me witless."

"I won't let go of you. Trust me."

It made her laugh. He had not let go of her once since she had stepped out onto the roof. Tatty's voice saying *to trust is good, not to trust is better* came and went in her ear so fast she could not catch it.

Daventry helped her to her feet and turned her in his arms so that he might kiss her again. The kiss escalated, robbing her of breath, sending her pulse galloping. He broke it and held her while they both regained their breath. Then he turned and took her hand to lead her.

She knew she held him back from his usual swift stride. She tested each step while he pulled her after him, with just enough force to coax, not drag. The cold wind blew between them and filled her ears, and she gritted her teeth to keep them from chattering. Her feet felt the icy slates through her slippers, and she tested each step gingerly.

Halfway across the roof, she heard brittle stones break above them like the ice of a pond cracking. At the sound he swung her in front of him with a sudden powerful pull of his arm. As she snapped forward, her grip slipped, and she went sprawling, thumping against the stones, unable to arrest her slide down the slope. Her heart had no time to break before he landed on her, covering her body with his own, in the same wild slide down the icy slope of the roof.

A darker shadow passed over them, and the roof shuddered at the shock of some giant blow and heaved up under them in a sudden explosion, lifting their feet and tilting them head downward, hurtling toward the balustrade. Daventry's arms framed Emma's head. They crashed against the barrier as a shower of dust and shards of broken stone rained down on them. Behind them the balustrade cracked and fell away. There was a heartbeat's silence then a deep thud in the drive below, the shock of it vibrating up through the building and Emma's bones.

Daventry's back had absorbed their collision with the low wall at the edge of the roof. His eyes were closed. His face shone palely, covered with dust. The duke's awful words came back to her. *He's a hard man to kill.* Emma reached a shaking hand to brush away the grit from his eyes and lips. He shook his head once and looked at her. They hadn't killed him, and it made her giddy with relief.

"What hurts? Anything broken?"

She shook her head. Her throat hurt. Her heart hurt. Mad laughter and tears threatened. She had doubted him for a black moment. "You?"

"Scrapes only."

Below them voices shouted and footsteps pounded.

"What fell?"

"The pots atop one of the chimney stacks. Can you walk?" He was shifting, rousing himself for action. "In a minute Adam Digweed will burst through that door. Let me get you inside first."

She understood him. He would protect her with his life. They got to their feet, shedding dust and fragments of stone.

Dav surveyed the damage. A four-foot opening in the balustrade gaped. There was a deep gash in the roof where the falling masonry had hit and shattered the tiles before it crashed through the balustrade and plummeted to the ground. Above them on the upper roof, the roofline had changed. A row of chimney pots was missing. He could not be sure the rest of the roof was safe. He had to take her back across the damaged section.

The voices below grew louder, and lights glimmered up from the drive. His brothers would be on the scene investigating as soon as the servants could alert them.

Dav took Emma's hand and led her back up to the inmost edge of the roof against the wall. He made her face the wall, and together they sidled along it back to the door. Inside he shed the velvet cloak and shoved it into her hands. With a low sardonic laugh he tucked her into the closet. "You're safe, Emma. Leave the cloak behind. I'll lead Adam away."

She touched his face once. She could hear a heavy rapid tread approaching.

"Tell no one you were on that roof." He kissed her and closed the door.

Chapter Sixteen

∽

DAV turned as Adam lumbered through the door, his nightshirt billowing around his giant form, a candlestick in his hand.

"Sir, wot happened?"

"A block of chimney pots tumbled from the upper roof. Let's go down. Is anyone hurt below?" Dav moved deliberately to the stairs.

Adam blocked his path. "You're not hurt?"

"No. The roof isn't safe, however; don't go out there."

Below in the drive, his brothers had gathered with a knot of footmen. Xander was giving orders. Will held up a lamp, examining the fallen masonry. Five chimneys in their enclosing plaster base had fallen. Looking up, Dav could see where the heavy block had come crashing through the balustrade.

Two groups of footmen went in different directions to search the grounds.

"Been ignoring home repairs, have you, Dav?" Will came to stand beside him.

"Were you up there?" asked Xander.

"Crossing the roof. There was a wire. I hit it with my knee and dove. The stack came down behind me, hit the roof, and tumbled through the balustrade."

Will swore. "Who knows you go up there?"

"And who has access to the roof?" Xander asked.

"Everyone in the house knows I go there."

His brothers waited for him to cast suspicion on Emma. He refused. Whatever falsehood he suspected in her, he knew the accident had taken her by surprise.

"Damn it, Dav, everyone in this house, except that girl, was hired by us with great care."

"Anyone watching from the woods might also know I like the roof."

"When was the last time you were there?"

"When Will was here."

"So we assume someone added the wire since then, but the work on the base of those stacks must have taken time."

"Weeks." Dav did not believe any of his people had been involved.

Will watched him. "You really don't want to blame that girl."

"The girl did not loosen the masonry or set the trip wire." He'd almost lost her. To think about it set his heart pounding again.

"You've got to stop hiding her if you want us to believe that." Xander made it a command.

"I won't have you grill her," Dav insisted.

"Someone needs to find out the truth about her." Will was caustic as ever.

"Someone other than me, you mean."

"You apparently can't think straight around her."

Xan put out a hand to cut Will off. "Come on, Dav, you can't let Wenlocke win. Not after all we've done."

"All right. Tomorrow, you'll meet her."

E MMA heard the voices coming. She would know Daventry's voice now anywhere. Even at a distance it seemed, something in the timbre of that voice resonated in her.

The voices stopped outside her door. Big Adam Digweed's voice took over.

"I ought to 'ave been checking the roof regular. I ought not to 'ave left my post."

"Adam, that masonry could have been damaged before we ever came to live here. The house has not been lived in for years. You've not let me down."

But she had. She had told Wallop that first day that Daventry walked on his roof. Maybe Wallop already knew it.

There was a pause. A door opened.

"But, sir, if time and weather loosed those stacks, why didn't the thing fall in the gale?"

Emma held her breath. She remembered the gale in early March. It had reached even Wenlocke and uprooted trees.

"It's enough that you're here on duty now, Adam. In the morning, we'll inspect the roof. Keep everyone off of it until we know what we've got."

"I'm not leaving you again, sir. Right here, I'll be."

"Thanks, Adam. Good night."

X ANDER let his wife take him deep into her body. Her hands stroked up and down his back urging him on. It was a call he was powerless to resist. In the aftermath, he turned them, so that her body nested in the circle of his. He knew she would drift off in minutes, weary from the demands of caring for their newest babe, but at his glance, she had understood his need for her without words.

Summoned from their bed by a servant, Xander's wakening had been doubly rude—the comfort of sleep disturbed and the comfort of the house. The house was supposed to be safe for Dav. They had taken every precaution in examining it and staffing it. Seeing the broken stonework in the drive reminded him of their enemy's reach and his willingness to unleash deadly forces against them. From the beginning Wenlocke had had bullyboys and henchmen easily bought and willing to kill.

As he stood in the drive, he had felt the blame descend on his shoulders again. He was the one who had lost his brother that night. He was the one who encouraged the legal action against the duke that had made Dav the marquess.

Cleo stirred against him, drawing one of his hands to cup her breast. "My love, you didn't make Wenlocke the bitter old man that he is. And you didn't fail to protect your brother."

"You think I'm taking too much blame?"

"You must see now how capable he is, how strong, how ready to take Wenlocke on himself."

"How does he take on an enemy that sneaks in the night to ambush him with the stones of his own house?"

"Directly."

"I almost lost you to an accident, remember?" he said.

She twisted in his arms and kissed him with a kiss that said she remembered, too, remembered finding his hand in the dark where her uncle had tried to entomb her and drown her. Hand in hand they had fled destruction together up to the rooftops of Bread Street.

"Wenlocke uses whoever will do his bidding. He used my uncle March and his crony Bredsell and even Dav's kidnapper, Harris. He must have another tool. Someone nearby watching the house."

"Or someone inside the house."

"An insider seems unlikely when you and Will have so carefully screened all the staff and when Dav has such loyal people as Adam Digweed and Mrs. Wardlow around him."

"The only person in the household we didn't hire is the new grinder, a woman; Emma Portland is her name."

"You don't think she chipped away the masonry around those chimney pots."

"No, but Will says she's the kind of woman to melt a man's brain."

"Because she's lovely, you're convinced she's false?"

"I haven't met her. I'm convinced she has Dav unable to think."

"Well, let Helen and I meet her, tomorrow, and give you our opinion."

A cool March wind fluttered the skirts of his mother and sisters-in-law. It was a sober party that examined the pile of stonework on his drive. By day it was plain that a wire had been attached to the five clay chimney pots that topped the stack above his favorite rooftop spot. Each one easily weighed three stone. Will studied the destruction on the roof itself. Lark climbed the stack to report on what he found where the chimney pots had stood. As Will suspected, tools had been used to loosen the masonry base. He would send his man Harding into the village to scout about who might have the skill for such a job and the need for ready if ill-gotten cash.

Those chisel marks meant Dav's grandfather had not given up the fight to destroy him. Whatever his brothers thought, he could not continue to hide at Daventry Hall expecting the old man to quit the game or die.

Tears streamed down his mother's face. She gave his hand a squeeze, begged his forgiveness for being a watering pot, and went off with her major for a drive. Xan and Will advised the major to go armed.

Dav moved them all inside for a round of sparring matches between the members of the group. They turned the hall into a ring for the occasion. Today, he would prove to Xan that he was ready for a match. Once he proved himself in the ring, his brothers would have to see that he was ready to take on Wenlocke.

Chapter Seventeen

✦

THE Royal Lodge at Windsor taught Charlotte once again the childhood lesson that even the Duchess of Wenlocke would be wise to recall. Getting what one wished for—say, an audience with the king—was not always a blessing. George's overheated rooms were even more of a trial than his delaying tactics. For this, her third visit, Charlotte wore a lavender muslin borrowed from her daughter though March frosts covered the park.

Charlotte wondered that Lady Conyngham, the king's long-time mistress, could endure the heat and the winks and nods of her fat lover.

Charlotte supposed that Lady Conyngham would not be counted harmful to the state by most observers. She had not used her position to interfere in government or military affairs but only to advance her complaisant husband and ambitious offspring. Yet she could be blamed, Charlotte felt, for reducing the king of England to a spoiled, cosseted child unable to support even the rigors of his duty. He was beyond stays now and beyond even the modest exertions required by his station—appearing at state events or meeting with ambassadors. Putting his signature to a pardon for Emma would be an effort for him.

Elaborately dressed servants led her to an anteroom and left her, and she was reminded of yet another challenge she faced. She must sweetly flatter in a way that went against her nature and against her long dominance at Wenlocke. She must let go of all command and be the bereaved mother begging for the life of a child. She must rouse him to believe that in signing her scrap of paper, he was performing a heroic act, a further defeat of upstarts and Jacobins everywhere.

Her influence had been greater at Bow Street, where she met with the magistrate himself. He had recommended a Runner named Jack Castle and assured her that Castle was as good a man as she could find for the job of finding Emma, for he had recovered Lady Bellingham's spaniel.

Charlotte had managed to hold her tongue and suspend her judgment until she met Castle himself, a small, neat man with a mop of brown curls above a long face and ears like mug handles.

He did not fear her authority or blink at the reward she offered. He did listen, and he agreed to help her in spite of the limits of what she could tell him. He remained her best hope for extricating Emma from Aubrey's hold.

An eel-backed equerry ushered Charlotte into the royal presence. The king sprawled on a red velvet sofa, his fat legs in white breeches splayed below his great mound of a belly, his swollen feet in tasseled black silk slippers propped on a regal red-and-gold ottoman. He wore a greasy green night turban and dirty blue silk jacket. At his side Lady Conyngham rested a bejeweled hand on one of his enormous thighs. He studied Charlotte and took up a glass of cherry gin, the scent of it ripe in the air. Charlotte tried to conceal the shock of coming face-to-face with all that laxity.

"Escaped that cold stick of yours, have you, Duchess?"

"Your Majesty is most kind to receive me." Charlotte dipped into a low curtsy as she had not done in many years. In the room, degrees warmer than the anteroom, an unaccustomed moisture beaded on her skin.

"We'll warm you up, I'm sure." The king winked at Lady Conyngham. "You've not visited before, so you must want something very badly, very badly indeed."

There was for a moment a shrewd glimmer in those eyes, the cunning of a child, who seeks to manipulate an adult to his advantage.

"There is no one else to whom I can turn, Your Majesty. Only you have the power to right a terrible wrong against a defenseless young woman."

He laughed, and it took his breath away. For several moments he lay back, eyes closed, gasping, while Lady Conyngham fanned him lightly. Charlotte looked away discreetly. The room was hung with portraits of great military heroes and of George himself in a hussar's uniform mounted on a gray.

"You must forgive me, Duchess, illness takes its toll, I'm afraid. I'm not the man I once was, leading the German Legion at Waterloo, you know, but I'm still ready to take on the enemy."

"I thought you would be, Your Majesty, that's why I came."

"Didn't come to see my giraffe, did you? I'll wager you

could look him in the eye. She could, don't you think, Lizzy?"
He turned to Lady Conyngham, who laughed politely at the
joke. "We should make an excursion to the menagerie."

Lady Conyngham flicked Charlotte a sharp look. Charlotte did not know who was more desperate to quash the
idea of an excursion.

"Oh dear, Your Majesty, let us not venture out into the
cold, today. Really, you have been gracious enough with
your time. I have just one small favor to ask."

The word *favor* brought an instant frown to the king's
brow, and he sipped his cherry gin again.

Charlotte removed the letter from her bag. "With your
signature I can rescue a dear child from a terrible fate."

"My signature, did you say?" The king's tone was quer-
ulous.

Charlotte could see a difficulty. She could not hand the
document directly to the king. He did not stretch out his
hand to receive it, and Lady Conyngham sat with her hand
occupied with the king's thigh. "It will be a heroic signing.
With the stroke of your pen, you confer freedom, but it must
remain our secret." She glanced at Lady Conyngham.

"May I tell you in strictest confidence, of course, the
identity of the young woman in question?"

An interested gleam lit the king's eye. "Our secret, eh?
Lizzy'll keep it." He nudged Lady Conyngham, who stretched
a languid hand to receive the document.

A HEAVY knock on Emma's door signaled the inevitable. She must dine with his family. She had avoided
them all day not simply from a fear of questions but from a
desire not to expose Daventry to speculation. She wore

bruises from her elbow to her shins. Ruth had seen them
and stopped her usual commentary. Without words she had
arranged a square black-bordered gold wrap to cover Emma's
arms where the puffed sleeves of her poppy gown might
give her away.

Daventry stood in the hall in his polite host guise with a
frowning Adam Digweed at his side. Adam looked as if he
wanted to pound someone with those great fists of his.
Daventry looked as if he wanted to push his way into her
room and shut the door.

Emma looked down at once under the heat of that gaze.
He offered his arm, and she reached to take it, and as she
did so, her shawl slipped. He frowned, his concentrated
gaze narrowing on a brown and purple patch above her
elbow. With a controlled move, he raised the soft fabric to
cover the blemish and tucked her arm in his.

"Ready, Miss Portland? I promise you I won't let them
attack you."

She nodded. His family should attack her. She had done
little to help Wallop, but the little she had done had already
endangered the man at her side. They should seize her and
cast her out in the darkness, and she should go, begin running. She had delayed as long as she could. Now if the law
caught her, Tatty and little Leo would still go free. By
Emma's count of days Tatty must have reached the coast
and the waiting messenger and sailed to freedom.

The journey through the long gallery to the south drawing room was accomplished in silence. Adam's heavy tread
followed them. Emma's skirts whispered and brushed Daventry's leg. The point of contact between them where her
hand rested on his solid wool-clad arm seemed the only
warmth. Emma felt the heat of him rise and draw her

closer. She did not think she had been warm since they had
left the roof the night before.

She had not allowed herself to sleep for hours after she
had heard him return to his room, fearing a nightmare. In
sleep falling chimney pots would be magnified and dis-
torted and joined to all the fears she kept locked away. By
day falling masonry assumed its normal size and dimension. By noon she had heard from Ruth how someone had
chiseled loose the heavy pots that topped the chimney stack
and set a wire across the roof to pull them down on whoever
crossed there. Only one person regularly crossed that stretch.
The accident had been intended to knock Daventry senseless or tumble him from the roof to the ground below.

His grandfather and Aubrey meant to kill him. She
could not now deny that she was a tool of his enemies, like
Wallop and whoever had climbed the roof. No one in Daventry's household had turned on him, she was sure, and
Wallop could never heave his bulk to such a height or come
unnoticed anywhere near the house. The boys could go to
the roof any time, and Lark was angry, but surely not angry
at Daventry, not enough to want to harm him. So Wallop
had someone else working for him, someone who had got-
ten to that roof.

The puzzle of it had consumed her as she had stripped
off her ruined gown, one of the ones the duchess had provided, and washed and brushed away the dust and stone
fragments from her hair, tossing the evidence on the fire,
and tended the scrapes to her hands, knees, and elbows.
She could not get warm.

"Anything to report from the schoolroom?" he asked.

She looked up, and his gaze sent a bolt of heat crackling
through her, not a mere spark from the friction of clinging

garments, but something swift and hot and jolting to her core.

It took a moment for the words themselves to register. "Finch," she said. "Finch has read his slate. Tomorrow or the next day I expect the others will follow his lead."

"Finch, huh. I'd have thought Lark would want to be first."

"In most things, yes, but he resists reading the most. I've blundered with him, you know. I can't blame him." She looked up at him. "He believes you'll send the boys away when they can read."

A shadow crossed his face. "I'll talk with him."

They reached the drawing room, and he leaned down to whisper assurance as Emma looked up. Their gazes caught, and it was impossible to look away. The candle and the candlestick.

He looked away first, and when Emma turned she met the lively green gaze of a woman in chestnut brown taffeta with white collar. Her knowing look reminded Emma instantly of Tatty, though the woman hardly resembled her cousin.

A tall, gangly youth with a head of untamed fawn-colored curls had the attention of most of the room's occupants. He had gathered three candelabras on one table and placed one candlestick on another, inviting them all to compare the light. His listeners joked and teased.

"Seriously," the youth claimed. "There's no escaping it; Xander's going to light the insides of your houses, too. It's merely a matter of who wants to be first."

"Gas flames in every house? You two will burn London to the ground."

The youth rolled his eyes as if he'd heard this objection before. He caught Daventry's gaze. "Dav, you should try the new lighting here at the hall, where there are no adjoining buildings."

They all turned at the appeal to Daventry and saw him with Emma. Talk halted with comical abruptness.

Daventry showed no sign of unease. "Can it be done in a house as old as this one, Charlie?"

"That's the point. Candles are the past. Gas lighting's forward-looking, the wave of the future and all. You don't want this place to be a mere museum."

"If Xan thinks it can be done, I'm for it." Daventry steered Emma toward a woman with a kind of beauty that could never be ignored. She was dressed in figured plum silk bordered with black lace with jet beading on the bodice. Her beauty must attract, must call attention to itself, must bewitch. At the woman's side was a lean, gray-haired man obviously devoted to her. Daventry introduced them as his mother and a Major Luc Montclare.

Emma did her curtsies. No one seemed alarmed to have the Frenchman in their midst, but Emma could not repress a little shudder to hear him named. Of course Daventry saw it.

Then she met an older, more severe version of Daventry, a man with broad shoulders, black hair, and an austere carved look to his face. He gave Emma a polite welcome. More polite introductions followed as they made their way through the room. Will Jones's wife, Helen, another beauty in an amethyst gown, with deep brown eyes and tawny gold hair, smiled at Emma and told her, "You are a favorite with Robin, you know. He says you can whistle and ride ponies and aren't afraid of mud or toads. High praise, I think."

Emma murmured her thanks at the undeserved kindness. Once the civilities had been observed she could watch Daventry in the midst of his people. His family was handsome and quick and stirred each other to ready laughter, and they all touched. But they didn't touch him. Everyone turned to him, talked to him, but no one touched him, nor did he touch them while Emma still felt the touch of his arm as they'd entered the room.

Later as they took their seats in the dining room, Emma looked from the dark windows to the blaze of candles within. They would present a lighted tableau to anyone outside in the dark. It seemed to her a mad indifference to danger.

Cleo Jones, the sister-in-law with the lively green eyes, leaned toward Emma and said, "Don't worry, Miss Portland, we've got Adam Digweed in the corner, and a small troop of footmen and grooms outside. After last night, my husband has posted servants to watch the house at all hours."

Dav took his place at the head of the table. He did not think his coolness toward Emma fooled anyone in the room except Charlie Spencer and Lark and Raven, who had been permitted to join the adult party. With Mrs. Creevey's help, he had arranged to have Emma seated between Charlie and Lark and across from Raven so that she would not be subject to grilling by either of his brothers or his clever, charming sisters-in-law. He had to be content to let Charlie engage Emma in conversation. Charlie, his head full of world-changing inventions and needed reforms for injustice, was not likely to notice the undercurrent in the room of suspicion of Emma.

It was more difficult for Dav to control his own wayward glance that wanted to stray to her end of the table and fix itself on her as if by looking he could satisfy his desire to touch her again. He thought he was perfectly attentive to Helen Jones on his left when she tapped him lightly on the wrist.

"Dav." Will called him to order. "We can't have our host woolgathering. Xan is about to announce his decision."

"*His* decision?"

"He's your trainer. It's always the trainer who says when a man's ready for the ring."

"He needs a name, doesn't he?" suggested Cleo Jones. "Don't all your famous prizefighters have names?"

"You mean, like 'Destroyer' or the 'Trojan Terror'?" Dav could see that Will was enjoying the moment. "I say everyone should propose a fighting name for the Marquess of Daventry."

Lark, Raven, and Charlie Spencer immediately took up the challenge. His mother cast a dismayed look at Xan.

Raven got a fair amount of applause for "the Masher Marquess."

But Lark objected that the name didn't fit Dav's style. Charlie suggested they needed a name that implied speed like "lightning bolt."

It was Nate Wilde who satisfied the crowd with "the Somerton Stinger."

"That'll do to put his name in," agreed Will with a salute of his glass to Wilde. "Xan, your announcement."

Xan rose and encouraged them all to take up their glasses. "To 'the Somerton Stinger.' There's talk of an amateur open around East Thorndon. We'll get the Stinger a bout."

"That's thirty miles from London. You'll have to stay in an inn the night before." His mother objected.

Dav smiled at her. "I can't hide here forever, Mamma."

"It's an easy coach ride, Aunt Sophie, and Thorndon's perfect if the magistrates get wind of it, because there are two counties to bolt to," Charlie added.

"Why am I not comforted by the lack of magistrates?" Sophie wondered out loud.

"Dav'll be fine if he keeps his guard up, shifts sharp on his feet, and brings that hard, fast left of his."

"What about Lark? He's ready, don't you think?" Dav asked.

Will turned to Lark. "Oh yes, and he needs his cork drawn to give some character to that face of his."

Emma turned to smile at Lark, and her shawl slid from her arm. She reached to retrieve it, and Lark reached as well. His narrowed eyes noted the bruise above her elbow and the scrape below it.

He frowned and turned back to the table. "Not me. I like the mufflers on. In a real bout, I want to be on the sidelines, making odds."

"Spoken like an entrepreneur," Xander Jones offered.

When the toasts and clinking of glasses subsided, Emma saw the major rise to speak. He lifted his glass. "Gentlemen and ladies." He turned to Sophie, took her hand, and faced the table. "Your mother has accepted me, and I respectfully request your blessings. We will be wed by Michaelmas in London."

The three brothers exchanged glances and rose from their seats, glasses in hand. Xander cleared his throat. "To our mother and her major, much happiness."

Sophie stood and signaled to the footmen to fill the glasses again. "If I had some sweet drug of forgetfulness, I might put it in all your glasses, so that past follies and trials were blotted out of mind. But how can I regret those follies when I see what they have given me—you as you are? My dear sons, know that I am happy in this new beginning with this good man." She toasted her major with brimming eyes and turned again to the table. "Be happy all."

Emma raised her glass with the others. She thought they would be happy, except Daventry. It struck her that his two families were breaking up. His brothers and even his

mother had found partners for their lives. His boys were
changing and rebelling. He remained alone, detached,
their angel warrior, a being set a part from others, meant to
protect them, but not to mingle with them.

L ARK spun Dav to a stop by his elbow before they could
    enter the drawing room to rejoin the women and the
younger boys.

"You took her to the roof," he hissed. The boy shook
with suppressed rage.

Dav didn't deny it.

"The roof is our place. She's not one of us." Lark's fists
were clenched.

"Taking her to the roof doesn't make her one of us."

"But you chose her over us." Lark pulled at his neckcloth,
undoing the knot, fumbling to uncoil the linen around his
neck.

Dav wanted to say that he had not betrayed them, that
old friendships could allow for new ones, but he could not
deny what he felt for Emma Portland.

"She doesn't change us."

"She's changed you. You aren't one of us anymore."
Lark tossed his neckcloth aside and stalked off down the
gallery.

I N the morning Emma gathered her charges in the schoolroom and handed each boy his slate. Lark and Rook were
missing. They had not slept in their beds or come for breakfast.

She was not surprised that Lark would absent himself
from the classroom today when the boys were going to take

the plunge and admit their new reading ability. He had tried to hold them back for nearly a fortnight. But it made her uneasy that they were missing in the wake of accident.

She would have to read their words herself. The other boys sat in a circle, their slates on their laps.

"Do you remember how it went?" she asked.

"The woodcutter's sons had to go out in the world because they had no food," Finch said.

"And no one gave them work," Jay added.

"And the ogre trapped them in his cellar," Raven concluded. "Because they had no words to say."

Robin looked up from his slate. "You're all forgetting the birds."

"The older brothers didn't feed the birds, but the youngest gave them his crumbs, so the birds came back and set up a squawk."

"Just where we left off."

The door opened, and Helen Jones entered. The boys made a space for her in their circle, scraping chairs across the floor. Emma passed her Rook's slate while Robin whispered what they were doing. Emma had each of the boys write a number on his slate.

"Ready?"

They nodded.

"As the birds swirled, the ogre swung his cudgel in the air. With great"—Emma pointed at Finch, who shouted, "Courage"—"the tallest brother smote the ogre in his knee with a stick. The ogre bent double, and with swift"—Emma pointed at Raven, who shouted, "Daring"—"the quickest brother snatched the keys from the ogre's belt and tossed them to the cleverest brother, who with"—Emma pointed at Helen, who laughed and read, "Skill"—"opened the cellar door. Out came the four brothers who had been locked inside, blinking

in the light of day. The ogre roared, and with"—Emma pointed
at Swallow, who shouted, "Decision"—"the oldest brother told
them all to scatter to the four corners of the compass. The ogre
began to chase the slowest brother, who with noble"—Emma
read from her own slate—"generosity led the ogre to the edge
of a tall bluff, while with"—Emma pointed at Robin, who
shouted, "Wit"—"the youngest of all summoned the birds.

"Then the great flock circled the ogre's head each with a
thread in his beak. When the birds finished circling the
ogre, his head was wrapped like a mummy in the threads of
their mother's dishrags. He staggered around, clawing at his
bonds. The brothers darted around him, shouting from the
edge of the bluff, and he spun, grabbed blindly at the voices
until he toppled like a mighty tree over the bluff with a crash
that shook the ground. He lay still as the brothers looked
down at him. Then with one final twitch, he died."

For a full two minutes the boys leapt and collided with
one another as they shouted their hurrahs. They only subsided when Helen Jones asked Emma to tell the happily-
ever-after.

Emma smiled. "What with the ogre's forests supplying
wood, the boys' skills at making furnishings, their mother's cooking, and the gratitude of all the people passing
safely along the road, the family lived happily ever after.
And twice a year they spread out a feast for the great flocks
of birds winging their way north and south."

The boys sat flushed with pride, and Helen Jones came
forward to congratulate Emma.

"They've resisted learning to read for three years, Miss
Portland; you are to be congratulated."

"Thank you. I think they've been afraid that Daventry
would send them away once they learned to do it. He is
their family."

"Then you are to be congratulated all the more—for understanding them. I understand that this is an afternoon off for you, but I wonder if you would let my husband and I take you as far as the village. I would like him to understand the good work you're doing in the schoolroom here."

Emma felt the smile freeze on her lips. Kindness could trap a person as easily as hatred.

Chapter Eighteen

❧

B Y noon carriages lined the drive and servants scurried
to load bundles and help the passengers embark.
Emma found herself sharing a carriage seat with the formidable Will Jones and a two-year-old with eyes as big and
dark as pansies. Her fear of being subjected to questioning
gave way to the recognition that Will Jones might frown
fiercely at her, but he would not test her in the presence of
his wife and children.

When he helped her alight in the village, he did tell her
that his man Harding would soon smoke out whoever in
the town was behind the sabotage of the chimney pots.

Emma smiled and encouraged him to act swiftly in his
investigation.

One of his dark brows quirked up. He laughed and
promised he'd do his best.

* * *

WALLOP had a beef and pigeon pie, a rasher of bacon, and a plate of cockles in front of him. His napkin wore the usual assortment of stains, but his manner was grim. He stared at Emma's well-covered chest and shook his head.

Behind him the cupboard door was open a crack.

Wallop must know that the attempt on the roof had failed. He could see for himself that the carriages full of Daventry's family had passed through the village. Daventry and his people were alone at the hall, and Ned's dog had never returned. Emma tried to think of something she could tell Wallop to divert his attention from the hall.

"Did you bring me the whelp's box?"

"I saw no chance to take it with his family about."

Wallop pulled his napkin from his neck and tossed it down. "The inconveniences is getting out of hand, missy. A businessman has to deliver the goods, you know. But here's the whelp surviving accidents like a cat. Here's his mother, the whore of Hill Street, dining in that fine big room with a thousand candles blazing on her jewels. Here's the biggest by-blows in London strolling the grounds like lords with riffraff running about beside 'em."

"His mother and brothers left today."

Wallop shot her a nasty look. "Always telling me wot I know, aren't you? Wot's 'Is Lordship to think? He's thinking you're an inconvenience is wot. He's thinking you're wearing silks and satins and sleeping in a soft bed and eating fine victuals and where's 'is profit? No profit in you, missy. You've got to do better, or you're wearing hemp."

"Daventry plans to leave the hall this week." It would be her last chance to escape. She had to be ready to take it. No lingering. No regretting Leo's pin or the ponies or the boys or the warrior angel.

"Oh, 'e does, does 'e? And where's he going, missy?"

"To fight in a mill."

Wallop rocked back in his chair. "So, he's going to do it. The whelp thinks he can face a real brawler? He won't last twelve minutes. No wonder 'Is Lordship wants 'im stopped. 'E 'as no sense of place. Always getting above himself like 'is brothers."

He stroked his side whiskers, watching her. "That open match in East Thorndon?"

Emma tried not to show him how right his guess was. She did not have to serve Daventry to Wallop on a plate.

"Only place that'd give a rank amateur a bout. It's soon, too." An ugly slow smile cracked his wide face and pressed its folds closed like dough being kneaded. "Josie Wallop knows the ways of the fancy. Josie Wallop knows all the milling coves. Wasn't Josie Wallop there at the Fives Court when the champion—"

He broke off and frowned at Emma. "Now the real work begins, missy. He's a raw one, to be sure, won't stand a chance if we get the right man against him, but you've got your part to do, mind. Daffy and doxies is what does a fighter in. You follow orders and you put those dairies of yours in his face every day, you hear me?"

A UBREY reminded himself that the old man would die. The timing was all. Right now, for instance, would not be a good time for his uncle's grand funeral. Right now was a good time to find his uncle standing by his library fire with something of his old air of icy command, prodding a giant log into place.

"Uncle, good to see you up, sir."

"What's the word, Aubrey? Have your tools produced any results?"

"What are you drinking, Uncle?" Aubrey looked for the good wine his uncle always kept. Wallop's plan had failed and probably alerted the inconvenient cub to the danger he faced. The girl had yet to prove of any real value. Wallop needed to apply more pressure there.

"Don't 'uncle' me, Aubrey. Just give me your full report and tell me that damned whelp is out of my house." The duke put aside the poker and turned his back to the fire. Aubrey saw that the troublesome leg was holding at the moment.

"You'll have to endure his irksome presence a while longer." He helped himself to a fortifying glass of wine and sank into a leather armchair so that his uncle could enjoy looking down at him again. He tasted the wine, French, the Beaune region. The cellar at Wenlocke was remarkable considering his uncle's acid nature, which hardly seemed the stuff of which wine connoisseurs were made. Aubrey really would have to cultivate that cool tone when he became duke to keep the Wenlocke tradition alive.

"What's happened that you lack the bollocks to tell me?"

Aubrey shifted in the chair and crossed one booted leg over the other. "Actually, Uncle, Wallop's had some success. I have his report here." He removed the papers from his pocket and placed them on the side table. "Wallop's man has penetrated the perimeter and brought down a row of chimney pots on the roof."

"Chimney pots!" A spasm briefly twisted the granite lines of the duke's face. "Don't expect me to rejoice in falling masonry, nephew."

"Wallop reports the pots weighed upward of twenty stone, put a sizeable hole in the roof, and smashed the balustrade to powder. Sadly, of course, they missed the whelp."

"What's the girl done for us? Has she bedded him yet?"

"The girl told Wallop about the cub's habit of roof walking."

"Anyone in the woods with a glass could see that he walks the roof." The duke worked his fist open and closed with quick, impatient starts. "She's got to do better than that to earn her scrap of paper."

"I agree. It would be most helpful if she'd get close enough to stab him in the ribs."

"Aubrey, don't attempt to humor me. We both know your interest here."

"Well, Uncle, if you are in good health, I'm prepared to let Wallop do his job." Aubrey lifted his glass to the duke.

"My health is fine, but I want more pressure on the girl." The duke moved to take up the papers on the table, tottered a little, righted himself, and scanned Wallop's notes.

When he looked up again, his face had gone queer, as if the left side had subsided, lost its underpinnings.

Aubrey put down his glass and came to his feet. "Uncle?"

"Tha whore wash in my housh." The cold voice had slowed to a thick slur of words. Wenlocke was opening and closing his fist again, and Wallop's report fell to the floor.

Aubrey seized the duke's arm, led him to a chair, and rang for a footman. *Not now, damn it, Uncle.*

A liveried servant appeared.

"Send for His Grace's physician. Now!"

E MMA wore the wicked gold dress to supper. Ruth did not say a word, but Emma heard Tatty's voice like a dozen warnings in her head. *Only practice seduction on a man you love.* She wanted to say that it was all part of the plan—patience, opportunity, and distraction. But that wasn't the whole truth.

Tatty's advice was wise, Emma supposed, but she knew something Tatty did not know. A person had to have someone to love. If life took those someones from you, took mother and father and grandmother and brother and cousin until you had no one, it was hard to begin again. And if you were so lucky as to find another someone to love, even if that person was the last person who could love you back, then you had to begin again to love as she had begun to love Daventry. If you didn't, you might as well let the crows have you.

With the family gone, Lark and Rook still missing, and the younger boys restored to the dining room, they were an intimate and listless party. Fewer candles were lit, and the room seemed to contract around the seven of them.

The dress did everything Emma expected it to do. It distracted Daventry more than she thought possible. He hardly listened to the boys, so he did not hear that she had finished the story. He would not guess that she would be gone by morning. On the surface he was his usual cool, polite self, but Emma felt the heat between them rise and shimmer like the air on a hot afternoon.

Dav wanted everything the dress revealed and everything it pretended to conceal. He had no idea what passed in front of him while he imagined taking her to his library, to the north drawing room, to the south drawing room, to the hall, to one of the guest bedrooms. He pictured furniture arrangements, doors, drapery, rugs, and tried to calculate how much time they would have and where they would be certain to remain undiscovered.

A cautious voice in his head distrusted the change in her

appearance, but need kept drowning that whisper of sanity. He who had noted so little of women's apparel knew the number of buttons on the backs of her dresses between the neckline and the folds of her shawl, and how the loops passed from right to left over those buttons. Tonight she wore no tucker, no scrap of lace across her chest, no shirt with a prim collar. Tonight the dress dipped low in front and in back. There could be no more than a single button above the band under her breasts.

Emma felt the change in Daventry's attention, but the boys took no notice of either their tutor or their guardian. Their concern was the absence of Lark and Rook. Even the excitement of Daventry's coming match could not make them forget their missing friends.

"Did they go in one of the servants' carriages, do ye think?" Finch asked.

"Quickest way if they wanted to get back to London." Raven ate with apparent unconcern.

Jay seemed to take the other boys' absence the hardest. He pushed his food around his plate without eating. Emma sent him a questioning look, but he wouldn't meet her eye. He blamed her, she supposed.

From the beginning she and Lark had been at odds, but she'd never guessed he would leave. His dissatisfaction was more about the boys' uncertain position in Daventry's life than her lessons, but she had not helped.

Finch tried to give the older boys' disappearance a happy cause. "Maybe they set off on an adventure, through the country, like the boys in our story. Boys always have to go and make their fortune in the world."

"Why must boys? Why don't girls have to go?" Robin wanted to know.

"Girls stay home and marry." Swallow spoke with authority.

Robin struggled to spear a turnip on his plate. "But Miss Portland didn't."

Swallow chewed an overlarge bite that swelled his thin cheeks. "She takes care of us, doesn't she? Same thing."

Robin turned to Emma with a bright look. "You should marry Daventry and stay with us, miss."

Swallow saved her the trouble of answering. "She can't. Daventry's a lord now. Lords must marry ladies like the misses at his party."

Robin's brow puckered. He cocked his head to study Emma as if he'd missed something. "But miss *is* a lady."

"No, she's a woman, a female. Ladies are like Dav's sisters-in-law and his mum."

Robin shrugged. Swallow's certainty ended the discussion. He managed to get the errant piece of turnip onto his fork. When his plate was clean, he turned back to Emma. "Maybe that's why stories are about boys. Boys have adventures. Girls . . ." He shrugged. "Don't."

Oh, but they do, Emma could have told him. They make hairsbreadth escapes from terrible dungeons and desperate dashes across continents and seas, until they are cornered and trapped and fall in love, but that was the one story she could not tell.

"Will we have lessons tomorrow?" Swallow asked.

"Yes, what will you teach us now?" Finch sounded eager.

"Will you start a new story for us?" Robin wanted to know.

The question woke Dav up from a contemplation of narrow bodice of the maddening dress. "You finished the story?"

The boys all turned to him when he spoke as if they had just remembered his presence.

"Will she be our regular grinder now, Dav?" Swallow asked.

Dav stared at her. She'd finished the story, worn a dress like no other, and used up her fortnight. His head rang like the clanging bells on a fire wagon. When the meal ended, it was the work of a minute to send Adam with the boys to the billiard room. What was she up to?

Dav ordered coffee for the south drawing room, picturing the room in his mind, as he tucked her arm in his. Desire crackled between them. It almost stopped him at the foot of the stairs. He took a steadying breath, and they began to climb.

He seated her in a red damask chair by the fireplace and took a seat next to hers. Tom, one of the footmen, lighted candles and brought in the tray of coffee. His quiet movements should have been calming, but Dav felt the tension winding tighter in him until he heard the click of the door closing.

Then he let himself look at her, unsure of what he saw, something reckless and determined in the lift of her chin. The dress was a deliberate provocation, a change from the way she usually concealed her femaleness. He did not know whether the dress was the truth or a lie. It was not the gown of the vicar's bookish daughter of those false papers.

He sensed that she had seized command with that dress, not of him, but of her own course. Only in the blue of her eyes could he find his pony-hugging, storytelling, nightmare-ridden would-be lover. He had wanted her in a shapeless gray gown in the desperate moment when she had told a story to save herself. But he had not foreseen that she could be this bright flame to his moth. The gold of the dress, like her hair, glinted in shades from rich amber to pale wheat. The bodice was merely a cord of twisted strands of gold and blue, no bigger around than his thumb.

He stood and doused all but one of the branches of candles. The room sank into rich shadows with only a flicker of light to make her skin glow and her eyes sparkle and the gold of the maddening gown gleam. He splashed a dash of coffee from the pot into each of their cups and extended a hand to her. Hers trembled in his.

"Here?" She glanced at the abandoned coffee cups.

"You're not backing out now. Not in that dress."

"The dress doesn't come with instructions."

"We can figure out what to do." He kicked off his evening shoes, and she did the same.

He led her into the shadows at the far end of the room, where a solid mahogany writing desk stood anchored like a ship in the calm blue sea of the carpet. He peeled off his jacket and laid it on the floor behind the desk. The gold walls and heavy red-velvet drapery made a shadowy cove, enclosing the space. Ordinarily he didn't put himself in tight places. He liked open doors, long vistas, and quick exits. He lowered himself to the makeshift coverlet and pulled her down on top of him. It made her squeal, a brief joyful sound, immediately stifled by his kiss. "Don't give us away," he warned.

She shook her head. He kissed her again, coaxing her to lie on top of him, her body pressed to his so that the meeting of their mouths extended to their twined legs. Her weight was insubstantial, but every place their bodies touched he felt her least move and rose to meet it.

He pulled her body up so that he could lift his mouth to taste her skin, her throat, her collarbone, her breasts down to the just-concealed peaks. With the span of his hands he could cover the exposed flesh. Everywhere else layers of linen, wool, and silk separated them. He wanted to tear off her clothes and his, but he would take what he could get and maybe more. The game invited cheating.

He distracted her with kisses while his hands pulled the yielding gown up over her legs and over her bottom, so that he could palm her through the fine lawn of her drawers, feel the sweet, firm flesh, the heat of her, as he had the night of her nightmare. He eased his own legs open so that she docked like a ship against his straining cock, bobbing there against him, as wavelets of desire rocked them both.

She broke the kiss to look at him, propped on her elbows, her hands framing his face. He touched her springy hair.

With one hand he found the little loop at the back of her bodice and slid the sleeves down over her arms. Her pale breasts cupped by her stays lay open to him. He lifted his head to kiss first one and then the other. Wool and lawn and the bunched fabric of her gown still separated them. He flipped her over onto her back so he could look and touch and taste more completely.

Kneeling above her, he straddled her as she lay back breathing hard, her breasts rising and falling. She brushed her fingers up the rise in his breeches and nearly set him off. He caught her hand and held it in his shaking grip.

He found the drawstring at her waist and loosened her drawers and stripped them away. She was open to him now below the waist, her pale limbs circled by silken blue garters above the knee, her golden curls a shade darker than her skin.

"Pretty." The word was all he could manage.

He found the place between her silken thighs where the hot slick center of her lay. He could not say why, but to possess her there, to cup that heat was a mindless pleasure. He had been denied it on the roof under the stars, but it was his here, now, in his jewel box of a drawing room. He slid one finger into the slick folds and felt her hips buck into his hand and his own body's answering jolt of pleasure. He stroked, learning the touch that made her writhe and whimper and shudder. With a sudden tight grip on his wrist she made him stop.

"Now you," she said. She came up on her elbows, and he distracted her momentarily by kissing her breasts again, but she pushed him back and sat up fully, her gown falling over her thighs as she reached for his breeches. His body went still anticipating.

With one hand hooked on his waistband, she worked the buttons of his fall, drew him from his linen smalls, and cradled his swollen cock in her upturned palms, stroking across the top with her thumbs.

He sucked in a shaking breath. "I'm waiting for your compliment. You can't say 'pretty.'"

She looked up at him while her thumbs still stroked, her fascination obvious. It made him laugh. She had cupped Robin's toad in her hands with equal wonder. "It's handsome."

"I don't know that I trust that compliment. I believe you found Robin's toad handsome." His voice was rough like gravel. Her touch lifted him to full, flaring arousal.

A fleeting smile passed in her eyes, and then they darkened. "It's true, but this part of you is as much you as any other part—proud, strong, maybe rude."

He laughed. "Rude will do."

He pushed her back down and held himself above her on his arms while he kissed and plundered her mouth. She strained upward to meet that kiss. Then he lowered himself to rub his length in the liquid heat of her, in flesh so lush and creamy he could hardly keep from crying out at the pleasure of it.

Emma was melting. She was hot wax in a flame. Tatty had it backward somehow about the candle and the candlestick. The stroke of Daventry's body against hers called for an answering move, a lift of her hips, and opening of her person. Her heart wanted to lie open for him like a book on his library floor, the pages bent back so that the spine lifted and the long secret seam lay exposed to his touch. She turned her head and pressed her mouth against his taut arm, smothering a cry of pleasure.

Just this, he told himself for mindless minutes. No more, but the next moment his cock pressed in, not slipping across, but pushing to enter, a move beyond his intention. She tensed, her body tightening around him, and consciousness faded. He fought his way back to the floor of the drawing room, the blue rug with its ancient pattern, the heavy desk, the faint smell of cold coffee.

Swallow's words at dinner came back to him. *Dav can't marry her. Lords must marry ladies.* He pulled back and pressed his slick yard to her belly and tried to make his mind work. *Not here. Not now.* He couldn't manage a more coherent thought.

Emma felt the connection between them snap, like ice on a puddle cracking under foot, without warning, an instant plunge in cold humiliation. She lay under him unable to move or to escape. She had offered him her love, and he had refused the gift.

She felt desperate to flee, but he remained pressed to her belly, and after a long moment, he reached for her again with his hand. Helplessly she arched and shuddered under his touch, and felt him move and find his own release.

He rolled away and they lay still catching their breath, staring at the high white ceiling overhead. He caught her hand and held it tight in his—regret or promise—she didn't know. Their breathing slowed.

You stopped.

Why did you wear that dress tonight?

I was trying to seduce you.

I got that. Why?

Dav was thinking again. It wouldn't last while he was in Emma's presence, so he needed to get her into her room away from him.

He used the soft linen of her discarded drawers to remove the evidence of their lovemaking and helped her to her feet. They worked to order each other's clothes. She stood behind him to retie the ribbon that held his hair in place. He inspected her in the shameless dress that now covered her breasts and limbs. No one would know that he'd stuffed her drawers into the old desk.

He kissed her again, once, thoroughly, before he opened the drawing room door. They started down the long gallery, walking side by side like cordial but indifferent acquaintances without touching. Daventry clasped his hands behind him. Emma twisted hers in the ends of her shawl.

He stopped and said something bland and polite about a painting.

Emma dutifully looked at the haughty face of a woman with powdered hair piled to an astonishing height above her pale face.

Don't touch. Don't touch. But he was so near, and the room was so long, and empty except for themselves.

He started walking again.

Emma looked at the carpet. Best not to remember her

step count now. Best to put one foot in front of the other. Her breasts, her secret folds still throbbed with the pleasure that had overtaken her. Her heart ached, raw from his withdrawal. She needed Daventry, to touch him, to kiss him, to taste him . . . To go the length of the room without touching was so hard. Without him it was going to be difficult to draw a breath in the world.

They had kissed on the roof and touched there and touched each other on the floor of his gilt drawing room. He had tucked her dampened drawers into a drawer of his desk. Each touch, each kiss had tuned their bodies to each other's being.

Emma stopped. As Tatty and Leo had been tuned to one another. That was why Tatty had to keep moving, running. All the kisses and touches had been taken away from Tatty; if Tatty stopped, she would probably die. And Emma would have to go on, like Tatty. Perhaps it was her good luck that he'd stopped. If she loved him, she should take herself away before they joined their bodies fully. If Emma stayed even one more day, they would become lovers. And when she left him, her betrayal would make another puckered scar somewhere deep in him.

They came to the end of the gallery and began climbing the stairs, their steps leaden. At her bedroom door, they faced one another, still not touching.

Then Daventry unclasped his hands and reached to lift her chin. "Emma."

The word connected them again. She opened her arms to him. It had been so long, and they kissed and clung.

Dav laughed at himself. He'd thought that the long, slow walk through the gallery beneath the portraits of his father's frowning ancestors would cool his body and restore his rational faculties. He thought he could solve the problem of

Emma's virginity and his position in the world. Both conditions called for a choice. Instead he could not stop holding Emma and kissing her. He pressed her against the door of her room, angling his head for access, holding her bottom so that her hips tilted up to meet his cock.

She pressed into him and made a little whimper of desire. He began to tug at her skirts, mad to touch her. Their clothes seemed heavy and irksome, but a tiny voice of reason intruded to remind him that he could not undress her in the corridor. He let her skirts go.

Footsteps and voices on the stairs made them break apart, breathing rapidly, and stand facing one another not touching. He laughed. He could solve this problem, and the sooner, the better.

"Call Ruth," he whispered. Aloud he said, "Good night, Miss Portland."

"Good night, Daventry."

He reached past her to open the door of her room. One candle glowed in the sconce. Emma made herself step inside and close the door behind her, leaning against it. She would call Ruth, as soon as she put herself to rights.

She would leave tonight. The snow and rain had passed. She had given Tatty as much time as she herself possessed. Once the household was abed, Emma would leave. She closed her eyes to think of her plan. She would leave through the back and circle round on the passing road. She knew each place where she could pick up a pair of shoes or a tin of food.

She drew a breath and opened her eyes. Her room smelled like cold ash as if the chimney did not draw. She pushed away from leaning on the door. She could do nothing until she dismissed Ruth and until she was sure that Daventry also slept.

She was halfway to her dressing room door when the chimney smell made her turn to look at the hearth. A black shadow flew at her and a scream died in her throat as a stranger slammed her back against the dressing room door. He pressed his forearm against her throat, cutting off breath. The scent of dead pipe surrounded her. Choking, Emma stared into cold black eyes under heavy brows like crows' wings. Her heart jumped.

"Ye want to save yer neck, girl, ye'd best not cross Wallop."

She could not breathe or cry out. She clawed at the arm pressed to her throat and kicked wildly at the man's shin. He was lean and hard and didn't budge. Her heels thudded helplessly against the door. She twisted and pushed the palm of her hand against his nose. Black dots danced before her eyes. She pushed harder. Her hands were losing their grip.

Her door burst open. Her attacker snarled and wrenched free of her hold on his nose.

"Emma!"

Daventry's hoarse cry made her attacker swing away. He shoved Emma to the floor. Daventry launched himself at her attacker. A knife glinted in the man's hand, and he slashed at Daventry, who dodged with a fighter's feint.

The two men circled each other while Emma gasped and tried to get her throat to open. Her windpipe felt crushed. Her lungs spasmed, and she coughed.

The knife in the stranger's hand winked wickedly in the candlelight. Daventry's gaze narrowed to the blade, his face intent, his movements quick, keeping himself between the stranger and the door, the fighter in him hardening his features. Emma pulled herself up against the wall. Her legs trembled weakly as she gathered them under her to rise.

When she got to her knees, the attacker turned on her, swinging his knife in a wide swathe. Daventry lunged between them, catching the man's free arm and flinging him away from Emma. Like a whip recoiling, the stranger whirled. His arm flew up, and he brought his knife down the length of Daventry's arm. Daventry let go with a curse, and the attacker turned and fled.

Dav heard the man's footsteps going down the long stairs. He seized the bell rope and pulled, and turned back to Emma. Her eyes had lost their blue again, black wells of fear.

He watched her fight it and come back to him. "You're bleeding."

He glanced at his ruined coat sleeve. Blood welled up over linen and wool. He didn't feel the pain yet. It would come. Kneeling, he took her in his arms. He could not crush her to him as he wanted. He'd burst into the room to see a figure like a black wing beat her down, and his heart had stopped and his other self had taken over, not Daventry but Boy.

The household began to stir in answer to the bell rope. He heard a swelling chorus of rapid footsteps and anxious voices, his people rushing to defend him.

"Come," he urged. "My room. Now." He hoisted Emma up with his good arm and helped her out the door, into his room, and across it to his dressing room. An hour earlier their footsteps had been slower than ivy growing.

He put her in a chair. Her hair was down, and she still labored to breathe.

He stripped off his neckcloth and began to pull off his jacket. She stood at once to help him with shaking hands.

"Miss?" Ruth called from Emma's room. "What's happened?"

Daventry strode into the hall. "A stranger attacked Miss Portland, Ruth. Get your mother and Ned Begley."

"You're wounded." Wide-eyed, Ruth stared at him, then bobbed a curtsy and was gone.

He turned and found Emma at his side. She tugged him back into his room. She didn't talk, but she made him sit and began to remove his coat, her face bleak.

"I was hoping you'd undress me." He flashed her a quick grin, turning and letting her pull the coat around his back to ease it down the injured left arm.

Mrs. Creevey bustled in with a pitcher and basin in hand. She took one look at Daventry and shook her head. "Well, we knew this day was coming. I've set Adam and Mr. C and the footmen to search the house and grounds. Ned's coming to have a look at you, and we'll have Dr. Bartling in the morning."

She turned to Emma. "You were attacked, Miss Portland?"

Emma nodded.

"Shall I have Ruth tend to you?" Before Emma could make her injured throat work, Daventry answered.

"No." His tone left no room for discussion. "Emma stays with me."

Mrs. Creevey didn't blink. "You'll help then, miss." Together they got Daventry seated next to the bathtub in his dressing room. His hair had come loose of its tie. His white shirtsleeve was torn and stained crimson from shoulder to wrist.

Mrs. Creevey cut away the ruined shirtsleeve efficiently, exposing the smooth curve of his arm and powerful shoulder. He looked again as he had when Emma had first seen him, a fallen archangel.

Blood flowed from the long, jagged wound, crimson on

marble. Mrs. Creevey instructed Emma to hold Daventry's hand steady while she poured a stream of cold water over the wound to wipe away the first blood.

Immediately bright new blood welled up. Mrs. Creevey gave Emma a fresh neckcloth to press against the upper arm, while she applied pressure to the lower.

Adam appeared with Ned, who took charge at once.

"Well now, let me look at that." Ned pulled up a bench and sat with the basin in his lap, Daventry's injured arm extended over it.

"Adam, hold the light, man."

Ned turned the arm from side to side, looking at the edges of the wound. "The worst of it is at the top here, but it's not too deep. The fellow didn't want to lose his knife, so he didn't get to bone or veins. Can you make a fist, Daventry?"

Daventry closed his hand while Ned examined the movement of his fingers and the muscles in the arm. "Looks clean. No bits of wool in you. Let's sew you up then. Dr. Bartling can look at you tomorrow. Laudanum?"

"Brandy."

"Tea, first, to warm you," Mrs. Creevey insisted. She made him drink while Ned prepared his implements. Daventry squeezed Emma's hand. Ned had him lie on the bench while Mrs. Creevey spread thick towels over Emma's golden skirts. Emma took the injured arm on her knees, her hand holding Daventry's.

"Your grandfather's men are getting too bold, Daventry," Ned commented.

Adam spoke up, "We found a broken window on the ground floor in your mother's room. No one heard a thing. Likely he came in while the servants were at supper."

"Your brothers won't like this. A second attempt on your life in a week."

Dav knew that, but he couldn't tell them that the attack was on Emma. Already he regretted his words to Ruth. If she talked about the episode with the others, they might wonder, as he did, who Emma Portland's enemies were and how they had found her in his house. He meant to demand answers as soon as he had her to himself again.

By the time Ned pronounced the wound closed and gave his instructions and Mrs. Creevey began cleaning up and shooing people out of the room, Dav's arm was a fiery ache from shoulder to finger tips.

He made Ned examine Emma's throat while Mrs. Creevey helped him out of his ruined shirt and into a dressing gown. He asked her to send up a plate of food and another pot of tea.

"She's going to be hoarse, and I'd have her drink cold water to keep any swelling down, but there's no bleeding. We'll watch her."

"She stays with me."

No one appeared shocked or surprised. So much for thinking he had fooled anyone about his desire for Emma Portland.

Adam opened the door, and Dav's people filed out and he was left with Emma. He held her hand in his good one.

She still wore the gold-and-blue dress. Only he knew that under it she wore no drawers.

"I should go." It was the first he'd heard her speak since the attack. Her voice was a hoarse whisper.

"Don't think of leaving me."

"But . . ."

"You have questions to answer."

She shook her head.

"I know you can't speak, but you can answer with a nod or a shake of your head."

Her eyes widened in response. He looked for the blue and saw instead deep wells of black. The black made him angry. He didn't want to love a woman who could be snatched from him at any moment by the evil that had followed her to Daventry Hall.

He lifted his head and drew a long breath. Who was he to complain? He had brought danger into the lives of his mother and brothers and their families, and yet they loved him. Emma Portland had brought danger into his house, and yet he wanted her.

He kissed her, a gentle touch of lips, not the ardent press he'd like to make, in deference to her injured throat. "I can't send Adam away."

"They are all on guard now." The low timbre of her voice stirred desires he needed to tamp down.

"Good. You're safe then. No one will harm you tonight. Tonight can be for us, can't it?"

Emma knew he was asking her to join him in bed. There was no leaving now. With the household awake and vigilant even Emma's skills would not let her slip away unnoticed. Her attacker had made it plain that she would die before she ever lived, while Daventry invited her to live, if only for one night. She would love him and betray him.

Emma told herself to be practical. The bed would never do with Daventry's arm. She looked away from it around his chamber with its somber earthen hues. No shadows lurked in the corners. His desk stood under the window as it had when she'd spied on him, still a jumble of books, papers, and writing implements.

Dav saw her glance at his bed. He'd lain in it for nights thinking of her in the next room and wanting the walls between them to dissolve. Now, she was here, and he had one useless arm. He could not make love to her as he'd imagined, but he had to have her.

"I want to undress you."

He turned her round so that he could undo her bodice for the second time in one evening. She made no protest. One-handed, his head feeling the brandy, he took his time. When he freed the last button, he spread the sides of the gown and pushed it over her shoulders. It slid in a silken rush to the floor.

He had wanted to undress her from the first day he met her, conscious of the irony in his dishonorable intentions, the one legitimate son of his mother, a gentleman by birth and yet no gentleman.

His own intentions should convince him he was not meant to be a gentleman. The night before he had danced with four indistinguishable young women of good birth and lofty ambition, whose names he could not remember. They might mistake his indifference for honorable restraint, but he could not imagine wanting any of them. Whatever came of taking Emma's virginity, he would face it. Perhaps he was one of the Sons of Sin, after all.

He kissed the top of her spine above the narrow wings of her shoulder blades where the white straps of her corset passed. He stepped back to examine the fastenings that enclosed her in layers of silk and linen, a challenge for a one-handed, light-headed man.

The tapes of her petticoats gave easily, and he shoved them over her hips so she stood with her feet in a froth of white linen. Her stays curved in at her waist and out over the flare of her hips, and her thin chemise barely covered her bottom. Her stockings ended mid-thigh in blue silk garters. He closed his eyes, dizzied with lust, and clung to her waist with his one good hand, steadying himself.

When he opened his eyes again, he took in the zigzag pattern of lacing that ran up her spine through what looked like dozens of eyeholes. A two-handed male with all his wits about him would have his work cut out for him.

"I was deceived by the gown," he told her. "The narrow bodice made undressing you, which I've been thinking about more than I should, look easy."

"Ruth could help." Her voice roughened by her injury did little for his condition.

"Ruth would be decidedly in the way here." He picked apart the knot at her waist. When the ends of the laces dangled free, he hooked his index finger under the lowest loop, and tugged. After the first few he had the knack of it. The rhythm of pulling the laces lifted her body toward him and away, mimicking his intent. His breathing grew ragged as the sides of the corset parted. With the last loop freed, he pushed the open wings of the corset apart and slipped the straps down her shoulders. The white garment fell away and landed with a soft huff like a breath. She took a deeper breath and swayed a little, and he held her elbow to steady her. Her balance restored, she looked over her shoulder at him.

"Now you," she said in that low whisper that already had him mindless. She stepped free of her rumpled clothes and faced him in her chemise and garters and stockings.

Emma stepped up to him. He smelled of blood and brandy and himself. The effort of undressing her had made him shaky. Mrs. Creevey had removed his pumps and waistcoat and ruined shirt earlier, so Emma could see a narrow swath of his chest and belly, its hard planes bisected by a line of dark, curling hair. She realized that their injuries gave her freedom. He was the knowing one, but he could not take charge as he had in all their previous encounters, and he seemed inclined to let Emma find her way.

Emma rubbed her palms over his shoulders and arms and chest under the silvery gray silk dressing gown. His belly sucked in at her touch, and she loosened the tie that held the silk gown in place. Under it he was beautiful to look at, living marble. She wanted to touch him every-where at once. She dragged her palms up his ribs, counting them.

"What are you doing?" His voice sounded strained.

She looked up. "Counting your ribs."

She brought her hands up to his chest, spreading her fingers out, grazing the brown coins of his nipples, sending hot sensation shooting to his groin.

He swallowed. "What's next?"

Her hands paused. "I'm counting your heartbeat."

She leaned her cheek against his chest, then her hands dropped to the waist of his trousers. His cock leapt in response. He counseled himself to patience. She believed herself in charge, but he looked over her shoulder at an old chair in the corner that he thought would solve the problem of his weak, burning arm.

Emma made herself work the buttons of his trouser fall one at a time. With the release of the last button, his sex jutted forward in its linen case. He caught her hand and pressed it to his length, and she had to pause and lean her cheek against his chest while her heart beat madly with wanting.

Just this to hold him so alive and wanting in her hand. She paused to fix the moment in her memory so that she could possess it forever when everything else was gone. But that was selfish. She could be selfish later.

She undid the buttons of his smalls and slid her hands under linen and wool to shove his trousers down over his hips and legs. He stepped out of his clothes as she had, the long silver robe gleaming around him. She liked the structure of him, the tight cage of his ribs, the flat belly, the neat architecture of his hipbones, the long muscled thighs, his sex jutting up from darker hair.

Dav took her hand pulled her toward the old chair. She hesitated, and he could see that she didn't completely understand his intention, but he sat and pulled her forward to stand between his knees. Then he showed her how to sit facing him, her knees hooked over the chair's low round arms. There were things he should tell her about the first time, but for a moment he forgot to breathe, lost in a vision of blue garters, white stocking-cased legs, and bare thighs. With his good hand around her bottom, he shifted her forward so that their bodies almost met. Her back arched up, and she was open to him.

The irony of it stopped him. At the same time she was giving, and withholding, herself. Her eyes were an ethereal blue he had not seen yet, a blue one could only see by looking straight up to heaven on a clear day. His palm pressed to her back, holding her firmly in place, he made himself test her.

"You are no vicar's daughter, are you?"

She shook her head.

"There are no Grimsby foundlings, are there?"

"None," she managed in that roughened voice.

"There's no Mrs. Merton."

"No."

"Tell me one true thing, Emma."

Emma was dying with wanting, with the feel of his legs rough under hers and the stretch in her thighs, and the aching pulse in her woman's place that wept for him. All they had done earlier in the drawing room had been leading to this moment, and he was torturing her for the truth.

She would torture him back if she knew how, but she only knew she wanted to love him. That was a true thing.

"I want to love you."

He swore. His breath was ragged and his lids heavy over the gray gleam of his gaze. He pulled her closer and draped her arms around his neck and dipped his head to take her breast in his mouth and tease and taste. Emma held on to his shoulders, her face pressed to his soft hair, while the pull of his mouth went deep and made her body contract in aching spasms of need.

He lifted his head and nuzzled her breasts, and his hand reached between them, cupping her and touching lightly until she pressed into his touch, and he drew his fingers softly over her flesh while she arched and spread and pressed. And then he parted her and began to stroke the slick sides of her folds. His fingers lifted a little fold of flesh and found a tiny part of her that he was teaching her to know, a bud, a pea nestled in a slick silken pod. He touched the tiny place and her awareness contracted to just that spot.

With a desperate effort not to yield to her release, she reached to pay him back, taking him hot and smooth and pulsing in her hand.

Emma, I want you.

I know. I'm here.

She bent down to press her forehead against his shoulder and nodded, and he shifted so that his male part met her place. Where his fingers had been, she now felt the smooth round head of his shaft, a different sensation. Her body opened to take him in, and he pushed up inside her with a strong thrust. She felt her barrier give, a brief twinge, and then he filled her. She felt him go still with it, felt them joined, a perfect fit, the yawning emptiness filled, her body gloving his.

"Did I hurt you?" he asked.

She shook her head against his shoulder. He hadn't hurt her, but she wasn't ready for his loving to end. Her body felt expectant, on edge, full of longing. Swollen as a mushroom in rain.

He began to slip out of her, and she tensed.

"Move with me, Emma." He spoke through gritted teeth.

She lifted her head and looked at him, brushing his hair away from his brow. His body wore a light sheen of moisture. His face had a drawn, anguished look so that she feared for his arm. But he grinned at her.

"Ready? We move together." He rocked his hips down and up, showing her. She drew a swift hiss of breath at the exquisite pleasure of it. He tilted his head back to look at her, one brow cocked. She caught his meaning. Cautiously, she began to move, flexing her thighs to get a lift and relaxing them to press him deeper inside her.

Together they found an angle and rhythm that wrung little sounds from her wounded throat and set her free and soaring as if she had sprouted wings to catch the air and rise on its currents. He dared her to reach for more, and she pushed for it and it eluded her, tantalizingly within reach, one more slide, one more stroke, she didn't want it to end, but she needed to reach the elusive sensation that hovered, until she succumbed to bright shudders of ecstasy and he followed her.

She closed her eyes and collapsed against him, her body warm and limp and boneless as oil. Thought came back as her body cooled and a shiver passed through her and sharp awareness of her body stretched awkwardly over the chair.

She would leave soon. She lifted her head and saw real pain in his face.

"Your arm—"

"Is on fire," he admitted.

Emma lifted her right leg and swung off his knees. She tugged at his good hand to pull him up out of the chair, but he resisted, looking up at her.

"I still haven't seen you naked."

She looked down at herself, surprised. There was a smear of blood above one blue garter. Underneath her shift she could feel the sticky moisture of their joining.

He came to his feet. "Come on.

He stripped off the silk dressing gown, and naked, he pulled her to his dressing room. Even one-handed he was efficient with towels and water, until they were both clean. He tossed her bloodied towel in the heap with the towels that had treated his wound, her blood mingling with his.

It was her turn to coax him into the bed.

Dav let her prop his injured arm on a pair of pillows and lay back with a sigh. She sat beside him, cross-legged, facing him, the covers about her waist. Her hands explored his chest and ribs and belly.

"Are you counting again?"

"Yes."

He pulled a curling golden strand at the side of her face, stretched it long, and let it spring back. "I have wanted to do that for some time."

She caught his hand and lifted it and kissed the puckered scar. "Tell me the story of the scar," she said.

He was silent so long that Emma feared he could not tell it.

"A man took me one night. Xan and I were walking to

dinner from a prizefight. Bound and gagged, I overheard another man telling the first to make me disappear. I thought he would kill me, but he moved me from room to room in London. Always my hands and feet were chained. I could not understand why my family didn't come for me. In time I learned to do what it took to stay alive.

"After my abductor died, I discovered that my family still looked for me, but it was too late. I was not the boy they were looking for. I had become someone else. If I doubted, I could look at my wrists. It made me feel too far from them to ever return."

Emma pressed a kiss to his jaw, and he began again.

"But Xan never stopped looking, and when he met Cleo, they found me. I had the boys, and I knew someone still wanted me dead and would kill anyone close to me. Will and Helen discovered that my grandfather was behind my abduction through a man named Archibald March.

"When I met March, he was holding a gun to Helen's head. When I heard him speak, I knew he was the man who had wanted me to disappear. I killed him."

Dav felt oddly light to have told her the story. She seemed to take it in to herself and consume its brutal, ugly details. Yet, she had such stories to tell, herself he knew, the stuff of her nightmares.

"Tell me about your brother."

It was her turn to pause. "He was wild, like my cousin, and fearless and funny and fine in his uniform. He loved her from the time they were eleven."

"And you?"

She shrugged. "As long as we had ponies, I could keep up with them. The grown-ups thought I made a good chaperone."

"Did you?"

"Not at all." She actually grinned at him, but there was a hint of darkness in the blue of her eyes. "I helped them to elope."

"He died then?"

"Shortly after." It dimmed the blue of those eyes for her to speak it.

He knew better than to ask in which uniform for which army in which battle her brother had died. He felt his eyelids droop, but he could sleep this night. He had her by his side, and guards stood on duty outside his room and house. An intruder could hardly get past Adam or the well-trained footmen around the house.

"You finished the boys' story without me." He ought to be troubled by the tidiness of that detail, but his mind hovered between the lazy drift of her fingers over his chest and belly and the pain of his arm.

She smiled a little half smile at the new topic. "Well, you know the woodcutter's sons defeat the ogre."

"But it's how they do it that matters."

"With the birds' help, of course."

"Tell me. I'm not going anywhere tonight."

She slid down to lie on her side next to him, her chin tucked in the gap above his shoulder. "Do you remember that the woodcutter's sons left their mother's dishrags behind?"

EMMA woke in darkness. Daventry lay beside her, restless in his sleep, making the noises of a dreamer. She imagined the pain in his arm and the dreams of knives and attackers that must be his. She dared not touch him.

She let her eyes grow accustomed until she could see in the light of the setting moon the outlines of his room. She slipped from the far side of the bed, her flesh instantly cooled and roughened from the cold. Clamping her teeth closed, she pulled her discarded chemise over her head. It was time to put her plan into action.

Only, she did not want to leave Daventry with nothing.

If she had Leo's pin, she could leave that, but she didn't. She had nothing to leave him, except her love. She had given that. He must know. He must have sensed what she gave him. He didn't speak it, but he saw and heard so much that others missed. He would know.

She judged her path to his door, estimating the steps, thinking about how to turn the knob soundlessly, a thing she had practiced on her own door. The moonlight fell across his desk and caught a paper lying there as if he had intended to write a letter. Emma stopped. The temptation was too great.

She sat and took up his pen and lifted the stopper from the ink bottle. Dipping the pen in ink, she wrote: *I love you.*

In the moonlight the letters lay like the shadows of bare twigs on frosty ground. A sudden thought bothered her. Only Daventry must find her message, not Mr. Creevey, not the doctor. Behind her Daventry stirred again, and fearing he would wake, she passed silently into his dressing room. A narrow shaft of moonlight illuminated the smaller room in which the bathtub hovered ghostly white, and the wardrobe yawned like black cave. But she needed no light to find his worn velvet coat that smelled of ash and stone and felt as soft and silken as skin.

She thrust her note into the right pocket. When he felt most betrayed, he would wear the coat and find her message and know its truth. She turned the doorknob with practiced stealth and slipped from the dressing room into the corridor. Adam for all his vigilance lay snoring, his legs sprawled across the carpet, his head against the wall. In her own dressing room she donned the layers of clothes she would wear and took the lightest of her bags.

Chapter Nineteen

❧

Dav knew Emma was gone even before he opened his
eyes. He felt her absence, not only in the bed beside
him, but in his house.

He threw off his covers, his injured arm in instant protest, and stalked across the room. Sharp morning light fell
into the room. He found no sign of her in that harsh light,
as if she'd never inhabited his house, and he'd dreamed her
only. Her feet left no prints on the rich gold carpet. Her side
of the bed lay smooth and still as a field of snow. His gaze
took in the floor where their clothes had fallen. For a
moment he dared to hope that she'd merely retired through
the open door to his dressing room.

It looked as it had the night before, the furniture arranged
for Ned's impromptu surgery. His wardrobe stood open,
which seemed odd, but probably Creevey had left it open
when Dav ordered everyone out. The careless moment when
he'd tossed the evidence of her lost virginity on the pile of

bloodied towels in the bath came back to him as a moment when he thought he'd claimed her for his own. How easily undone his conquest. He felt his nakedness then, his burning arm.

But the fire in his arm was nothing to the ache in his chest. He could, with an act of his mind, separate the pain in his arm from the rest of his body. But if he so much as breathed, the other pain claimed him.

He summoned detachment. He knew how to shut down pain and cold and hunger, whatever made one weak and unable to act. Emma Portland's betrayal was just another discomfort he could endure. He pulled a pair of trousers from his wardrobe. His old coat hung there, and for a moment he considered putting it on, but he remembered holding her in its folds on the roof.

He turned back to his own room. A pen lay across his desk. He touched the nib, which left a black dot on his finger. She had written him a message. Instantly his heart leapt at what it might mean. He glanced around for the note on the desk or the floor. He crossed to the bedside table and found nothing. His mind narrowed to her sitting at his desk writing something while he slept while she planned to leave him. He should not have believed that message was for him.

In the hall Adam was awake and obviously unaware of Emma's leaving.

Her room gave nothing away—not the table with its porcelain pots and dainty papers, nor the untouched bed. The blue walls, an echo of her gaze, pained him.

In her dressing room she seemed to have left behind everything she'd come with. The trunk, the silk dresses, slippers, ribbons, shawls. He realized what he should have known all along that nothing she'd left behind had any connection with her true self, the self he had known naked in bed in the act of confessing to one another. He'd not lost her to another man but to the nightmares of her past from which she still ran.

A search of the woods turned up Ned Begley's dog, Hector, with its throat cut. After the burial Dav encouraged the boys to spar in the hall to lift their spirits.

With Lark and Rook and Emma gone, Adam had to shout encouragement. "That's it, lads, left, right, left."

Dav's mind drifted from the pain of his arm to the puzzle of her escape. He had to call it that. In the night it had made no sense to pursue her attacker, but he should see to it now. The man had been lean and agile, a fellow capable of killing a dog, scaling Dav's roof, and tampering with the masonry.

Someone cleared his throat at Dav's elbow. "The town constable is here, sir."

Dav turned. He did not know how long Creevey had been standing there.

"Says he has a communication for you. Shall I show him in?"

Dav nodded. In a minute Creevey returned with George Lockwood, the constable, a stout, worthy fellow of four and forty, not to be trifled with. He carried a notebook.

"Yer brothers were making inquiries in the town, Your Lordship, so I thought it my duty to warn you of a suspicious female hereabouts."

"What's the report, Mr. Lockwood?"

"Well, Your Lordship, we've had two reports, one from the landlord at the Bell, and one from a Mr. Wallop, a brewer who came to Somerton to look at our maltings."

"And what do these reports say?"

"A young female, very young, sir, not one and twenty, they say, passing herself off as a decent woman in order to defraud gentlemen of their generosity."

Dav raised a brow. It was an oddly vague report to cause alarm in an official breast. "What does this suspicious young female look like?"

"She has a gently bred air they say. Hair either gold or dark brown or a mix of both, you know."

Any of the young misses Dav had danced with during his family's visit would fit that description. "What color are this woman's eyes?"

Lockwood checked his notebook. "I find no mention made of the eyes, Your Lordship."

Not Emma Portland, then, for who could miss those eyes?

"Our informants do say she wore an unusual crowned brooch, like a talisman. It says here, a 'filigree of gold.'"

Dav stiffened. However vague the description of the woman's person, the significance of the brooch struck him. He had not seen the thing she lost, but it could have been a brooch.

"The thing is, Your Lordship, the description of the suspicious Somerton female fits that of another female who's been the subject of a search since January. That female is described in the same way, including the brooch. Might your notice advertising for a tutor have reached Reading?"

"Reading? Reading seems a far way from Somerton."

"A hundred miles, but the same newspapers reach Reading. And you hired a female person as tutor to these young boys here. I thought you might have been imposed upon."

Dav contained himself. Imposed upon, what a tame expression. *Seduced. Betrayed.*

"In Reading she passed herself off as a nursemaid to a babe. But a sergeant of the ninetieth ended up dead in the taproom at the Kings Arms there after this female was seen drinking with 'im."

Dav looked at his visitor. "You're saying this woman is under suspicion of murder?"

"I am, my lord. The sergeant was stabbed in the back, an upward thrust by someone who knew her business."

"Or his. Any witnesses?"

"None except the tapman who saw them drinking together. The mistress of the house found the sergeant at the table slumped over as if he'd had too much, but when she couldn't rouse him, she discovered the truth."

"What happened to the babe?"

"The babe?"

"Where did the gentlewoman go who was supposed to have hired this suspicious female as a nursemaid to her babe?"

The constable checked his notebook. "I've no word of them, but I would like a word with your tutor, my lord."

So would I. "She's not employed here any longer, Lockwood. She left the hall yesterday at the end of her trial period."

"Why did she leave?" Lockwood's suspicion was obvious.

"She no longer needed or wanted the position."

"And where did she go?"

"That's her affair, not mine."

"You don't know."

"I don't." Dav found it convenient to assume the authority of marquess, letting Lockwood see that the interview had ended.

When the constable left, Dav found Finch at his side. "Is Miss Portland in trouble?"

"I believe she is, Finch."

"Do you think she didn't like us?"

He looked down into Finch's troubled face and summoned the truth. "No. I think she liked us very well."

"But she lied to us, didn't she?"

"About some things, she did."

"Not all?"

"Not all."

"Well, which ones?"

"I wish I knew."

Will arrived with his man Harding shortly after Lockwood left. Harding had tracked down the source of Emma Portland's references in the town of Grimsby. According to Harding a fine gentleman hired a widow who made her living writing to answer inquiries according to his written instructions. She was to burn the instructions after she complied. The scribbling widow did not know the gentleman's name. A go-between had passed her information and funds. She'd been grateful to get them. There had never been such a school, but the woman had put her heart into the project, enjoying the fiction that such a place existed. When Harding checked all the inns in town where a gentleman was likely to stay, he found no obvious ties to Wenlocke. Whoever the widow's gentleman had been, he had covered his tracks well.

Will had fared better in town. He had discovered that the Duchess of Wenlocke was looking for Emma Portland. She had sought Bow Street and engaged Jack Castle, Will's old friend on the force, to find the girl.

Furthermore, Will had taken a gown from Emma's trunk and tracked down the modiste who produced it. She claimed it was one she had made. The woman recognized her work as something she had made over a year earlier for a young actress, who was then in the keeping of the Earl of Aubrey.

"It's plain as day, Dav, your tutor is connected directly to Wenlocke. The duchess is looking for her, and Aubrey supplied her with a singularly seductive wardrobe and likely with her false papers as well. Aubrey's probably the fine gentleman in Grimsby. Her presence here is a threat to you. Dismiss her today, and Harding and I will see that she's returned to Wenlocke."

"I can't dismiss her."

"You bleeding won't, you mean." Will's temper flared.

Dav drew his brother aside. The boys were still close by. "She left. She escaped in the night."

Will looked stunned. "Good. Let her go. Don't go after her."

"I won't." Dav turned away. "I've got a match to prepare for."

Before supper the boys summoned Dav to the chapel. He entered annoyed with himself for the instant recollection of his first meeting with Emma Portland.

"We have to tell you something," Jay announced. Leadership had fallen to him now.

Dav steeled himself.

"We stole a pin from Miss Portland."

Robin added, "We didn't mean to make her leave."

"You didn't make her leave," Dav told them.

"Lark told us to give this to you to prove she lied, but she didn't lie to us, did she?" Finch spoke from behind his hand again as if all the progress he'd made had vanished.

"She didn't lie to you." Her papers had been false. But her way with the boys had been genuine. Her earnest delight in their progress had been real. She had been honest with Dav about her failure with Lark. Her nightmares were real whatever they were. Whatever made her lean against a pair of shaggy ponies and touch the empty pocket of her skirt was true.

Finch held out his hand with a folded paper wrapped around an object. Dav took it. The note was brief enough.

Miss Portland lies.

Dav regarded the pin in the note. It was smaller than most of the coins in a man's pocket. A filigreed gold crown slightly bent topped a fat crescent moon with a Latin motto etched on the edge. A loop of frayed and faded red ribbon enclosed the pin's clasp.

He had no doubt the pin was Emma Portland's missing keepsake. Her brother's, she had said. If her brother was a parson's son who'd gone off to war and perished, the pin had not belonged to him. If the pin had belonged to him, neither she nor her brother had been the child of a country parson. Dav had seen such pins lining the breasts of royal dukes at the king's coronation, where his brothers had each been on duty, Xander as a knight, and Will as a policeman.

Light as it was, it felt heavy in his palm, a piece of her true self Emma Portland had left behind. The mix of truth and lies in her swirled in him like a whirlpool that could suck him down.

Five worried faces staring up at him brought him back to the present. He closed the pin in his good fist and lifted it for them to join him in a pledge. Five fists joined his. "We'll keep the pin safe for Miss Portland until she returns."

* * *

D on't be stubborn about this," Will advised at the end of yet another practice round.

"You're telling me not to be stubborn." Dav laughed at his reckless middle brother.

Will grinned. "Just let the old man die first, then take your chances in the ring."

"I'd rather meet Wenlocke face-to-face."

Will helped Dav out of his practice gloves. "He'd never fight fair. He never bleeding has."

"Still, I'd like to take him on directly."

"That's what this mill is about, isn't it?"

Dav raised a glass of cold herb tea that Mrs. Wardlow insisted would heal his arm. "It's what you'd do."

"Well, at least you're going to Thorndon prepared. And you're not going alone."

With a week of Will and Xan's workouts Dav had gained good movement back in his arm. His body was tired, but he relished the weariness and the aching muscles.

He lived like a man swimming below the surface of a cold lake. He could see the sun and sky and those who inhabited the airy regions, but their words and actions didn't touch him. The only thing he seemed to feel were the blows his brothers landed in their practice bouts.

His injured arm still tired sooner than Xander liked in their practice bouts, but Dav knew he was ready for the match. He had but one more thing to do before he began to fight for those who were his own in the world. He climbed to his own roof. The fields and woods wore the lightest green now.

He carried the sword up with him. It felt familiar in his hand, and his good arm could swing it easily. He knew himself ready for the match, not because his feet and eye were quick and his arm was strong but because he knew the kind of world he truly lived in. He would not let Wenlocke shape his life any longer. He had to strike the next blow. He raised the sword over his head and brought it down against the edge of the balustrade with a shattering blow. The long blade snapped, and a jagged piece plummeted to the ground. He took the broken hilt and hurled it in a tumbling arc out over the lawn. From now on the fight would be face-to-face and his weapons would be real ones—his fists and his mind.

Chapter Twenty

෯

FOUR days into her journey Emma dared to walk through a town by day. It was south and east of the hall by many miles. She had trusted no one and accepted no rides even from carters who offered, and so she did not know how far she'd come, but it was beginning to look as if she had escaped. A few more days, a few more miles, and she could begin to think of starting a new life.

She would only have to stop thinking of Daventry every minute and wishing he did not hate her. It was a true thing that one paid dearly for seducing an angel. She wondered when he had found her note, and she passed far too much time composing imaginary letters to him full of all the reasons he should be glad she had left. He had his boys and his family, and he could make them all happy by choosing some good English girl to marry.

The day was warm, but she pulled her shawl close around her three layers of dresses. She entered the inn behind a crowd of passengers off a stage and ordered tea and a bun. It was as she left that she saw the flyer for the match. *Open rounds for amateurs. The Somerton Stinger challenges the Copthorn Croaker to fifteen rounds.* He was going to do it. He was going to go openly where his enemies could get at him.

Wallop's words had nagged at her every step of the way. Daventry believed her to be his betrayer. He hated her, but she could not hate him. Tatty had no saying that Emma could remember about being stupidly in love. Apparently, if you had the worst luck in love, if you loved someone who could not love you back, you still loved.

She told herself that Daventry's brothers would be with him, that he was strong, that Wallop and Aubrey did not have the power to control a prizefight. But she read the announcement again. It did not say where the thing would be because the organizers would not want any constables to arrive and spoil the event.

It made her angry that he would risk himself.

A parson in a broad-brimmed black hat saw her standing in front of the broadside and stopped and tore the flyer down. "Ye'll not be thinking of such doings, miss."

He went on his righteous way, and Emma came back and scooped up the torn flyer.

L ARK could hear a hum over the rattle of carriages in the road. It sounded almost like Oxford Street, different because of woods and fields instead of cobbles and bricks, but with the same, restless, surging rise and fall of sound a decent crowd made. He grinned at Rook and picked up his pace. He'd missed crowds in the country.

They had spent the night in a barn. In the morning they'd

filled their pockets with apples stored in a farmer's hayloft and departed before he came to tend to his cows. They'd trudged along the dark road half dozing on numb feet until the sun rose. Then they'd looked at each other and stopped to knock and slap the straw from their clothes and hair.

Now they turned into a churned-up path across a common headed for the buzz of sound. Greening woods circled the open expanse. If Dav kept to his plan, he'd be among the millers today. Lark hadn't decided whether he wanted Dav to see them or not. Mostly he blamed Dav for spoiling everything. Once or twice a stealthy thought sneaked into his mind that he and Rook were not cut out for the respectable dull life Dav wanted them to have.

One thing was certain. If Lark wanted his old town life back, he had to get tough again. Their eight nights on the road had shown him just how soft he'd become sleeping in beds under roofs with a full belly as he'd done for three years since Dav had taken them to live with his family. He and Rook had tried sleeping back-to-back for warmth. They wore boots and coats and waistcoats and stockings, and still their teeth chattered and sleep did not come easy. It was a sorry state for a pair of street rats.

A fine curricle pulled up beside them, and a swell toff hailed them. "Where have you lads escaped from? Eton, I'll wager. You'll be flogged for it, but hop on up, I can bring you closer."

Eton? Rook's brows shot up, but Lark accepted the ride with his best accent and scrambled into the carriage. The driver had a friendly face, a head of fashionably cropped black curls, and a gold ticker, as fat and round as a turnip, dangling where a gold ticker had no business dangling if it wanted to stay long with one owner.

Lark looked away from the watch. "What are the odds on the Somerton Stinger?"

"The Stinger? What, is he your favorite? You'll lose your shirt and your boots, too, if you lay your blunt on the Stinger, lads. Everyone in Thorndon favors the Croaker. He's made mush of five hopefuls since he came into the ring."

Lark figured the gentleman got to keep his ticker only because he'd done them a service. He let them down at the edge of the crowd where pie men and peddlers circulated, shouting their offerings to knots of spectators who hadn't yet joined the main press. Legs called out the odds and collected bets.

Rook's gaze watched a pie man go by, but Lark pulled him along by the elbow and made him look at the restless, shifting crowd.

"What do you see?"

"Coves. 'Undreds of 'em."

"By my count maybe two hundred. What don't you see?"

"Ladies?" Rook turned a puzzled frown Lark's way. Rook would never go to the head of the class.

True, there were few women present, drabs and hawkers mainly, they looked to be. No ladies, though Lark glanced at the carriages to confirm it. He had heard that sometimes wicked ladies came to mills for to see the men strip down and bloody one another. Before Nate Wilde had told them of it, Lark had thought only Bread Street doxies had a taste for blood and battle.

Lark gave Rook a cuff with the back of his hand. "Wot you don't see is constables. That's the beauty of a mill. No one invites the beaks. There are probably fifty tickers and a hundred purses, and not a constable for miles. And, wot's more, we look like toffs. *Eton* the gentleman said."

A slow satisfied grin spread across Rook's face, and a larcenous gleam lit his eye. He nodded his head. "They're all ours, ain't they?"

"As many as we can hold," Lark confirmed. "Then we lay some money on Dav, and clean the pie man out of his wares."

"And 'ave a good chop and cucumber and ketchup, too."

"Done." Lark shook his partner's hand and slipped into the crowd.

EMMA wore black. Today she was a soldier's widow on her way to her husband's family in Poole. The disguise worked well with strangers, but there were few women on the Thorndon common, and it would be easy for Wallop to pick her out in the crowd. She was sure he would be here planning an accident for Daventry, and she didn't want Wallop to find her before she pointed him out to Dav's people.

She hadn't meant to come, but the flier had changed her plans. She meant to be miles farther west by now. But Tatty and the babe would be on a ship bound for America now, out of reach forever of the past. Emma could not lose Tatty now, only Daventry. If Aubrey and Wallop found a way to destroy Daventry, they would. And if Daventry did not exist, what kind of world would it be for Emma to live in?

She felt light-headed with hunger and shaky on her feet, but it was best to stay in the thick of the crowd. Moving among the throng of spectators was like rowing on a choppy sea. Around her coarse men shifted and shoved each other for position. They staggered against her or trod on her feet, buffeting her with rough shoulders and ripe smells. The higher orders kept to their vehicles above the churned-up mud of the field. Emma's boots were caked with it.

She could not take a step without thinking she had delivered Dav to his enemy, and he would not know it until the enemy struck, until falling stones or a knife-wielding attacker hurtled at him. She did not know how Wallop would use the prizefight, but she knew he would. Daventry would not recognize Wallop as his betrayer, but he would know Emma. She could expose Wallop by her mere presence.

The ring looked honest and open, a square of grass perhaps fifteen feet in either direction enclosed by ropes. It lay at one end of a long, wide hollow. She had expected an accident along the road, but she could see now how much more exposed the ring would be. Once Daventry emerged from his closed carriage, he would be in the midst of hundreds of men. Any rough character in the crowd could be a tool of the duke with a weapon.

She spotted the boys with Will Jones and his young protégé, Nate Wilde, in an open carriage next to an elegant black vehicle, closed. The boys looked giddy with excitement. She looked down, shielding her face with her bonnet brim, as Will Jones's alert gaze raked the crowd. It comforted her to see Will there. Daventry had made it safely to the match, and his brother was looking out for him.

Around her men talked of the odds. Those offering three to one on the Croaker did a brisk business, but all of them studied the two closed carriages on opposite sides of the ring in a cheerful, bloodthirsty way. Everyone expected an easy victory for the local champion with plenty of blows and blood. The Somerton Stinger was an unknown. They assumed his defeat. Emma smiled to herself. No one knew Daventry at all.

Now that she'd found his supporters, Emma looked for Wallop's purple waistcoat in the tide of brown and black coats. In the ring itself four men stood conversing, indifferent to the rising hum of the restless spectators. Slowly, she swept her gaze over the carriages until she spotted Wallop. He had a slouched hat pulled low on his brow, but the bulge of his purple waistcoat was unmistakable. He leaned down in conversation with a white-haired man in a loose brown frock coat and dirty linen neckcloth.

The man at Wallop's side left him and slipped through the ropes drawing the attention of the fellows in the middle. A brief conversation caused two men to dash off toward a closed carriage on the opposite side of the ring from Dav's carriage. The remaining two officials marched over to Wallop. Wallop descended from his carriage and opened the door of a third closed carriage next to his.

For the next quarter hour Emma watched the men come and go, consulting with one another as the crowd murmured and stirred. One of the group went to talk with Will Jones, who then opened his brother's carriage. At last the four reassembled in the center of the ring and got the attention of the crowd.

"The Copthorn Croaker withdraws. The Langley Leveler will meet the Somerton Stinger." The announcement rippled through the crowd, darkening the mood, and setting off waves of furious negotiations over bets.

A dark-haired man of about thirty emerged from the third closed carriage and tossed his hat in the ring. His seconds stripped him and brought him to the weighing stand. The crowd watched the big man closely. What one saw first was the black eye patch. Otherwise, he had a heavy black-stubbled square jaw in a long, angular face that might be called handsome under close-cropped hair. He was oddly top heavy with a great pink barrel chest covered with dark hair and tree-limb arms, but a thin waist and frog-like legs.

* * *

Dav's brothers reported the change of fighters to him with grim faces. According to the vinegars the attending physician had pronounced the Croaker too ill to fight. Another fighter from the field of contestants had agreed to take his place. If Dav agreed to meet the Langley Leveler, the stakeholders would sponsor both men, and the match could proceed.

Dav agreed with Will and Xan that the whole thing smelled fishy. But no one outside of his family knew that the Somerton Stinger was the Marquess of Daventry. No one knew that he'd left the hall to participate in this fight.

He wasn't going to back out of the match in spite of Xan's urging. It was what he'd wanted since he was a boy, a contest that pitted him against an opponent he would have to outdo in body, wit, and spirit. He wanted blows he could feel in his ribs and belly. And if his grandfather had somehow manipulated the game in his favor, Dav welcomed the confrontation. He pointed out that if they paid attention, they could expose his grandfather's hirelings.

At the boys' urging he had worn his old black velvet coat. As he stepped down from Xander's carriage, he had to admit that a bit of theatricality added to the occasion.

Will stood at his side, looking at the white-haired fellow who had reported the Croaker's illness. "That fellow's a physician as much as I'm a bleeding lady's maid."

"Do you think he 'treated' Croaker?"

"I don't doubt it. He won't be treating you, however. Wenlocke's got to be behind this change."

"Is Wenlocke here?"

Will looked annoyed. "We don't think so. I have Wilde

scouting about. Listen, Dav, don't do this thing. There will be other matches."

"You think the Somerton Stinger can walk away from this crowd?"

Will cast his shrewd gaze around at the throng of men pressed against the ropes. "We're watching every minute. Any foul play, I'm stopping it."

Dav thought the Leveler looked appropriately menacing. Not too much hidden there. The man's reach and his fists were more of a match for Adam Digweed than Dav. The Leveler was punching the air in his corner of the ring, doing a little dance with his feet for the spectators' notice.

Dav thrust his hands into the pockets of his old coat. His fingers encountered a puzzling scrap of paper. He drew the folded thing from the depths of his pocket and froze at its message. No punch from the Leveler could knock him so.

I love you.

Emma Portland had betrayed and deserted him. But she'd sat at his desk, taken his pen, and confessed her love. He'd been confused about her for days, weighing her sweet lovemaking against the evidence that she came from Wenlocke and reported to Wenlocke's man in the village. Now his ears filled with the restless noise of the crowd.

He stripped off the coat, tossed his hat in the ring, and let Xan strip him down for the weigh-in procedure. He could feel the crowd's eyes and their judgment, but he was somewhere else, apart from the scene. He noted the scramble to change odds when the onlookers got their first glimpse of the gash in his arm. With the Croaker out of the picture, the old bets were off, the odds would change with each round. None of them were likely to favor Dav.

From his corner he looked out over the crowd, a restless mass of browns and grays, nothing to arrest the eye except the occasional checkered neckcloth or vivid waistcoat. A purple expanse caught his eye and nagged his memory, but the boys cheered for the Stinger, bouncing in their seats, making the carriage rock on its springs. He raised his fist for them. His eye paused again on a woman in a black bonnet looking down, but she did not lift her head, and he was deceiving himself to imagine any resemblance to Emma there.

The umpire called him to the mark, and he gave his attention to the Leveler. He had wanted this encounter chained by Harris, hounded by his grandfather, trapped in the gilded palace his family wanted for him. It was not the dream it had been on the night Xander had taken him to the Fives Court to see the champion in that exhibition match, but it was what he must do.

Emma watched Daventry as he stood in his black velvet coat. A breeze lifted his hair, and the sun flashed in it. His wide stance spoke of easy confidence, but he appeared detached as if he inhabited some untouchable space. He had not believed her note. Her love had not reached him. He shoved his hands into his pockets.

She watched him draw a folded thing from his pocket, open it, and freeze like a man stunned.

Across the ring Wallop climbed heavily up into his carriage. The Leveler was clearly his man, but the Leveler would only be a part of the strategy. If Aubrey and the duke were behind Wallop, there would be other enemies in the crowd. She asked the man next to her who the white-haired man was who'd gone into the ring.

"Sawbones," he said. "Gotter 'ave one on 'and." That was not good. The man didn't look like any physician she would trust. She would go to Wallop and let Will Jones spot her there. She would expose the truth, and the crows could have her.

Chapter Twenty-one

❧

EMMA watched three rounds, working her way through the dense crowd. At first the two adversaries eyed each other and moved to position themselves to advantage. When Dav got in a body blow, the Leveler glanced a blow off his opponent's head. In the second round the Leveler came out with a whirlwind of blows while Daventry seemed to hoard his lightning strikes. Emma could not determine who gained the advantage, but the odds makers still called out three to one for the Leveler, who bloodied Daventry's mouth when he slipped on the wet grass and took a heavy fist to his jaw as he went down.

It wasn't until the Leveler connected with Daventry's ribs in the fourth round that Emma recognized that something was wrong. The blow sounded wrong and Daventry reacted oddly, but she had spotted Lark and Rook. Lark could take a message to Daventry. He would believe Lark. She pushed harder to make her way through the crowd during a furious exchange in the fifth round, enduring curses from men intent on the action.

Lark was shouting himself hoarse when she touched his elbow. He swung toward her, nearly knocking her senseless.

"You!" He turned back to the fight as Daventry and the Leveler went to their corners.

"The Leveler is the duke's man," she told him.

Lark whipped back to her. "Wot do you mean?" he hissed.

She pointed out Wallop. "That man in the purple waistcoat he reports to the duke's nephew. He's been in Somerton for weeks collecting information about Daventry, trying to do him an injury."

"You mean the roof?"

She nodded.

"How do you know that?"

"I spied for him."

Lark swore at her and turned back to the ring as the fight resumed.

"The Leveler's cheating in some way, isn't he?"

Lark watched the fight. "He has loaded hands."

"What?"

"He's got something in his fists to make them heavier."

"Tell Daventry."

"He knows." Lark turned his face away from her.

Emma could see that Daventry was somewhere else, in a state of alertness that blocked out everything except the Leveler. Lark was right. Daventry was good at noticing things, the smallest details. He wanted the challenge. He wanted the match to be as brutal and punishing as it could be. He wanted the Leveler to be a dangerous opponent.

The round was Daventry's. He worked out a way to invite wild sweeping shots from the Leveler that he could block with an elbow while his right fist flashed at the Leveler's jaw. But the tactic opened the gash on his arm, which bled freely. The third time Daventry connected, the Leveler swayed on his feet, a man dizzied by blows. The big man shook his head and spit out a tooth. With a roar he lowered his head and rushed Daventry, his shoulder catching Daventry's ribs, driving him against the ropes until he'd trapped Daventry where he could pummel his side with those fists.

Daventry went down on the slippery grass, and the Leveler drove a punishing fist into his back. Daventry arched under the blow. Xander Jones shouted at the umpire, but his words were lost in roar of the crowd. The boys screamed. Adam Digweed lunged forward, slicing through the crowd, held back only by the ropes. Daventry struggled to heave himself up. He had one foot under him, ready to push up when the Leveler moved in to land a blow to his ear.

Adam's hand shot out over the ropes and caught the Leveler's right wrist and yanked it back. It shocked the crowd silent for an instant. Lark screamed madly, "He's got loaded hands." Adam twisted the Leveler's arm until his fist opened and three round brass cylinders fell out. It stunned those closest to the ring. The umpire rushed forward to push the Leveler away from Dav.

Dav's ears rang. His eyes stung with sweat and blood, and his breath was a harsh, hot rattle in his chest and throat. The umpires had a hold of the Leveler, pulling him away. The man's hands hung limp at his sides. His barrel chest rose and fell like a great bellows, and his bloodied face looked alarmed.

Will stepped into the space between the Leveler and Dav and said something that Dav couldn't hear over the roar in his ears. Then his brother dashed off.

The white-haired physician took Dav's bleeding arm. "Let's treat that, son." He reached to press a cloth over the wound.

"No!" The cry came from the crowd.

Dav twisted out of the man's grip, turning to see who had shouted, and his gaze found Emma Portland, standing openmouthed in the crowd, the blue of her eyes was clear and sweet and true as the sky. He had thought her a sweet clever lie from beginning to end, but his understanding underwent a complete reversal.

I love you.

He knew it was the truth.

As he watched, the crowd swallowed her as if a muddy pond had closed over her. Dav started in her direction when Xan caught his good arm and pulled him around to face a large man in a purple waistcoat, caught in the grip of a pair of stout vinegars.

AUBREY descended from his carriage at a discreet bend in the road where a stand of beeches concealed his business from the masses. An evil-looking fellow in a workingman's cap and dusty tan corduroys pointed a wicked if ancient pistol at a kneeling Emma Portland, her black bonnet askew, her hem crusted in mud. Aubrey savored the image.

For sheer effrontery the chit deserved every bit of what was coming to her. The little vein in his forehead throbbed in a mildly disagreeable way, and it was her fault. She had cost them the best chance they'd had in months to rid themselves of Sophie Rhys-Jones's inconvenient brat. With

Wenlocke's health in question, they could not afford lost chances.

Behind him his servants went about their business as they were trained to do, readying his horse and carriage. Already an ambush was in place for the Joneses' carriage as it returned to the hall. Mates of the man in front of him would wait to finish the injured.

It was unfortunate that Aubrey had had to take matters into his own hands. Wallop's people had proved quite hopeless. And Wallop himself, who was supposed to be the master at providing accidents, had failed dismally, not only with the chimney pot fiasco but now with the sham fight and the phony physician. Aubrey had been lucky to find a gang of footpads preparing to work the crowd. The man's pistol never wavered. He did not look the sort to find blue eyes appealing.

Aubrey came to stand over the kneeling girl. The temptation to nudge her with his boot passed quickly. His boots would not benefit from contact with her soiled skirts. "Miss Portland, you disappoint me."

She made no answer. She neither trembled nor appealed.

"We gave you every opportunity to prove your worth, and you failed."

He used the tip of his crop to tilt her face up. The blue eyes had something in them he had not seen before. He dismissed it. If the girl didn't mind murder, she should not have quibbled at mere spying.

"We save you from the law and dress you in silks and ask only a small favor in return. Instead you thwart our efforts. You repay us by false information and an ill-judged flight into wretchedness." He brought his riding crop down on her shoulder.

The girl flinched, but did not cry out.

"I suppose I should have expected as much from an unnatural woman, a murderess. As things stand I have no choice but to turn you over to the mercies of the law.

"Take her to Horsham. They'll know what to do with her. I want her in jail tonight. Don't let her out of your sight."

Emma recognized her usual luck. She knew a bad guard when she met one. This man would spit in the soup. Aubrey's man shoved her into the carriage and took a seat opposite her and settled a long, wicked pistol across his lap. He grinned.

Chapter Twenty-two

☙

D<small>AV</small>'s ear opened, and he heard Xan say, "We've found a man of Wenlocke's named Wallop."

It was the name the constable had given for the brewer who shed suspicion on Emma. Wallop had been in Somerton recently. Dav turned to the vinegars holding a fleshy fellow in a purple waistcoat and plaid trousers and experienced another moment of dislocation.

Xan's hand on his shoulder, the din of the crowd, and the purple silk expanse of the stranger's midsection created a shift in time and place, a narrowing of his vision. He was momentarily a boy again on a November night, excited by his first mill and the champion's victory, throwing wild punches in imitation of his hero as the crowd streamed out of the Fives Court into Leicester Square. That night Xan's hand on his shoulder had kept him from punching a man in a purple waistcoat, who had given them a fixed stare.

"You." A jumble of images tumbled through his mind, and another piece in the puzzle of that long-ago night fell into place. His head cleared. "You were there. You pointed me out to Harris, didn't you?"

Wallop's broad face kept its genial lines, but his eyes shifted, looking for an escape.

"Who pays you? Wenlocke?"

Dav grabbed Wallop by his wilting neckcloth.

Wallop twisted to look at Xan and Will. "Your boy's a bit confused. His first match, isn't it? Promising lad. My apologies about the Leveler. I was quite misled. Wanted to see a match go forward."

Dav hit him. Hard. In the diaphragm.

Wallop doubled over gasping like a fish on sand. The vinegars jerked him upright again.

"Who pays you?"

Wallop gasped, his mouth working soundlessly, his eyes squeezed shut in the folds of his fleshy face. Dav waited for it. "Lord . . . Aubrey."

"Dav! Dav!"

He turned at the shouts. The boys swarmed into the ring. They jumped and pointed, out of breath and frantic. Dav collared Swallow and made the others hush.

"A man with a pistol put Miss Portland in a coach. Another fellow, a swell toff, hit her with a riding crop and rode off on his horse."

Dav spun back to Wallop. "Who took Emma just now?"

Wallop tried to straighten up. "Now, boy, this is no way to treat a friend of the fancy. Josiah Wallop doesn't know such things."

"You're no friend to anyone. You tried to kill us. You frightened her."

"She gave you up, boy. Anything we wanted she told us."

Dav smashed Wallop's nose. Blood gushed over his fleshy chin and his soiled linen and spattered the purple silk.

"Who's got her? Aubrey?" Dav knew his grandfather would not be mounted on a horse.

"Don't . . . know."

Dav hit him again.

"Aye, Aubrey was here."

Dav looked at his brothers. "I'm going to get her."

"It's another trap, like this match. Aubrey's likely got hired fists or guns waiting." Xan spoke quietly. "Let us go."

"She's their lure. They're using her to draw you in." Will protested.

It made sense, but the bits and pieces of Emma's story collided in Dav's brain and fell into a kind of rough order. "They've got some hold over her." Dav shoved Wallop, who was slumped over his neckcloth, bleeding freely. "What's the duke's hold on her?"

"She needs a paper, a pardon. Wenlocke has it."

"A pardon? For what?"

Wallop still breathed in short, pained gasps, but he smiled a sly, malicious smile, ensanguined by the blood on his teeth. "She murdered some poor bloke. She'll swing for it."

His brothers' faces wore shock. The boys were sober and uncomprehending.

Lark stepped up to his side. "She came to warn you."

Dav detached himself from the urgent pleading voices in his ears. Everyone wanted him to believe that Emma was a murderer. Emma, who hugged ponies and rejoiced in grubby boys reading and admired toads. Emma, who yielded her sweet self to him when she had nothing left to give. He knew better. He'd got it backward when she'd disappeared. He'd thought her love was a lie, but her love was the truth. Everything about Emma Portland was a lie except her love. *I love you.* That was the truth. She wasn't a vicar's daughter or Wenlocke's spy or a murderer. He didn't know who she was yet, but he knew her, the woman under the layers of disguises. He loved her, and he had to get her back from Aubrey.

His immediate surroundings came back into focus. The vinegars and the umpire formed a loose circle around Dav and his brothers in the middle of the ring, but beyond them the crowd voiced its displeasure at the breakup of the match. They'd missed seeing the bloody spectacle they'd come for. Hotheads in the crowd started a chant of "Cheat, cheat, cheat!"

"In case you haven't noticed, Dav, a bleeding riot is brewing. These fellows came to see a match." Will cocked his head in the direction of the crowd.

Dav turned to him. "Then give them a match. You and Xan. School them. And empty Wallop's pockets for starters. Get the boys to spread some of his blunt around. See that every workingman gets a day's wage."

"And what are *you* going to do?" One of Will's black brows quirked upward.

"I'm going to Wenlocke to get Emma's pardon."

"You can't go to Wenlocke without us."

Dav nodded to Adam Digweed, who began to clear a path through the onlookers with brute size. "Catch up when you can."

"Wenlocke will kill you."

"Or die trying. It's much the likelier outcome."

"Wenlocke won't give you her pardon."

"I think he will when he hears what I'm offering. I think he'll give me everything I want."

*   *   *

STANDING in the corner of the ring, Lark tasted gall, a bit-
terness that made his mouth go dry. He could not move for
a full minute as he watched Dav go. Dav did not look back.
His mind was on the girl. He had left them behind to enter a
world where they could not be his mates. They would not
scramble together to the top of some roof to share the spoils of
the day. Dav thought he had stayed one of them, but he hadn't.

Around Lark Dav's brothers began to turn the crowd
from disappointment to interest in the new match. Xander
Jones had stripped for the ring, and already the legs were
offering odds. Will Jones held a purse high over his head,
encouraging wagers that he could land a hit over his brother's
guard. No one was watching Lark and Rook, which was a
good thing. Their bulging pockets would not bear scrutiny
at the moment. Rook looked decidedly uneasy. Any minute
now some persons in the crowd were bound to discover
their pockets had been lightened and to begin to complain.

It was time for Lark and Rook to slip away. Lark nudged
his companion. As he held the rope up for Rook to duck
under, Lark spotted Dav's old velvet coat on the ground. He
snatched it up and dragged it with him through the ropes.
They moved quickly then while the crowd laughed and
shouted at Xander and Will Jones in the ring.

A steady pace took them up the hillside bordering the
green into the wood. In the concealing shelter of beech trunks
Lark stopped and donned the worn coat. It smelled like London, like smoke and stone. A little loose in the shoulders, it
hung down to his ankles and he had to turn up the cuffs.

"Wot're ye doing with 'is old coat?" Rook wanted to know.

"Starting a new career. Let's head for London."

Rook grinned.

Chapter Twenty-three

❧

ANCIENT oaks that cast long shadows before a bend in the road allowed Dav a full view of Wenlocke Castle from the carriage window. He had never cared to possess it, and he knew he could count on his grandfather's reluctance to surrender its splendor into unworthy hands.

Mounted on a hill above the surrounding countryside, Wenlocke was meant to daunt rather than welcome visitors. Whatever defenses it had possessed through the dark centuries of wars and plagues, over time it had undergone an architectural transformation that made it less a battlement than a rich man's palace of stone modeled after the grandeur of ancient Greece and Rome.

Dav had realized something about his grandfather on the way to Wenlocke. The old man had never cared for a direct fight. For seven years Wenlocke had sent his lackeys and hirelings against Dav, paid tools of malice. Dav felt he had the advantage in a direct fight.

The carriage halted in front of a massive central block like a tricked-out temple from an ancient acropolis. Six fluted columns supported a pediment and frieze of warring figures clashing in battle. Stone urns and torches bristled along the roofline against the blackening sky. From the center block imposing wings branched out to the north and south. Wide steps compelled the visitor's gaze up to the entrance. Dav guessed the place had five hundred rooms or more, but he only cared about one of them, whichever one held Emma prisoner.

As he opened the carriage door, a flock of crows took off in raucous flight at the edge of the woods. He hoped Emma could not hear their harsh cries.

He stepped down. A raw evening wind tugged at him and blew his loose hair back from his face. The stinging touch of the breeze set his wounds throbbing. His right eye did not open fully, and he could imagine its plum hue. He tasted blood every time he moved his lips. Yet he felt oddly exhilarated at the prospect of confronting his grandfather at last.

Adam lumbered down to stand beside him and untucked two pistols from his belt. They crossed the drive, Dav confident that some vigilant soul inside would soon note their arrival. The crunch of their footfalls, the rustle of the breeze, and the driver tending to the spent horses sounded loud in his ears. The crows flew off as they advanced.

As they reached the foot of the steps, the castle's grand door opened, and a pair of shaggy orange and white setters exploded from within. All lean muscle and energy, the dogs barreled toward Dav, hair flying, teeth bared.

He stood his ground and stared them down, and the beasts dropped panting at his feet. A long moment passed filled with the flapping of his open coat and the dogs' ragged pants. With a wave of his right hand, he freed the dogs to dance and cavort around him.

A solemn butler watched the display from above, flanked by three liveried footmen on either side. Dav let the servant phalanx take his measure while the dogs barked and danced. Then he gave Adam a nod, and they strode forward.

The footmen shifted uneasily on either side of the butler, looking to him for a signal and casting wary glances at Adam with his pistols. Dav took the steps and halted on a level with the waiting men.

"I've come to see the old man." The stiff butler's high collar kept his chin angled upward and forced him to look down a long nose at Dav, but the man's eyes were alive with recognition.

"Regrettably, sir, His Grace is not at home to uninvited guests."

Sir was calculated for politeness and a refusal to recognize Dav's claim to his title. Dav let his gaze sweep the assembled footmen and return to the butler. "Ordinarily, Mr. . . . ?"

The dogs chased each other back up the stairs and halted panting at Dav's side.

The butler flicked them a disgusted glance. "Vickers."

Dav nodded. "Ordinarily, Mr. Vickers, I would not interrupt His Grace's enjoyment of his vast possessions, but as he's taken one of mine, I must. He'll see me when he reads this." Dav produced the folded paper with the terms he'd conceived for Emma's release.

Vickers took it as if he handled live ammunition. With a slight bow he stepped aside. "You'll be pleased to wait in the hall, sir."

At a signal from Vickers two footmen went running in opposite directions, one up a stone staircase, and one through a door to their left. Dav exchanged a glance with Adam, alerting him to be ready for whatever was thrown at them next. Adam nodded. The dogs trotted in with perfect unconcern for the human drama around them, their nails clicking on the marble tiles.

H IS supper interrupted, Lord Roderick Philoughby stood in the narrow stone cell in the women's wing of the jail looking at a disheveled young woman in black with mud on her hem. Philoughby thought it no wonder that she kept her head bowed. The place reeked of confinement and helplessness, submission and abandonment. What appetite he'd had for his supper deserted him.

Foley, the constable, rattled his keys. The girl lifted her face, and Philoughby looked into eyes of the purest, sweetest blue he had ever seen. Eyes of truth, he thought.

The day had little light left, slanting down through a grating in the wall, catching a strand of the pale culprit's untidy hair and lighting up the cell with it. It was unlike Foley to speak up on behalf of the wretches who ended in Horsham Jail, particularly when the accused had been taken up on a charge of murder, but looking at the young woman before him, Philoughby understood Foley's unease.

Philoughby could not imagine a more unlikely murderess in spite of the dirt and bewildering contrast between her thin face and well-padded person. She appeared to exist in some other realm than the sordid cell with its iron bed and reeking chamber pot.

"You did well to summon me, Foley. This whole affair smacks of unseemly haste."

"Thought ye'd want to know, Yer Worship, Colonel

Crutchfield is over at the Swan. Says 'e's got a jury ready to act in the morning. 'E's spoken for the executioner's cart."

Philoughby frowned. Juries were meant to deliberate before deciding. Crutchfield was acting above himself to rush this case. Earlier Philoughby had received a brief on the case with a message from the Earl of Aubrey to move the proceedings to tomorrow's court session and put all other cases back. The disorder in this abrupt change and the demand for haste aroused suspicion in Philoughby's well-ordered soul. The terse request from Aubrey irked him, try as he might to regulate his temper.

Open-and-shut case. Proceed to administer justice with all dispatch, the note read. Philoughby disliked being told to hasten his proceedings by a person with no connection to his court. He had no intention of donning his black cap and condemning a prisoner for any lord's convenience.

He already knew that the woman in front of him had no counsel to speak for her. Furthermore, witnesses were not to be present for cross-questioning. Aubrey wished their earlier sworn statements to be read as evidence of the facts.

Philoughby cleared his throat. "Do you have any family nearby to assist you, Miss Portland?"

"None, Your Worship."

Philoughby looked around the comfortless cell. "Did you have a proper supper to sustain you in the night?"

The girl shrugged as if indifferent to the matter of supper. Philoughby recalled his own abandoned supper spread with care on white linen in the private parlor reserved for him at the Queen's Head. The prisoner's disinterest in supper struck him as a further sign that she inhabited some other realm in which he could offer no assistance.

"I do have a request, Your Worship."

"What is it, Miss Portland?"

"That my gowns might be sold."

"Your gowns?" It was almost black in the cell. Philoughby was sure he'd misunderstood.

"Yes, Your Worship, for the burial cost. When I am hanged, I wish to be cut down quickly and buried." She spoke as if she made the most ordinary of requests.

Philoughby leaned toward to the girl, uncertain he had heard correctly.

"Is it not possible?" she asked. Her voice had dropped to a faint whisper.

Philoughby straightened. "Of course you may expect common decency."

"Thank you." The girl smiled at him, a sweet, grateful smile he could see even in the dim light. "I do not wish . . . the crows to come."

Philoughby could not move. The interview was at an end. His promise, slight as it was, went beyond the requirements of justice and common compassion. A pastor might tend to the girl, but as a judge Philoughby's duty was to administer the law. Nevertheless, he felt he had left the business unfinished.

Foley cleared his throat, and the keys at his waist jingled.

Philoughby bowed and left the cell.

Everything against the girl must be a lie. Philoughby would comb the evidence. He would read it again and again if it took all night. Surely, he would find where the details contradicted one another, the places where the case failed to make sense.

Chapter Twenty-four

❧

D AV regarded the pair of Roman busts at the foot of the
duke's grand staircase, white as snow and as the soaring marble columns that drew the eye to a lofty alabaster ceiling. The entry was like a cave of ice. The frowning Romans
and the sharp-edged stone certainly must discourage boyish
sliding on banisters. He could not imagine his father being a
boy here. He could not imagine his lads or any boy enjoying
the cold stone staircase. Nothing he saw moved him with a
desire for possession. The duke could keep Wenlocke.

A footman came down the stairs and held a quiet exchange
with Vickers.

"Sir, if you consent to leave all weapons behind, I will
show you to His Grace."

Dav nodded and submitted to a search of his person by
a pair of fumbling footmen. His injuries made themselves
known as the nervous pair poked and prodded him for concealed daggers and guns.

Adam frowned and crossed his broad arms over his chest with his pistols pointed outward.

When the footmen stepped away, the dogs made to follow Dav, but he sent them back to lie at Adam's feet.

His footfalls echoed on the marble. He had been fighting his grandfather for a third of his life. The old man had won their first match when Archibald March had arranged for Dav to be kidnapped by Timothy Harris. Dav had been young and weak and taken by surprise into captivity in London's meanest streets until Harris died unexpectedly. He had lived on his own for nearly two years until his brothers' courage and sacrifice had persuaded him to come home. Together they had taken on the old duke in the courts.

Dav had won that second match played out over three years in the courts with the help and support of all his family and at the cost of most of his mother's small fortune and some of his brothers' wealth as well. In November he had been declared the Marquess of Daventry, his father's son, his grandfather's heir.

But his grandfather had continued to plot his destruction. Today Dav understood the full extent of his grandfather's treachery, a treachery that had made Emma a tool of Aubrey and Wallop. For that alone, for the pain he'd caused Emma, the duke deserved no mercy.

So, weaponless, Dav would meet the old man face-to-face for a third and decisive match. Outside the heavy oak door, the butler paused, and Dav nerved himself to meet the man who had been trying to kill him for seven years.

The Duke of Wenlocke easily dominated the long oak-paneled room, a tall figure in black. Even a stone fireplace grand enough to roast an ox seemed less powerful. Gold gleamed on the spines of hundreds of books. One of the duke's hands clutched the gold head of a black cane. The other pointed a lethal-looking pistol at Dav.

It came to him that his grandfather had given orders from this place, from rooms so vast they could hold whole tenements, that led to Dav's being chained to a bed in a room on Bread Street.

He looked about him for how he might win the fight, and saw that the duke's pistol hand wavered with a slight palsy. In the next second he spotted a weapon among the assortment of priceless objects on a mahogany gate leg table. He palmed a small bronze of a hunting dog, the size and heft of a decent cobble, and laughed to himself as the feral instinct of the street came alive in him.

He had not expected his grandfather to be a dragon with scales and horns or fiery breath and great fangs, but he had not guessed that he bore any resemblance to the old man. He now saw his own nose and his straight brows rimed with white on a face of cold severity. It was like looking into the frostiest of mirrors. He and Wenlocke were nearly a match in height. He might even give his grandfather the edge, for the duke leaned some of his weight on that gold-headed black cane.

The old man said nothing. He gaze raked Dav frankly. Dav hoped the old man saw his scrapes and the purpling colors of his cheekbones and knew them for the signs of a fighter.

"So, you've escaped Aubrey and his man." The voice burned with cool hauteur, the way an icicle could burn and stick to the tongue.

"I wanted to have a look at the man who has been trying to arrange my death for seven years. At least the pistol is direct." Except that in the duke's unsteady hand a bullet was likely to go anywhere.

"Don't push me, boy." The duke put down the wavering pistol and took up Dav's paper in his fist, shaking it. "What is the meaning of this?"

"A chance for you to take back Wenlocke. It's what you want, isn't it?" With the pistol on the desk, Dav dropped the bronze piece into his coat pocket.

"You can't be serious. No one throws away a dukedom for a mere chit, a murderous one at that." He tossed Dav's note onto the vast desk.

"What I want and what you want have never agreed."

"Don't try to dictate terms to me, you baseborn blight on the house of Wenlocke." The old man's voice shook with rage.

Dav said nothing. He understood now the terrible hold that stones and acres and centuries of a name had on the old man.

"You've wasted a fortune fighting me for what is mine. Now you want to throw it in my face?"

"I want to make a trade, the safety and security of my family, for your vast acres and gilded pile."

The old man gave a snort. "You have no idea of the value of Wenlocke."

"I know the value of what I want."

"A girl? You would throw away Wenlocke over a girl? If I'd known your price earlier, we could have avoided all the expense and delay."

Dav gave the magnificent library a slow perusal, the miles of leather-bound books, the rich carpet, the velvet drapery, the high vaulted ceiling, the priceless relics of ancient empires. His gaze came back to the duke. "Keep it all. I want Emma."

"What touching sentimentality over your doxie. You're just like your father, a fool for a tart."

Just like your father. The bitter words hung in the air. The duke himself seemed shaken by his own backhanded acknowledgment of Dav's origins.

"I was content to be Kit Jones. I might never have known my father's name if I had not gone to that boxing match. But after that night I had years to ask myself who hated Kit Jones enough to give him over to Harris. I could not think what Kit Jones had done to offend anyone that much."

"Your existence was an offense to me."

"A thousand bastards in London no more trouble their fathers or grandfathers than flies on dung. Why did I trouble you?"

"You took his name."

"Not while he lived."

"You had no right."

"I had the right of blood. The same right as any son. He'd captured my mother's heart, and for him she consented to be a wife."

"For Wenlocke you mean. For a title and riches that avaricious whore stole my son, destroyed him."

The icy voice grew brittle, cracking like a frozen pond. The old man sank into a leather chair. "Why did he go to India? Why did he die?"

Dav saw that it was pointless to reason with him. The past had him in its grip. The old man had never stopped blaming Sophie and Dav for the death of his own son. Dav waited until the old man's eyes again saw him.

"Take the name back," he advised his grandfather. "Give Wenlocke to your nephew if you will. Kit Jones will do for me, but leave Emma and my mother alone if you want your dukedom back."

Behind him the door clicked open, drawing the old man's gaze. And it occurred to Dav that the old man had been stalling. He pivoted to his right and found a new man, solidly built, about Dav's height but at least twice his age with a pistol leveled at Dav's belly.

"Troubled by an intruder, Uncle? Shall I shoot him?" The man was dressed for travel with the dust and mud of a hasty journey on his long drab coat. A raised vein bulged on his broad forehead.

"No need, Aubrey. The fool's prepared to give up everything."

"I wouldn't believe it, if I were you." Aubrey advanced into the room.

Dav kept his gaze on him. "Where's Emma?"

Aubrey's lips thinned in a cruel smile. "You are a most inconvenient fellow, you know. You were supposed to return to the hall, yet here you are, where you're least wanted."

"Where's Emma?" Dav took a step toward the door. Aubrey held him back with the pistol.

Dav glanced at the duke. "Without Emma, I make no deal."

"Aubrey, you've spooked the boy. You need to see his terms."

At a jumble of steps and raised voices outside the door Aubrey stepped to one side, his pistol still aimed at Dav.

A tall, spare woman, elegantly attired in pewter silk, with gray hair coiled about her head, burst in, and the dogs bounded past her. She called them to heel and turned to Aubrey.

"Aubrey, a weapon? What's the meaning of this? What have you done? There's a wounded man lying in the hall, claiming you're out to kill my grandson."

"Aunt, calm yourself. We have an intruder." He tipped his head toward Dav.

She turned and caught sight of Dav and gripped a chair

back. Her hand went to her mouth, stifling a cry. Her eyes filled with tears. She dashed them away at once. "Wenlocke, tell Aubrey to put away his pistol. You will not permit Aubrey to shoot our grandson."

"Aunt, I beg your pardon. This man is not your grandson. He's a base imposter the Jones bastards have been using to trick uncle out of his fortune."

The duchess shook her head and appealed to the duke. "Look at his hands. Look at the shape of his head. He *is* Granville's son, our boy's son."

"I see nothing."

"Stubborn, pig-headed old man. See nothing then, but I know him. I know Granville's heir when I see him." She addressed Dav, her voice strong. "My dear, dear boy, why have you come here among your enemies?"

"For Emma, Your Grace."

"Emma Portland? My Emma?"

"Your—?

"My dear friend's granddaughter. How do you know her?"

"The old man can explain. I believe he has a pardon Emma needs."

The duchess glanced at the duke and back at Dav. She shook her head. "Emma's not here. Aubrey took her away over a fortnight ago."

"We did you a favor, Aunt. We couldn't have the Duchess of Wenlocke harboring a murderess, could we?"

"Emma is no murderess." The duchess turned to Dav. "You can't believe that of her."

"I don't."

She looked at her husband. "I've been to see the king, Wenlocke. He signed Emma's pardon."

"That's unfortunate, Aunt. Emma is no longer of use to us."

"Wenlocke." The duchess looked at her husband. "I warned you not to harm Emma. Call Aubrey off."

The duke and his duchess exchanged a long stare. Dav gripped the bronze piece in his pocket.

"Oh, you stubborn man." She spun on Aubrey and dealt him a ringing slap to the face. At the duchess's sudden move, the dogs sprang up, tangling themselves between the two. Aubrey swung his pistol arm at the duchess, and she went down with a cry under the blow. The baffled dogs yelped and leapt over one another, knocking a table over. Aubrey backed away, cuffing the milling dogs with his pistol.

Dav lunged for duke's cane. Aubrey freed himself from the dogs' chaos first. Once more he aimed at Dav.

"Now listen, everyone, and listen carefully. Don't move, Aunt. No one leaves the library. We have an intruder to be dealt with."

"Wenlocke," the duchess cried. "Stop him."

The duke leaned against the desk, looking down at his fallen duchess. His mouth had a twisted look and his left hand worked spasmodically open and closed. Aubrey watched him, waiting for a sign.

Dav held the cane along his left side, concealed from Aubrey. It felt light as a foil in his hand after months with the heavy sword.

The duke turned from his wife to his desk. As if suddenly unsure of his purpose, he picked up the paper with Dav's terms.

"The pistol, Uncle. The pistol! Shoot him!" Aubrey cried.

The duke dropped the paper and fumbled the pistol from his left to his right hand. The hand didn't seem to cooperate. But as he turned, he steadied the gun, his brow furrowed, his puzzled gaze on Aubrey.

"For God's sake, Uncle, shoot."

Dav hurled the bronze piece. It knocked the duke's pistol aside. The gun went off.

The dogs howled.

The gun slid from the duke's grip. He tottered to one side and collapsed in his chair. A harsh tremor shook his body.

Dav had already shifted the cane to his right hand. He lunged for Aubrey, whipping the heavy crown of the cane down on Aubrey's wrist. He heard a snap and the pistol's discharge. Aubrey staggered back, the pistol slid from his lax grip while his other hand clutched for a hold and found only air. He collapsed on the floor, his smooth face contorted, his gaze fixed on the missing toe of his boot. Blood oozed from the blasted leather. The room filled with the acrid smell of blood, spent powder, and burned leather. Aubrey shouted curses.

Dav stepped over Aubrey and lifted the fallen duchess.

Shouting voices filled the corridor, and footsteps pounded nearer.

Aubrey clutched his boot below the knee. Dav stood over him and pressed the tip of the duke's cane to his throat. "Where's Emma?"

Aubrey moaned. Dav pressed harder on the man's Adam's apple until he choked. Dav released the pressure.

Aubrey swallowed. "Your little murderess is in Horsham Jail."

The duchess gasped.

"The local magistrates have orders to see that she gets swift justice. She'll hang by nine tomorrow."

A murderous tide of bile and hatred rose in Dav. It burned his throat like molten coal in one of Xan's gasworks furnaces. He swung the gold head of the cane up for a blow that would smash Aubrey's head, but Aubrey's face had the look of satisfied malice he remembered seeing on March's face. Killing March had been necessary to save others; killing Aubrey would not save Emma. Emma was all that mattered. If he saved Emma, he beat Aubrey.

He turned and hurled the black cane down the long room. It smashed against the tall windows, shattering glass.

The duchess touched Dav's sleeve. "Come. It's forty miles of good road. We'll reach her."

Vickers stood in the doorway with two footmen. The duchess spoke first. "Vickers, His Grace needs a physician." She nodded to a footman and sent him running with an order for her carriage.

The voices in the corridor came nearer, and Dav recognized his brothers' voices among them. The next instant Xan and Will shouldered their way through the gawking servants.

WILL took in the carnage at a glance, the Earl of Aubrey moaning on the floor, clutching one bloodied boot, and the Duke of Wenlocke frozen in a chair halfway down the long room. Pistol smoke and blood filled his nostrils. A pistol lay on the carpet beside Aubrey, and another lay to the right of the duke in a pile of glittering shards from one of the great windows. *Damn it, but Dav was a bleeding dangerous fellow.* There was a cool detachment in him that neither Will nor Xan could match.

Will had no sooner registered these details than Dav headed for the door. Will caught his arm but his brother's sharp glance made him let go at once.

"Aubrey's put Emma in jail."

"You're unhurt?"

Dav nodded. "Emma."

Xan immediately protested. "You can't leave us behind again."

Will put his hand on Xan's shoulder and spoke to Dav. "Go. We'll handle the damage here and follow when we can."

And Dav was gone. Will could only wish him speed and luck. He exchanged a look with Xan. They both knew what it was to have the woman you loved in danger from Wenlocke's hirelings. He turned back to the magnificent library and the huddled duke.

The man seemed to have been seized in some way. He sat frozen in his chair. Will put a careful hand on his shoulder. The duke's eyes turned to him, a puzzled frown on his brow. He opened his mouth. Will could see the throat working, but no words emerged, just a strangled moan.

Vickers, the butler, came up beside Will. He gently took the old man's hand. "Your Grace?"

Again the duke's throat worked. His mouth opened and closed. No sound emerged. Will smiled grimly at the justice of it. Vickers turned an agonized face to him. "His Grace can't speak."

Chapter Twenty-five

⁓

L ORD Philoughby gazed at the crowd. He straightened his black robes and long judicial wig. The effects of his uneasy night still troubled him. When he'd retired for the evening after studying the documents in the fair prisoner's case, he had attributed his unease to a bad bit of beef at supper. He had spoken to the landlord and given directions about the future of meat during his stays at the Queen's Head. In spite of the landlord's profuse apologies and a stomach-soothing tea, Philoughby's unease had persisted through the night.

The constable entered the court, leading the prisoner, while the onlookers strained to get a look at her in a way that troubled Philoughby. She did not look up. Her manacled hands hung down as if she had no power to raise them.

If ever a prisoner needed someone on her side, it was this sad girl who wished to sell her gowns to bury her corpse. It was rather the common practice for anatomists to take possession of the bodies of the hanged. Philoughby's queasy stomach rebelled at the thought as the constable read the writ.

The accused, one Emma Portland, did willfully stab to death Sergeant Jeremiah Bowley, an officer of the king's army in the pursuit of his duties, the night of January twenty-second in Kings Arms tavern common room in the county of Sussex.

The reading of the evidence in court seemed to incite the crowd to more bloodthirsty curiosity but made the case no less troubling. The court turned immediately to the evidence Lord Aubrey had provided. The dead man was reported to be a recruiting sergeant for the Ninetieth Regiment of Infantry, but another place in the documents listed the dead man as unnamed. Philoughby slowed the proceedings repeatedly to Crutchfield's annoyance, to make sure the jurors noted contradictory passages. In Philoughby's experience no regiment sent an unnamed man to recruit. There were other anomalies as well concerning where the man was likely killed and where his body was discovered. In one place the testimony described the sergeant as a man of great bulk and in another place, the undertaker observed that the dead man's uniform was too large for him. Again Philoughby asked a question to call attention to the discrepancy.

But Crutchfield had admitted a noisy crowd to the hall. The spectators' benches were jammed, and onlookers continued to squeeze into the standing room at the rear of the hall under the gallery, their noise unseemly for a courtroom.

Philoughby banged his gavel. He was a tough judge disinclined to leniency, but he found the bloodthirstiness of a mob distasteful. He had been quite a young man when France had convulsed in the violence of the guillotine and the drownings at Nantes. Reports of those events had made a strong impression, and he had favored English restraint over continental excess ever since.

Restraint seemed particularly necessary in this case where the accused was a stranger. The townspeople of Horsham had a reputation for enjoying a hanging or two. And Philoughby knew how keenly the sympathies of the spectators could be felt in the courtroom. Crutchfield had made very sure that Philoughby's black cap was on the table next to his gavel.

They were an hour into the proceedings when it became clear to him that the girl could not have done the murder. She could not have overpowered a large man in a public room or moved him from a private one without aid. He settled his wig more firmly on his head. He was ready to demolish the case.

The doors at the rear of the hall burst open, and a disturbance rippled through the crowd, displacing people and raising a buzz of noise.

Philoughby banged his gavel sharply, but the commotion grew as it came closer. A tall young man with a blackened eye and an open shirt emerged from the crowd. In his upraised fist he clutched a paper. People gave way before him as he strode to the bench.

Philoughby blinked. His gavel stopped mid-swing. Almost he expected to see a fiery sword, not a battered face and sealed document. Cool gray eyes met his. The man's authority was palpable. The crowd grew quiet.

The stranger slapped the paper on the table. "The king's pardon for Emma Portland." He did not look at the prisoner.

Whispering erupted into a loud babble.

"Wait a minute now." Crutchfield drew himself up. "Who might you be to interrupt these proceedings?"

"Daventry. The Marquess of Daventry." The young man did not so much as flick a glance in Crutchfield's direction.

The babble died. The crowd seemed to hold its breath now, straining to see the young man. Philoughby felt the weight lift from his shoulders. He took the offered document, broke the seal, and read. A full pardon with the king's own signature and seal, a hard thing to come by.

Philoughby looked up and raised his gavel high. He let it fall one last time with a resounding bang. "This court is dismissed."

The stunned spectators did not move at once. But Philoughby signaled to the constables to move the crowd along, and a grumbling exodus began.

The young man with the gray eyes turned to the dock. "May I release the prisoner?"

"You may." Philoughby removed his wig, noting an immediate relief to the churning of his unsettled stomach.

Emma stood in the dock watching him. Dav thought the blue in her eyes was like the first hint of dawn, a promise of the day to come. "They didn't kill you."

He climbed over the rail into the dock with her and lifted her ironbound wrists to kiss her hands. "Forgive me." He dropped to his knees.

The iron at her wrists clinked as she lifted her hands to his bowed head. He felt her fingers uncurl to touch his hair. "I thought they would kill you because of me."

"Never because of you."

"I tried to let you go, but I couldn't keep away. Wallop knew you would go to that fight, and I thought . . ." He felt the shudder run through her.

"If you had not come, if you had not cried out, I would never have known the truth." *I would have lived without knowing you loved me. It would have been no life at all.*

The constable fumbled the key, but at last the manacles opened.

The crowd outside the town hall let them pass through and kept a distance from the duchess's coach. Her liveried footmen and outriders had a stern magnificence that silenced onlookers.

Dav laughed as they stepped into the light, and scooped Emma up off her feet and carried her into the morning sun. It made them both blink. One of the duchess's servants opened the carriage door at once, and Her Grace stepped down.

Dav put Emma on her feet, and the duchess dipped into a deep curtsy. "Your Highness."

In the duchess's gesture and Emma's response Dav realized another truth about Emma Portland. He had known it and denied it from the first moment of noting her regal posture in the shabby gown in the bare schoolroom. The king's pardon was the courtesy of one royal person to another. He had assumed she was a penniless waif, his for the taking. He'd been wrong.

Dav could not ask the question burning on his tongue. He reminded himself that she did love him. The situation was not hopeless, and he could not let her go back to Wenlocke. Even with his victory there, Dav would not trust Emma near the duke or Aubrey. But a gentleman would command two rooms at the inn, not the one bed he had immediately imagined them sharing.

Emma reached to pull the older woman up. "Oh no. Just Emma, Your Grace. You must not think otherwise." Emma swallowed. "Malfada is past."

Malfada. Dav caught the name of her kingdom. It had to be tiny and insignificant in the tangle of European politics, but he could guess its history, swallowed up by France under Napoleon.

"My dear girl," the duchess held Emma's hands, "I would not have had you suffer like this for the world. I had no idea how to find you."

"You are not to blame. You have been our one friend in the world, Tatty's and mine. Have you had any word from her?" Emma's love for the duchess was clear.

"No word yet, my dear, but when word comes to Wenlocke, I'll send it on to you at once."

The duchess turned to Dav with quiet dignity. He spoke first. "I must thank you, too, Your Grace, for giving me Emma back when I thought I had lost her."

"Ah, you've won her completely, have you?" The duchess smiled at him.

"If I haven't, I will. I am not a man to give up on the thing I want." He took one of Emma's hands in his.

"That, I think, you have inherited. I must go back to Wenlocke, but I am your grandmother, if you will have me."

He had not thought to have a kindly grandparent. "I will, Your Grace."

"I have no right to ask you to keep his name, but I hope you will. I hope you will keep my dear boy alive in you and never give up your birthright. Wenlocke will be a different place someday because of you."

He was surprised at the impulse to embrace the duchess. He so rarely touched another person, but without the duchess there would be no Emma standing with her hand in his.

"I would like to tell you about your father someday, if I may."

Dav nodded.

He and Emma saw the duchess off in her carriage and turned to the inn, where the landlord outdid himself in civility. Nothing like a crested ducal carriage to draw the notice of ostlers, postboys, chambermaids, and waiters. When Dav made his wishes known, the whole household sprang into motion from the lowliest chambermaid to the hostess herself. Fires were lighted, beds aired and warmed, baths drawn.

Dav led Emma to one of a pair of adjoining rooms, gave her a quick kiss, and left her to the care of the inn's people.

Chapter Twenty-six

❧

DOWNSTAIRS he found the landlord again willing to take orders. His host ushered him to a pleasant enough room where he sat at a dark oak table under an old mullioned window sending messengers and messages across the town and across England. His mother and his brothers must be told. The boys would need to hear from him. He and Emma must have fresh garments to wear. As he put his mind to simple, necessary tasks, the other part of his brain, his imagination, was free to hurry Emma through all the attentions showered on her.

He delayed as long as he could in the landlord's private room, certain that he had given her time to bathe and change and eat and above all to think. He could not ask questions about her future while any trace of the horror of the morning still lingered in her eyes. To see her in the dock, a manacled thing, the blue of her eyes extinguished, had daunted him as facing his grandfather had not.

He thought of the accusation made against her. He had
known it was false from the moment he first heard it, but he
had also known the chilling likelihood that the truth, whatever it was, would not save her from the law. Betrayed and
wounded by her, he had done nothing to save her in her
time of peril.

By the logic of stories, he did not deserve to have her.
No tale ended with a bystander, a do-nothing, winning the
princess. Since Dav had failed to act to save her when she
was in terrible danger, he could not claim her now. But
deserving and wanting were such very different characters.
Deserving was a mild, polite boy, waiting to receive his
due. While wanting, the way Dav wanted Emma Portland,
was a ragged, restless boy of the London streets whose
eyes and hands were quick to spot and steal a treasure,
whose heart would keep the stolen treasure forever.

The law was harsh on such boys. He had pored over the
tomes in his library for months, reading the cases of beg-
gars and thieves, whipped and transported and hanged for
wanting what chance denied. He wondered what kind of
life sentence he might be handed for the act of stealing a
princess.

He set himself to fill another hour with his own acts of
self-restoration. At least he could meet her looking like a
marquess. A bath, a shave, and fresh linen would help.
Nothing would disguise the scrapes and bruises, the signs
of his true nature, but that could not be helped.

He escaped the landlord's solicitous attentions and
climbed the stairs to the room set aside for him. When he
opened the door, Emma stood there unchanged. The blue of
her eyes was as uncertain as the sea under shifting clouds.

"What is it?" He was across the room in two strides.

"Why did you order two rooms?"

"Not from any wish to lie apart from you."

"Then why?"

"I think you know, Your Highness. Should I kneel?"

"No." She shook her head. "Just Emma."

He lifted a brow. "I doubt the Duchess of Wenlocke bows to a mere Emma."

"Stop. You must have the truth. You deserve it."

"About Malfada or about the dead man, Emma? Your cousin killed the spy, didn't she?"

"How do you know?"

I know how you touch things and hold them and how you love.

"All we wanted was to be free. We didn't want to kill anyone, but he was going to kill the babe. He was going to kill little Leo."

"Tell me." He stepped forward and led her to a bench under the window where she could sit in his embrace to tell her story. He had wanted the end of Emma's story from the first hour he had known her. He wanted to say the words that would free her from the ogres of the past.

"Tell me."

She sighed and twisted in his hold to sit upright, facing him. "We were in prison off and on for seven years, Tatty and Leo and I, after the French came. When we were of no more value, they hanged Leo, and Tatty and I escaped.

"Escape was easy at first. We disguised ourselves as boys. But when the babe came, there were delays. We expected to be followed, of course. Tatty took a knife. But when we crossed the Channel, when we left the Continent behind, we thought we'd outrun our pursuers. We had only to get to Bristol to meet a boat that would take us to America.

"We stopped at that inn in Reading. We'd come so far we felt we must be safe. It was a bitter cold evening, and we feared for the babe, little Leo. There was no time to sell another jewel to raise some funds, so we only had enough for our room and Tatty needed to eat to keep up her strength to feed the babe.

"A soldier was drinking in the taproom, and he invited Tatty to join him for a drink and a meal. We hadn't eaten that day, and there seemed no harm in letting him pay for a meal. I put the babe to bed in our room and went to see if I could assist the landlady in return for a meal.

"Tatty's sergeant went on drinking. He was a great hulk of a man. In time he wanted to take Tatty upstairs. She signaled me for help. I rushed ahead to the room. When I opened our door, a stranger was standing over the babe. I knew at once he was Malfada, our countryman, a spy. He wore the same boots as all our guards.

"My throat closed up. I couldn't scream or cry out. I signed to Tatty. She told the sergeant to wait downstairs for her. I moved around the bed to make the spy look at me. Tatty got behind him with her knife. I pleaded for the babe's life, and the Malfada laughed. It was a terrible laugh. Tatty heard it and used her knife, stabbing up and turning her fist, the way Leo taught her.

"The spy crumpled. I saw in his face the shock of his death. But I made myself grab little Leo. When Tatty saw what she'd done, she shook and shook, but I gave her the babe to hold, and she quieted. I knew what we must do.

"We shoved the dead man under the bed, and I sent Tatty back to her sergeant to bring him up to our room. He was quick to strip off his clothes, and he fell asleep as soon as he hit the mattress. We put his clothes on the dead spy, and put the spy in the sergeant's chair in the taproom with his head on the table. We could not let news of the spy's death get back to others who might be on our trail.

"We were gone before first light. We weighed the spy's clothes down with rocks and sank them in a pond and hid in a wood for most of the day. We were so afraid. We argued. I said we must send to the duchess, our grandmother's friend. We could trust her. But Tatty didn't want to wait for the duchess, so we put walnut dye in our hair, and she took the road for Bristol to meet the agent who had arranged our passage to America. I went north to find the duchess, hoping any pursuers would follow me, not Tatty.

"At Wenlocke I thought I was safe. The duchess was so sure that no one would come there to take me away."

She sagged against him. He knew the weight of her burden had worn her out. But she pulled herself up and met his gaze.

"So do not call me princess. I am a woman who does what she must to survive in this world. They took everything from us, from Leo and Tatty and me. The French ate our ponies. They cut off their heads and left them on the road, and the crows came. We ate fish soup even when the guards spat in it and tore our dresses to shreds and sold our jewels. And when they hanged Leo and the crows . . ."

Dav took her in his arms in a tight hold. "I have your brother's pin. The boys did take it. Swallow gave it back to me after you left."

"Oh." He heard one sob. Then she pressed her face to his shoulder. He held her and stroked her back and let the storm of tears spend itself against him. When her grief subsided at last, he recognized what was different in their embrace. She sat up, wiping her eyes and hiccuping. He handed her a napkin from the table with a kiss. Their lips held and clung. His honorable intentions dissolved.

"I love you," he told her. "Are you wearing stuffing?"

She laughed, her tear-washed eyes sparkling blue. "Three

gowns. I was to take one off each day, so that I would be hard to trace, but after I left you, I could not get warm."

"Turn around." His hands searched her back for fastenings. "Let's get you out of them."

The first dress was black and stiff and fitted tightly over the layers underneath. He peeled the sleeves off of her and undid the buttons at her wrists and the ties at her waist. At last the black shell fell away, and she stepped out of it.

"Are you going to marry me?" she asked.

"How can I when you're a princess, and I'm a street rat masquerading as a peer?" He started on the second gown, a fawn wool, plain and worn. He was gaining skill in undoing her clothing.

"I think if you're going to undress me in a private chamber at an inn, you should have honorable intentions."

"I love you. You know that now."

"Not what I asked."

He went to work on the third gown. He recognized it, the shapeless gray muslin of the day he met her. He was impatient now with scraps of linen and scruples, but he would give her one last chance. "You think you can marry a man whose rank in life is decidedly beneath your own?"

"It's you. You don't want to marry a woman who told you two lies to every truth."

The last gown fell away. He took a deep breath as she stood revealed in her linen shift, no corset, no stays. He knelt to remove her shoes, letting her dwell in doubt while he admired her sweet limbs.

"How many lies did you tell? Could you even keep track?"

"It was a challenge—lying to you and to Wallop."

"A thousand lies don't matter. As long as your love is a true thing, the rest doesn't matter."

He kept her turned from him with a hand on her shoulder while he took a minute to free himself from some of his own trappings. Then he turned her round to face him. He pulled her close, hoisting her off her feet and letting her body slide against his. She gave a sweet laugh that ended in a teary hiccup, her arms around his neck. He lowered her to his bed.

Emma leaned back on her hands, and her legs fell apart. She had no will to press them closed. Standing with his hands working at her clothes for what had seemed hours had made her impatient for this. Her chemise rode up so that it lay across the juncture of thigh and hip, leaving her body open to his gaze. He stood and watched her for a moment in her sudden boldness. He bent down and untied her plain garter ribbons, breathing in the scent of her, kissing the silky sweet flesh of her inner thighs. He circled each leg above the knee and peeled her muddied stockings off one by one. When he tossed aside her second stocking, he stepped forward and pulled her to him so that his sex met hers. He cocked his hips and rocked against her, sliding slickly. His arms enclosed her in tight possession. He would never let her go. Emma's body wept and ached and opened to his. Her heart rose as if powerful wings beat the air, lifting her into the pure ether. For a moment she clung to sense, fighting her soaring release to tell him one more thing.

"Here is a truth. I want to be Emma Portland for you, new baptized."

"Then we are even again. I will be Daventry for you, if you will have me."

"I will, my love, now and forever."

Chapter Twenty-seven

∽

A MODEST reception followed the wedding of Sophie Rhys-Jones to Major Lucien Montclare at Woford House, the temporary home of Sir Xander Jones, his wife Cleo, their young children, and Cleo's brother, Charlie, the future Baron Woford. At their mother's wedding her three sons, the Sons of Sin, danced with every woman present repeated times. They whirled their mother and their wives and Dav's bride-to-be in giddy waltzes until the fiddlers demanded a respite.

In one of the lulls in the gay party, Dav, glancing at his watch, led Emma into the garden. It was a night of indigo skies sparkling with stars, a rare night. The garden was damp and fragrant with dog roses. The trees and bushes shed cool drops from a rain that had passed earlier in the day. Dav took Emma's arm in his to make a stroll of the circular gravel path. She was happy he knew. Plans for their own wedding were well in hand. She was no longer a fugitive from English law or from the primitive revenge of factions from Malfada.

She was no longer a prisoner, locked in, but a treasure, guarded as something precious is guarded and kept safe, guarded by a mortal angel, who would avenge any wrong against her with a fiery arm.

Only one shadow sometimes still darkened the blue of her eyes. Tonight he knew, surrounded by his family, the shadow came in moments when she remembered hers. She was good at bearing her losses. She now wore the pin he had restored to her openly, and she waited with a kind of held breath for news from her cousin. The Duchess of Wenlocke promised to send word as soon as it came to her, and she had, so Dav led Emma to the back of the garden.

She teased him that he no longer needed a ruse to be alone with her. But he led her to a gate in the high wall at the back of the garden. There a woman stepped from the shadows with bright hair, a babe in her arms, and a red-coated soldier at her side.

E MMA clutched Dav's arm. "We can save her, can't we?"
   The girl passed the babe to the soldier, who took the child with easy assurance. The boy, a round-cheeked cherub of near a year, patted the soldier's cheek, then stuck his thumb in his mouth to gaze at the strange proceedings of the two women.

"He's not taking her to prison, Emma," Dav assured her.

The two women embraced and lapsed into their own tongue, a bright flow of words interrupted by tears and laughs and hiccups and sniffles. Dav offered a handkerchief.

The officer deftly switched the babe in his arms and offered his own square of linen.

"She married him," Emma told Dav.

He knew. "The duchess sent word this morning."

"And he's taking her to Canada. He's posted there."

"She'll be safe."

Epilogue

⚜

MORNING CHRONICLE

Married in St. George's, Hanover Square
London, September 4.

—*At St. George's Church, Hanover Square, yesterday, the Marquess of Daventry was married to Princess Giovanna Saville of Malfada, daughter of their late majesties Leopold and Louisa of the house of Saville, Duke and Princess of Malfada. The ceremony was witnessed by the Duke of Wellington, the Duchess of Wenlocke, the Foreign Secretary, Sir Robert Peel, and many members of the Government, the Diplomatic Corps, and the Metropolitan Works Group. Charles Spencer, Lord Woford; Sir Alexander Jones and Lady Cleopatra Jones; Sir William Jones and Lady*

Helen Jones; Major Lucien Montclare and Mrs. Montclare comprised the bridal party.

Fine weather brought out the crowds to see the "fairy princess," as Her Highness has been dubbed, wed the "secret heir," as the marquess is called. Loud cheers accompanied the pair leaving the church.

The marquess is the grandson of the Duke of Wenlocke, who was not in attendance due to poor health. The porch of the church was lined by Life Guardsmen and by officers of the Bow Street Magistrate's Office. The bride wore magnificent lace, sapphires, and pearls. The reception at the Duchess of Wenlocke's town house, which followed, was thronged with high society. Illuminations such as London has not seen since England's victories in the late wars lit the London night.

Read on for a special preview of
the next seductive historical romance
from Kate Moore
Coming soon from Berkley Sensation!

L YLE Massing, Baron Blackstone, was losing at cards, a situation he could only attribute to the rise and fall of the ship under him. The HMS *Redemption,* a naval vessel of questionable seaworthiness, had been pressed into service to bring Blackstone and a few other survivors of the Greek misadventure home.

He tried to concentrate on the cards in his hand and not think about home. At the moment he didn't have one. Blackstone Court, the ancestral seat he'd inherited from his father, had been mortgaged to pay his ransom to the warlord Vasiladi. The house was now leased to a wealthy maker of crockery. Blackstone's widowed mother and sisters had removed to a modest town house in Bath. His mother made no complaint, but in the first letter to reach him after his release, his sister Elena had double-underlined *thirty feet*—the distance between his mother's two drawing rooms in Bath. When he thought of his mother in such narrow circumstances, he grew a little reckless with his cards, and already a pile of his vowels littered the table.

Beating its way across the channel to Dover, the *Redemption* lurched and shuddered, making the yellow light waver in the smoky compartment. Lyle blinked at the unforgiving cards in his hand. His opponent, Samuel Goldsworthy, a large mound of a man with thick red hair and beard and a green silk waistcoat that glowed in the swaying light, grinned at him. The fellow seemed incapable of ill humor or of losing. The endless card game and the rolling seas had claimed the other two passengers. Only Goldsworthy and Blackstone remained at the table.

The big man could not conceal his satisfaction with the situation. "Lad, those cards you're holding are worthless. Let me offer you a way out."

Blackstone felt an unsettling prick of wariness, as if the man could see his hand. He made a joke. "Is this the moment when you suggest that I marry your quiz of a daughter?" If Goldsworthy had such a daughter, Lyle might do it. He had few options to recover his estate.

Goldsworthy gave a head-splittingly hearty laugh. Lyle had suggested such a marriage in jest, but as if in protest at the idea of his marrying, his careless memory threw up a flash of laughing black eyes and soft, creamy breasts. He shook it off. That opportunity had long since passed. No doubt the chit had married while Blackstone was in the hands of Vasiladi's bandits.

"Nothing so clichéd, lad. All I ask is that you enter my employ for a year and a day."

Lyle wondered how calculated the phrase was. A year and a day, the amount of time he had been a captive; a year and a day, in which Byron had died and the freedom fighters who had sought to throw off the Turks had fallen into rival factions, apt to cut one another's throats.

He peered again at Goldsworthy. The man looked ordinary enough in spite of his oak-like size and the absurd invitation to employment. He was taller than Blackstone by four inches or more and wider than any of the berths offered on the ship. Blackstone put his age at somewhere between forty and fifty. He looked like a great leafy tree with his russet coat, walnut trousers, and the green waistcoat. For all the stirring of Lyle's instincts at the man's turn of phrase, the fellow probably had a warehouse on the Thames stuffed with bolts of muslin or sacks of coffee beans.

Goldsworthy and the *Redemption* had appeared in Koron harbor at that singularly delicate moment in Blackstone's negotiations with the bandit when the money was about to change hands and there was suddenly no reason to suppose that Vasiladi would follow through with the release of his hostages, including a score of young girls and boys who had been pressed into slavish roles by the warlord's army.

"I suppose you're a cesspool cleaner or a pure collector."

"Nothing so fragrant or so tame, I assure you, lad. Something rather more suited to your talents." Goldsworthy took a long pull on his ale.

"We didn't meet in London, did we?"

"Not at all."

"You can't have a high estimate of my talents based on our little game."

"You are a charming fellow—"

Blackstone shot Goldsworthy a skeptical glance. For a moment there had seemed a sharp gleam of cunning behind the genial mask. "I've hardly charmed you."

"Still among your own, among the ton, you move with

grace and ease, wear a well-cut coat, show a pretty leg on the dance floor, and perhaps off it, drive and ride to an inch."

"All of which hardly recommend me for anyone's employ." His companion's knowing look, like a school-master's, was becoming annoying.

"Except mine. You'll be invited everywhere, and I want you to attend as many of the season's events as you can."

Maybe there was an ugly daughter after all. "And for submitting to the endless social whirl?"

"I will pay off all your debts, including the mortgage on Blackstone Court."

"I beg your pardon." Blackstone stared hard at the man who seemed to know more of his business than anyone out-side of his solicitor.

"Come with me to my club, and I'll explain."

"Your club?" The blunt fellow did not strike Blackstone as a clubman.

"The Pantheon Club on Albemarle Street. I've a post chaise meeting the ship. It will take us directly there."

Not to Bath and his mother's reproaches, but to London and a chance to repair his fortune. Goldsworthy certainly knew how to dangle temptation. He didn't he trust the man. A year and a day had the suspicious ring of a catch some-where, as if one were staking one's soul.

"Who are you?"

Goldsworthy frowned. "You can't have forgotten already."

"Not your name. Who are you? What's this mysterious position you're offering? Am I to sign a contract in blood?"

Goldsworthy grinned broadly. "No bloodshed required, lad. Your word will do, and I'll explain at the club. You'll like the coffee, and the floor won't pitch under your feet."

If the fellow called him *lad* one more time, Blackstone thought he might lean across the table and choke him.

The pile of scraps on which Blackstone and his luckless fellow travelers had pledged their funds to Goldsworthy lay on the table. He glanced from them to the dismal cards in his hand. Luck was certainly against him.

The ship paused on a peak. Then the treacherous ocean shifted, and they fell into a stomach-seizing nothingness, as if the world had vanished. Goldsworthy calmly clamped a hand around his ale pot. Blackstone caught the lamp. Everything else hit the low ceiling. In that moment of free fall, nothing to grab, nothing to lose that wasn't lost already, Lyle saw the flash of laughing black eyes and wanted against all reason to see them again, which was madness.

The long fall ended as the *Redemption* slammed into another wave, shuddered mightily, and decided not to splinter into driftwood.

"I'll do it."

"That's the good lad. A year and a day, then you'll be free and clear."

JOANNA BOURNE

presents her stunning and award-winning debut novel

THE
Spymaster's Lady

**She's never met a man she couldn't deceive . . .
until now.**

She's braved battlefields. She's stolen dispatches from under the noses of heads of state. She's played the worldly courtesan, the naive virgin, the refined British lady, even a Gypsy boy. But Annique Villiers, the elusive spy known as the Fox Cub, has finally met the one man she can't outwit.

"A FLAT-OUT SPECTACULAR BOOK."
—*All About Romance*

"Love, love, LOVED it!"
—Julia Quinn

Now available in trade paperback

penguin.com

**Enter the rich world of
historical romance
with Berkley Books . . .**

Madeline Hunter

Jennifer Ashley

Joanna Bourne

Lynn Kurland

Jodi Thomas

Anne Gracie

Love is timeless.

berkleyjoveauthors.com

Photo by Loren Moore

Kate Moore ...ated
author of ...lifor-
nia with ¹ ...e at
¹ ...¹

They are the "Sons of Sin"—three brothers whose mother is an infamous London courtesan. Though Xander, Will, and Kit may not be legitimate in the eyes of the aristocracy, their mother made sure that they each received a gentlemen's education and knew how to make their way in the world...

The youngest of the Jones brothers, Kit, has just been made the Marquess of Daventry—heir to his vengeful grandfather, the Duke of Wenlocke. As Daventry, Kit is a warrior angel trapped in a gilded cage who wants to free his family with a decisive defeat of the old duke. In a daring move that breaks all the rules of his well-guarded life, he hires the beautiful Emma Portland to tutor his young wards while he makes his plans.

But everything about Emma is a lie. Alone, pursued by enemies from her past, and falsely accused of a murder she didn't commit, Emma must spy against Daventry for his grandfather. For if she doesn't play by the duke's rules, she'll hang. So Emma passes herself off as a tutor as she plans her escape. What she doesn't plan on is falling in love with the man she's been sent to destroy...

PRAISE FOR THE NOVELS OF KATE MOORE

"Fast paced, exciting." —*Booklist*

"A stunning trilogy."—*Library Journal*

"Very enjoyable."—*San Francisco Book Review*

ISBN 978-0-425-24369-5

5 0 7 9 9

EAN
S

9 780425 243695

www.penguin.com

$7.99 U.S.
$8.99 CAN